CAGE

DARK OPS DADDIES
BOOK 1

KATE OLIVER

CONTENT WARNINGS

This book is a DD/lg romance. The MMC in this book is a Daddy Dom and the MFC identifies as a Little. This is an act of role-playing and/or a lifestyle dynamic between the characters and falls under the BDSM umbrella. This is a consensual power exchange relationship between adults. In this story there are spankings and discussions of other forms of discipline as well as heavy age play.

Additional content warning

Death of a parent
Abandonment by a parent
Murder of bad guy - It was deserved
Heavy age play

Please do not read this story if you find any of this to be disturbing or a trigger for you.

This book is dedicated to my amazing readers who deserve to live out their deepest fantasies... Or at the very least, read delicious books about them.

I love you all.

XO, Kate

PROLOGUE

CAGE

22 Years Ago

If it weren't for the stench of body odor, mildew, and urine, plus the constant shouting, this jail cell wouldn't be so bad. In fact, I'd consider it one of the best homes I've ever had. I can't count how many times I've been here, but every time I walk through those heavy metal doors in handcuffs, I know I'm going to get three meals a day, and no one is going to lay a finger on me. There will be no abuse, no starving, and no sleeping on the floor in a closet.

"You have a visitor."

One of the juvenile detention officers stares at me

through the bars, his round stomach hanging over the waistband of his pants. He chomps loudly on a piece of gum, waiting until I rise from my thin, uncomfortable mattress. It doesn't matter how crappy it is, though. It's my own bed and it can't be taken away from me.

I don't even glance up from the book I'm reading. "Not interested."

Whoever is here to see me, I can guarantee I don't want to see them. It's either someone from the state or my most recent foster family. Either one can fuck off. My social worker has continued to place me in abusive, neglectful homes even though she knows they aren't safe. My most recent foster parents are no exception. And it's a wonder why I'm always running away and getting into trouble.

"Not a choice, kid. Let's go," he demands, sliding open the metal door with a loud clank.

Irritation prickles down the back of my neck. This asshole thinks he's the top cop or something—when in reality, he probably failed the academy, which is why he's stuck here. Babysitting a bunch of fucked-up kids who can't stay out of trouble.

I toss my book aside and follow him toward the visitors' area. It's always depressing as hell. Parents sobbing because their precious kid did something stupid and ended up here. Boys crying because they want to go home with their families once they realize they aren't cut out for being locked up. Guess they think their parents aren't so bad after being in here for a night or two. At least they have people who give a shit about them.

Instead of going to the large room at the end of a long hallway, we stop in front of a door on the right. The officer opens it, then motions for me to go in. I eye him warily as I slowly approach.

What the fuck? I've never seen anyone go in here before. I assumed it was a supply closet.

My stomach twists when I cross the threshold, glancing back as the officer closes the door behind me. A second later, the heavy lock slides into place.

White-painted cinderblock walls that are filthy and cold create the small space. Smack dab in the middle of it is a wobbly laminate table that looks like it was in a school back in the eighties. Dusty flickering fluorescent lights hang above it from the stained ceiling panels that look like they could fall at any second. No cameras or windows. It's damp in here, a copper smell lingering in the air. Blood. I'd know that smell anywhere. Is this some kind of interrogation room? Fuck, is that blood splatter on the wall? When I finish scanning it, the hairs on my arms rise as I glance at the person waiting for me.

I have no idea who he is, but sweat gathers at the back of my neck as I take him in. I'd guess he's in his fifties, but he's exceptionally fit for his age. His salt-and-pepper hair is the only thing giving away the fact that he's older. A huge scar running from his temple to his chin adds to his intimidating appearance. Add in the black cargo pants, boots, and a black T-shirt that hugs his muscles; he looks like a soldier. A deadly one.

"Sit," he instructs sternly.

Swallowing heavily, I lower myself onto one of the chairs across from him. I don't say anything. It's obvious he's here to do the talking since I have no clue who he is.

"My name is Deke Black. I'm here to make you an offer." His voice is cold and direct. I can't imagine this guy cracking a joke or laughing.

When I don't reply, he opens the thick file folder in front of him.

"All of your tests over the past five years track you as exceptionally gifted. On top of that, you're also violent and carry several traits of a psychopath, though I'm not convinced you actually are one."

What. The. Fuck. Who is this guy? A psychopath?

"I can see you think I'm an asshole, and you're correct about that. I'm also your only lifeline to get out of this world you've been living. I'm giving you a chance to start over. To be able to use your abilities without ending up here repeatedly."

I raise my eyebrows and cross my arms over my chest. "My abilities," I repeat with a huff. "Who the fuck are you?" I slam my fists down onto the wobbly table.

His expression stays relaxed. He's not the least bit bothered by my outburst. I'm not used to that. I might barely even be a teenager, but I'm bigger than most kids my age. I've always been tall, and in the past couple of years, I've built some muscle, making me look menacing to most. This guy isn't fazed.

"I work for an organization called The Agency. Specifically, I'm building a group called The Elite Team. It's a team of young men like yourself who are recruited. Once they join, they start a whole new life. A new identity. No more foster homes. And eventually, endless amounts of cash in their pockets."

I narrow my gaze. "I might be young, but I'm not dumb enough to believe you're some magic fairy coming to grant me three wishes. There's a catch."

Deke Black smiles, and it looks like it pains him to do so. "Smart boy. There is a catch. In exchange for all of that, you would become a lifetime employee of The Agency. Once you're in, you can never get out."

"What the fuck? Like ownership?"

He studies me for a second. "No. Like family. The Elite Team would be your family. And unlike the social services system, family is forever at The Agency."

Family. It's a common word. People say it all the time. Most of them never think twice about it. I'm not most people, though. I've never had anyone to call Mom or Dad. I've never had any siblings. The only life I know is being passed around from one foster home to another. And I still long for something, anything resembling a real family. The kind I see on TV. The ones who sit around the dinner table every night and talk or fight but still love each other afterward. It's something people tend to take for granted when some of us want someone to actually love us.

I lean back and stare at the man in front of me, the weight of the world suddenly weighing me down. "So I'd be exchanging one sentence for another; only your sentence lasts forever."

"Yes, but my sentence also gives you everything you've never had. Security, family, money, and the opportunity to use your abilities."

"My abilities. There you go with that again. What does The Elite Team do exactly?"

"The short explanation is they do special operations for different organizations. It's dark ops, meaning it's all done in secrecy. We are who the CIA or the FBI calls when they need a problem handling that they can't do without bringing negative attention to themselves. Most of the time, it's all for the greater good of the world. We also take contracts with different mafia syndicates and anyone else who offers enough cash."

That sounds like some kind of movie shit. Stuff that doesn't actually happen in real life.

"The CIA and FBI have you do jobs for them, but you also do stuff for the mafia? So you're a crime organization, but why would government agencies work with you, especially if they know you work with criminals?" I ask, glaring at him in disbelief.

"Believe it or not, we're not a crime organization. We do bad things, but we have the clearance to do so. The letter agencies depend on the mafia, and the mafia depends on the agencies. All of it is meant to keep peace in the world and our country safe."

"I'm confused. I'm only thirteen."

Deke nods and looks down at the papers in front of him. "Yes, but on paper you're a genius. Well beyond your years in that respect. I've watched you on the streets, and with training, you'd be ready to start doing missions within the next three years."

"Wait, so I'd have to train for three years?"

"Yes. We put our guys through rigorous training. Twelve hours a day of physical, mental, and emotional conditioning, two hours of technical, an hour for each meal, and seven hours of sleep. It's grueling but rewarding. By the time you go on your first mission, you will be a deadly trained machine able to handle any situation that could arise."

Part of me wants to laugh, and the other part wonders if I've gone insane. This isn't real. It can't be.

"Where would I live? Would I have to kill people? Could I get killed doing these so-called missions? And what if I want to have a life of my own someday? Maybe I want a wife or kids at some point. Are you saying I couldn't have any of that?"

"You would live in a compound, on a secure piece of land, with the young men who would become your brothers. You would train together, eat together, live together, and be a family together. As far as killing people, I think the question is, would that really sway your decision? Because the guy in the alley, who bled out from his throat, was pretty dead by the time you'd finished with him."

My heart pounds so hard I'm afraid it might break a rib. My hand closes into a tight fist. "That piece of shit was raping a woman at knifepoint. I don't regret killing him even if I spend the rest of my life in here. He deserved it. It's even better that he was killed with his own fucking knife."

Deke smiles again. He appears relaxed, but everything about him is in control. "Which is why you'd be a great asset for The Elite Team. You don't hurt people for the sake of it. You do it because they deserve it. To answer your question, there are no rules against having a family. However, you would still be on the team, and you would still live with your brothers; your future wife and kids would live safely on the compound."

This guy is really serious. The detention center wouldn't have allowed him to be here if he wasn't who he says he is.

"You're smart enough to know if you keep living like this, you'll be dead or in prison by the time you're twenty-five. Statistics don't lie. So the question you have to ask yourself is, do you want a lifetime of bouncing from place to place, prison to prison until you finally end up six feet under, or do you want to have a family while being able to help make the world a better place."

How is it possible for someone like me to make the

world a better place? Most of the time, I think it would be better if I weren't on this earth anymore.

"You keep saying *brothers*. Are these guys already on the team?"

"Over the next six months, I'll be recruiting agents. The Elite Team is a new unit so you would all grow together."

I narrow my eyes. "And you? You're on the team?"

Deke's eyes crinkle at the corners as he lifts his mouth into a smirk. "No. I'm on The Elect Team. It's the same format as The Elite. The Elect Team is taking a step back as we're getting older. Once trained, The Elite Team will take over the fieldwork, but we will remain active as a resource for you guys. I would be your guardian and handler within The Agency."

"Did you get recruited in the same way?" Now I'm curious about Deke Black. Who is he? How did he get here? How did he find me?

"I did. I was a little older than you when I was recruited. I didn't have a family, I was pissed off at the world, and I was already committing crimes that could have put me away for a long time. I was a lot like you. Then, a man showed up at the juvenile detention center and made me an offer. The same one I'm giving you."

"And do you regret it?"

He smiles, his Adam's apple bobbing. "Not for a second. I'd be dead by now if I'd turned him down. Either on the streets or in prison. The Agency saved my life, and I'm proud to serve for them."

"You have a family and all that?"

"I have a *Little* girl. And my brothers. It's all I need."

I'm not sure why he emphasized the word Little. I guess it doesn't matter. I don't know this man, but for some reason, I trust him. He came here to change my life. What do I have to lose?

"You really think I can do this?" I ask.

"Yes." It's all he says. Just yes. As if he doesn't have a single doubt about it.

"I'll do it."

Deke rises from his seat, and is even taller than I expected, then holds out his hand. "Welcome to The Agency."

1

EMBER

"Are you listening to me?"

No. I haven't been listening for the last twenty minutes. Not since he told me he's sending me away with some sort of bodyguard assassin. I'm not going to say that out loud, though.

My father leans back in his leather chair and laces his hands over his stomach, his face a mask of calmness. Sitting across from him, I want to pull my knees to my chest and curl into a tiny ball. Instead, my entire body trembles.

I look around the large office, wishing someone would jump out from behind a piece of furniture to tell me I'm being pranked. It would be an awful joke, but at least it would mean what my father is saying isn't real.

"I don't understand. If you think the threats aren't

anything to be worried about, why do I need a bodyguard? And why do I have to go to a safe house?"

None of it makes sense.

"Because you're my daughter and the most important thing in my life. I'll do whatever it takes to keep you safe."

I stare at my father, blinking rapidly. I want to laugh at that; surely it was a joke. Yet, he looks dead serious. If I weren't his daughter, I'd probably believe him. But I've lived with him for twenty-two years, and I know when he's lying.

Like when he goes into congressional meetings and lies his ass off about whatever it is he's trying to get passed. Or when he speaks at press conferences and answers questions with complete baloney. He's wearing the same confident yet friendly, *trust me and vote for me* expression right now as he does then.

"Why are they threatening *me*? I never appear with you. I'm not involved in anything political. I'm surprised they even know I'm your daughter."

He steeples his index fingers and rests his elbows on the desk. Then he sighs like this conversation is exhausting him. "I don't know why they are threatening you, Ember, but they are, and I'm not having you here unprotected. I've arranged for one of the best men in the country to keep you safe until we find who it is."

I lower my face into my hands and rock back and forth while trying to keep myself calm. It's getting harder to breathe with every second, and if I don't get it under control, I'm going to have a full-blown panic attack.

"Ember, are you listening?" he asks again.

Part of me wants to stomp my foot and yell at my father that I'm an adult and can decide for myself what I want. The other part of me wants to hide under my bed with Spike, so the scary people can't ever find me. Although that might not be the best hiding spot. They'd probably check there first. Maybe my closet would be a better place.

This isn't the first time my father has received threats. He's a congressman. It comes with the job. But it's the first time he's received a threat to harm me. And the scary part is, he doesn't know why they want to kill me.

"I know you're scared and don't want to go away, but it's for your safety. You'll be fine. It's only going to be for a short time until we find whoever is making these threats."

I twist my fingers together, feeling so small. I don't want to go. I want to stay here where it's familiar. I've spent enough time in strange places over the years.

When I don't say anything, he sighs heavily again. "Go pack whatever you need for a couple of weeks. My security team will get you to the bodyguard safely."

My heart stops, and my hands go cold. "I have to go right now?"

He huffs and for the first time, I notice stress lines on my father's face as he pinches the bridge of his nose. "Yes,

Ember. Go. Now. I'll be here waiting to take you to him. We need to be there in an hour."

T ears run down my cheeks as I carry a shoulder bag stuffed full of clothes, necessities, and Spike down the grand staircase. I've tried to get myself together three times already, but each time I think I'm done crying, it starts all over again.

My father is already standing by the door along with his security detail. When he sees me, he strides to the bottom of the steps, his face etched with what looks like actual concern. "It's only for a little while, Ember. A couple of weeks at most."

Yeah, but why do I feel like my father is always sending me away? Whether it was boarding school or summer camps, I've spent most of my life living elsewhere. I was shocked when I told my father I wanted to go to college locally and he agreed without too much argument. It's not that I'm especially attached to this house or living with him, but I was so tired of having roommates and never getting any alone time. I didn't want to live in a dorm. All the noise and mean girls and petty drama was too much for me.

I don't say any of this out loud, of course. Even though I want to shout and ask him to be a loving parent for once. To be present and involved in my life instead of sending me away for someone else to deal with me.

He studies me silently for a moment before he reaches into his pocket. "When you get back, things are going to be different, Ember. I know I haven't been the best dad, and it might be too late to rebuild our relationship, but if you're up for it, I'd like to try."

My mouth drops open. Did I hear him correctly? It feels like my mind is playing tricks on me. Then he pulls a necklace from his pocket, the silver twinkling under the foyer lights.

"I've got this for you. It's a compass with the coordinates for our house engraved on it. A reminder that, no matter what, this is your home, Ember." His voice is rough, like he's having a hard time speaking.

"Dad," I say tightly, trying to keep from bursting into a ball of sobs.

"I have a lot of making up to do and this is just the beginning. This will all be over in no time, and then we'll be able to start over. What do you think?"

As I stare up at him, my heart squeezing with a mix of uncertainty and hope, I hate that I can't tell if he's genuine or not. He's so good at getting people to believe him. Is this a ploy to get me out of his hair to agree to go with this bodyguard? It sucks not to know, and it sucks even more that every part of me hopes that he's telling the truth. That he really wants to have a relationship with me. Even though he hasn't been a great parent, he's still my dad.

"Okay." I swipe at my cheeks and nod. "I'd like that."

He smiles and fumbles with the clasp of the necklace. "Turn around, I'll put it on you. It's an expensive necklace, so make sure not to take it off until you're back home. I'd be devastated if you lost it. It's so special."

Bringing my fingers to the dime-sized compass, I blink several times, a watery smile on my lips. "I won't take it off, Dad. Thank you. This... It means a lot to me."

When he takes a step back, I let go of my hair and turn to face him, trying to put on a brave face. "Okay. I'm ready."

2

CAGE

"Stop wiggling."

"But you're not doing it right!"

I can wire a bomb with meticulous accuracy, but for the life of me, I can't do a Little girl's hair. At least not in her opinion. I think it looks fine.

"They're uneven," Rowie whines as she tugs one of the pigtails.

Somebody woke up on the wrong side of the bed today—I'm not quite sure if it's her or me. Some days, Rowena is an angel, and some days, she truly tests our patience. Today, I happen to be the lucky one she's testing.

"Sweetheart, they're even. They're in the same spot on each side of your head."

When she twists to look up at me from where she's

sitting on the floor, she scrunches her face. "Nuh-uh. They don't *feel* even."

I stare at her, my eye twitching slightly. Arguing with her will get me nowhere on days like today. The best I can hope for is that when she wakes up from her afternoon nap, she'll be less cranky.

"If you don't like them, you can pull them out, but I don't have time to start all over again. I have a meeting to get to."

She sighs, long and dramatic. "Theo always gets them right."

"Well, Theo isn't here, and if you don't stop complaining, I'm going to take away one of your Good Girl Points."

Rowie's face drops into disbelief. "That's so mean, Cage. I think I should take away one of your Good Boy Points for being so grumpy this morning."

Jesus.

"I don't have points because I'm in charge and you're the Little girl. Now, go find Cassian and tell him you need breakfast." And make his life a living hell for the next hour or so instead of me. I don't say that, of course.

Even though my palm is tingling and I'm already drained from Rowie running circles around me, I still love her to pieces. I couldn't imagine how mundane and lonely our lives would be without her in them. The innocence and peace she brings balance us out. She's the bright light to our darkness, and she loves us despite who we are and what we do.

I hold out my hand to help her up. When she's on her feet, I pull her in for a hug. "I love you, Little one. I'll be home tonight. Be good, okay? You're so close to having enough points to get the dolly you want."

She wraps her thin arms around me and snuggles into my chest. It feels like yesterday, instead of twelve years ago, that she was too afraid of us to speak. It took a long time to gain her trust. Even then, it took years for her to come out of her terrified shell. Now, we can barely get her to be quiet. I wouldn't have it any other way. She's the sister none of us ever had.

"I love you, too. Be safe, please." They're the same words she says to us whenever we have to leave.

"Always."

She nods and skips off toward the kitchen, her pigtails bouncing along with her. I don't care what she says, they're even. Brat.

Before I forget, I pull out my phone to send a quick text.

> **Cage:** Rowie's in a mood this morning. Proceed with caution.

> **Cassian:** Noted. Sugary cereal it is.

> **Jasper:** I don't think she slept well. I saw her tossing and turning on the baby monitor a few times.

Theo: Don't give her cereal. Jesus. The last thing she needs is to be hopped up on sugar if she's already tired. Make her some toast and eggs, then turn on a movie for her and give her a stuffie. She'll probably fall back asleep.

Cage: It's all you, Cass. I'm headed out for a meeting.

Jasper: I'm leaving and probably won't be home tonight. I have some loose ends to wrap up in Mexico.

Theo: I'm going to try to be home tonight, but this mission has been exciting so might not be until tomorrow.

Exciting is never good in our world. I guess it's a good thing we are who we are and can handle anything.

Cassian: Fuck. She's having a meltdown over her toast. It's too well-done.

I snort. Yeah, it's going to be a rough day at home.

For the entire flight to DC, my phone has been blowing up with texts from Cassian, Ghost, and Rylan pleading to be saved from the wrath of Rowie.

It's funny because, for a bunch of deadly bastards, we're pathetic when it comes to her. In a life where we do everything possible to have no weaknesses, no soft spots, she is exactly that for all of us. Which is why we keep her so protected. No matter how many jobs we have going on, at least three of us stay at The Ranch at all times because of Rowie. Unfortunately for those three assholes, today is their day.

> Cage: Good luck with the Little one, brothers. Glad it's you and not me.

> Ghost: Fuck off, bro.

> Cassian: I hope your dick falls off, man.

> Cage: That's harsh. I like my dick.

> Rylan: Probably a little too much.

I snort and put my phone away as the plane comes to a stop. Time to get to work and see why I had to fly all the way to fucking DC for a meeting with one of our CIA handlers. It's never a good sign when they ask to see us in person because it's an indication that the job is dangerous and extremely complicated.

"Thanks, Captain. I'll be ready to fly back in a few hours," I say, saluting one of the pilots we keep on payroll.

He lifts his chin but doesn't say anything as I start down the airstair.

An armored SUV waits for me nearby. I spend a few minutes checking for bombs and bugs before I climb in and start the ignition. Can't ever be too careful. Especially in our line of work. We never know who might decide to come after us.

By the time I make it up to the top floor of the modern, state-of-the-art government building where my meeting is, I'm irritated. And the handler is already waiting for me.

At least it's Ruth. Though she's already glaring at me as I walk in. She's one of my favorites of the bunch. She also seems to favor me out of the rest of my brothers, so maybe this job won't be so bad after all.

"Cage," she greets warmly as she stands and holds out her hand.

I've known this woman for twenty-plus years, but she still shakes my hand every time we see each other. That's where our formalities end, though. Especially when we're alone like this.

Her sky-high heels click on the shiny tiled floor as she strides over to me and drops a file on the table. I don't know how she walks in those fucking things.

"I have a job for you," she explains bluntly. "I'll be honest, though, it's a bit different than the type of stuff you normally do."

I shrug, unfazed. Just because it's not my usual job doesn't mean I'm not trained for it. Whatever she needs me to do, I'll complete the mission successfully because that's what The Elite Team does. That's what *I* do. Failure is not an option in dark ops.

"A congressman has reached out to me and asked for someone I trust. His daughter's life is being threatened."

Leaning back in my chair, I nod. "So, track down who is threatening her and eliminate the threat. That's no problem, Ruth. I don't think I needed to fly out here for that information, though."

The older woman stares at me and then rolls her eyes. "Cage, shut the fuck up and listen."

I chuckle and hold my hand up for her to go on. Ruth is the perfect name for her because she can be absolutely ruthless when she needs to be.

"It's a bit more complicated than that. And no, I don't need you to find out who the threat is. We have that information already."

"Then what the fuck am I doing here, Ruthie? This meeting could have been an email."

Her lined face turns into a scowl. Amusement spreads through me as she glares at me. I don't know why it's so fun to ruffle her feathers, but it is. Maybe because, around everyone else, she's nothing but professional.

"Do you want me to shoot you, Cage? Because I will if you call me Ruthie one more time. And this meeting couldn't have been an email because it's classified information, but you won't shut up long enough for me to tell you everything."

Okay, I guess the trip was worth it. Messing with her is always a blast.

,

"Yes, ma'am. Please proceed," I reply with a smirk, only irritating her more.

She sighs and rubs her temples. "I don't know why I like you as much as I do. You're a true pain in my ass."

"It's the flowers I send for your birthday each year," I answer confidently.

Her scowl softens. Ruth's husband died nearly twenty years ago. Ever since I found out that he never missed getting her favorite flowers on her birthday every year, I've been sending her a bouquet. I'm not sure why I started doing it; it felt right at the time. The tearful phone call I got from her afterward cemented it as a new tradition for me.

"As I was saying." She lowers herself into a seat across from me. "The daughter is in danger. Her father wants someone who has what it takes to protect her."

That has me sitting straighter. "What exactly are you getting at, Ruth?"

"Your mission is to protect his daughter. Take her into hiding and keep her there until this situation is resolved."

"I'm not sure when the last time you looked at my resume was, but I'm not a bodyguard."

She shoots me a bored look. She's used to my sarcastic comments. I'm pretty sure she loves them, too, based on the way her eye is twitching.

"I know you're not a bodyguard, Cage, but I promised him the best. That's you. He's concerned because whoever is threatening her claims he's taken something valuable of theirs."

I raise an eyebrow and lean back, threading my fingers together in my lap. "And has he?"

Ruth shakes her head. "No. He's a family man who lost his wife well over a decade ago and has been serving his country since then. He's put forward a substantial sum of money for his daughter's protection. You may not be a bodyguard, but for the amount he's offering, it might be worth your time."

Money means nothing to me. I have heaps of it. But if the man is prepared to pay such a large sum to keep his daughter safe, he must feel that she's in true danger.

"How old is this kid?" I ask. "I'm not a babysitter."

Rush shakes her head. "She's old enough to take care of herself. All you have to do is keep her alive."

"No limits on that?"

She smiles at me. "No limits. You have the freedom to protect her how you see fit and use your own facilities and safe locations. The less I know, the better. He would prefer she be far away from DC, though."

I let ideas roll around my head for a moment. I could take her to one of the safe houses we have in Idaho, so I'd still be close enough to Bend if I needed to go home for some reason or call in some of my other brothers to assist.

"You're still forgetting one thing, Ruthie. I'm not a fucking bodyguard. I run missions to stop terrorist attacks, to find serial killers, and to spy on other countries for delicate information. Not babysit some spoiled rich kid."

"Well, that's too bad for you because I already told him you'd do it." Her cheeks are stretched with how hard she's grinning.

Motherfucker.

Of course she did.

I pinch the bridge of my nose and count to ten. Killing a CIA handler would be bad. Very bad. Don't do it, Cage.

The mantra I repeat in my mind helps, and when I look back at the woman, I smirk. "Whatever you need, Ruthie. I'm here for you, ma'am."

My slight digs make the corners of her lips twitch, but she doesn't say anything. Instead, she gets up and glides to the door of the conference room. "She'll be at the airfield in an hour. Don't let me down, Cage."

I scoff and lift my head to ask her when I've ever let her down, but she's already gone when I do.

Fuck.

The only information in the file is a name. I scan it several times.

Ember Elizabeth Adams.

Cute.

If she's the daughter of a congressman, she's not using his last name because I don't know who her father is based on her surname. Fucking awesome. It's already complicated.

3

EMBER

The city passes by in a blur as I stare numbly out the window. My father has been on a call since we left the house. I've managed to stop crying, but now I just want to curl up in a ball and sleep. And I'm dying to snuggle Spike. I can't pull him out in front of my dad and his guards, though. I can't handle hearing my father tell me I need to grow up. Not again, at least.

I hesitated to pack Spike at all, but I couldn't leave him. I just couldn't. He's my best friend. The poor guy probably can't breathe being stuffed in there. I'll have to give him CPR. Thank goodness dragons have nine lives.

What if this bodyguard is mean? Where is he going to take me? Is my life truly at risk? Why would anyone want to come after me? I have nothing to do with politics or my father's career. I think most people forget he has a daughter because of how few times I've ever been seen with him in public.

As soon as the SUV comes to a stop, I blink several times to get my eyes to focus. I hadn't noticed where we were going. Why does it matter? I don't seem to get a say in any of this anyway.

Oh my God. Why are we at an airport?

I shake my head, my body trembling at the same time. This is not happening.

"Dad," I whimper.

"Ember, it's fine."

"No. No. I don't like planes."

He shoots me a look of annoyance and pulls his phone away from his ear. "You don't have a choice. It's a perfectly safe private jet."

My eyes burn with tears. This can't be happening. It's been nearly two decades since I've flown, and I planned never to get on one of these death traps again. I squeeze my hands together, the urge to have a meltdown simmering just below the surface.

One of the security detail opens my door and steps to the side so I can climb out. There's no way in hell I'm getting out of this car. My entire body is frozen as I stare at the enormous, shiny, white airplane with the steps lowered. My heart races. It's getting harder to breathe.

"Ember." He's using his disappointed voice, the one that always guts me and makes me feel like a terrible daughter. It won't work this time.

I turn to him, my bottom lip quivering. "I don't want to go on a plane."

Ignoring me, he presses on my seatbelt release and then gets out of the car. When he comes to my side, he and the security detail look at me expectantly.

"What's the problem here?" The deep voice comes out of nowhere, sending a shiver down my spine.

Both of them turn to face the man who's approaching. My gaze travels between them. When my eyes land on the stranger, I gasp. I'm not sure if he's as tall as he appears or if it's all his muscles that make him look huge, but the man is imposing to say the least.

"You must be Cage?" My father tilts his head back to look at him.

He nods and holds out his hand. "Cage Black."

This is my bodyguard? Why is he dressed like he's about to go into combat?

"Zeke Griffin," my father replies as they shake hands. "This is my daughter Ember."

I can't take a breath as Cage's gaze moves to me. Heat creeps up my body. Wow. He's intense. Those eyes look like they know too much. There's no way I'm going with this man.

Unable to hold his stare, I look away and cross my arms over my chest. It's a double-no for me.

Plane.

Nope.

Scary dude.

Nope.

"Ember," my father hisses.

"No," I answer between clenched teeth. "I'm not going."

"This isn't an option. It's not safe for you here. You're going with him."

"No. I'm not getting on that plane."

"What's wrong with *my* plane?" Cage asks, his eyebrows drawn together in disbelief as he looks back at it. Is he seriously offended because I don't want to go with him? "It's the safest plane on the market. I've inspected it myself."

My head snaps toward him. "Planes aren't safe. I'm not going."

The men all look at each other for a moment as if none of them are sure what to do.

"I was told there are no limits to keeping her safe." Cage turns his attention to my father for a second. "She's in my care now?"

"Yes. She's all yours," he replies.

Cage smirks and takes a step between my father and his security detail. "Great. Excuse me, gentlemen."

The next thing I know, Cage reaches into the car and plucks me off the seat with ease before tossing me over his shoulder like a bag of freaking potatoes. Then he grabs my bag, slinging it over his other shoulder, and heads toward the plane.

"You know how to get in touch," he calls out, giving a quick wave with his free hand as he starts up the steps.

"Let me down!" I scream as I pound on his back.

"I'll let you down in a minute. Just take a breath and stop kicking me."

I don't stop flailing. I'm not going to make this easy on him.

"You're kidnapping me! What kind of person kidnaps a woman?"

"Not kidnapping you, firefly."

"I don't want to go!" I squeal.

He chuckles. Actually freaking laughs at me. Jerk.

"It's cute that you think you get a choice, firefly."

I pound on his back some more, though it probably feels more like a massage to him; he's so dang big and muscular.

He's not even winded. Why is he in such good shape? It's not fair.

When he flips me into a plush leather seat, he grins and holds onto the armrests, blocking me in. "There ya' go. Nice and comfy. That wasn't so hard, was it?" he asks, his voice dripping with sarcasm.

Snarling at him, I reach out and pinch his forearm, twisting as hard as I can. He doesn't flinch.

"Keep doing that, firefly, and you might be flying with a hot ass."

I gasp and let go of him, biting back a slew of insults. Who does he think he is?

He looks so pleased with himself as he takes a step back before I can kick him right in the balls. It's not fair that he's so good-looking because he's a real asshole. As soon as I get off this death trap, I hope it does crash.

I'm halfway up when I realize the plane is already moving. Oh, God. Dropping down again, I grab the safety belt and fasten it, tightening it as hard as I can while Cage walks around the cabin like nothing is happening. Doesn't he know he's about to die? That we're going to die in a minute?

"Ready for takeoff, Mr. Black," one of the captains calls from the cockpit.

"Thanks." Cage casually sits across from me. He doesn't buckle up. Even though I hate him, I don't actually want him to die.

"You're supposed to fasten your safety belt," I say in a small voice.

He looks at me, his eyes dark and studying. "You don't like flying."

I stare at him, unblinking. Is he an idiot? Was it not completely obvious to him?

My irritation quickly disappears, replaced with cold-hard, sweat-induced fear as the plane picks up speed on the runway. I grip the armrests of my seat so hard that my knuckles turn white as I wait for the moment this tuna can drops to the ground after lift-off.

"Ember." His voice is deep yet gentle, bringing me out of the spiral of panic I'm tumbling down.

When I look at him, he isn't smiling anymore. No, he looks concerned. And maybe even a little regretful.

He leans forward and stares at me like he's trying to figure me out. "Why don't you like flying?"

I blink as sadness takes hold of my heart and squeezes so tightly that it actually hurts. Bringing my hand up near my chin, I rub my thumb just below my lip. "My mom died in a helicopter crash when I was five."

Almost as if I've slapped him, he sits back abruptly. "Fuck."

That's it. He doesn't say anything else.

After a few minutes, when the pilots let him know that we're no longer climbing altitude, he gets up and heads to the front of the plane, returning a moment later. "Here, this might help with your anxiety." He lowers a warm blanket over me, and almost instantly, my panic eases.

Okay, that was nice of him. Maybe he's not the worst person in the world. Maybe this time away, wherever we're going, won't be so bad.

Unfortunately, that comfort only lasts about twenty minutes until one of the pilots announces over the intercom, "Mr. Black, we have a plane following our tail."

4

CAGE

I'm not a fucking bodyguard.

I don't deal with people. Or emotions. The only woman I can handle is Rowie, and even she's a test of my abilities sometimes.

The problem with dealing with humans is that nothing is concrete. I can calculate how long it will take for a grenade to explode or the distance I need to hit a specific target within a centimeter, but emotions have never been my strong point. Reading the room is a challenge, even on my best days. When I dropped Ember into her chair and saw the color drain from her face, I felt like the biggest asshole in the world. That was before I actually registered the look of pure fear on her face. If Rowie ever looked at me like that, I would die.

As bad as I feel, I can't think about that right now. There are bigger issues at hand. Like, why the fuck is someone tailing us, and who are they? If they're the people threatening Ember, it means they've been watching her this entire time. And if they have a plane of their own, this isn't a simple threat. They have money, which means it's not money they're after. So, what could it be?

Shit.

Why do I feel like Ruth didn't give me the full magnitude of this job?

Ember pales. She looks around the plane as if she wants to bolt, but there's nowhere for her to go. Not that I'd let her anyway. I'd have her captured in a heartbeat. Then I'd have her over my knee for trying to run away.

If we continue to Idaho, we'll be leading them right to the safe house. That's not an option. I quickly look through my GPS while formulating a plan.

"Land at the airstrip in Illinois. I'll work on getting a car to meet us there."

Without wasting a second, I grab the untraceable phone we all carry around and call Ghost.

"Speak," he answers, knowing this isn't a call for pleasantries.

"I need an armored SUV at our airfield in Illinois. And a dozen armed men to escort me plus one from a plane."

"How long?"

"One hour, five minutes."

"Ten-four."

As soon as Ghost ends the call, I find Cassian's name.

"Speak."

"I have a plane tailing me, and I need to know who the fuck it is."

Cassian is already typing in the background. "Can you see what kind of plane? Any numbers or colors on it?"

"Stay put," I tell Ember sharply as I rise to go to the cockpit. She startles at my tone. Shit, I'm an asshole. I probably need to be more gentle with her. She's terrified. Right now, though, I have a more pressing issue to handle.

The next few minutes are spent trying to find anything identifiable on the other aircraft, but we come up with nothing. Whoever is flying it is smart. They're keeping a distance and staying in a blind spot almost constantly.

"I'll work on this and get back to you," Cassian says, then abruptly ends the call.

"If they get closer or do anything other than keep our tail, let me know," I tell the pilots before I turn and stride away, a feeling of urgency to return to Ember settling in my stomach.

"What's happening?" she whispers, her dark eyes sparkling with tears.

I kneel in front of her, hoping to comfort her in some way. In any way. I can't stand seeing her like this. Mad, sure. Scared and sad, I don't like it. Not one bit. She won't stop shivering despite how warm it is. She blinks, sending a stream down her cheeks. Fuck, I'm such an asshole.

"I'm not sure yet. I'm putting things in place so we can land safely and get into a car. My brother is trying to figure out who is following us. Do you know anything about who is threatening you, Ember?"

She shakes her head and for the second time since we've been on the plane, she starts rubbing just below her bottom lip with her thumb. It reminds me of when Rowie sucks her thumb. Something she does when she's stressed or frightened. Maybe stroking her chin is soothing for Ember?

"I don't know anything. My father told me an hour ago about all of this." She sniffles, and I can't help but notice the smattering of freckles on the bridge of her nose. Adorable. Too damn innocent for someone like me.

"We're going to crash and die, aren't we?"

Her voice is so fucking small, and she's curled herself up into the tightest ball that her safety belt will allow. I want to layer blankets over her just to get her to stop shaking. The problem is that won't work. She isn't cold. She's fucking terrified. I bunch my hands into fists to keep from pulling her onto my lap to comfort her. She's a client who I'm meant to protect, not coddle.

"No, Ember. If anything went wrong with the plane, I have parachutes available for emergency evacuation."

When her skin turns green and her eyes bulge, I curse under my breath. I don't think that was the best answer to give.

"No matter what happens, you're not going to die with me. My job is to protect you, and I never fail. Understand me, firefly?"

She studies me for a few seconds before she gives a slow nod. "I don't like planes."

I huff and lift one corner of my mouth. "I'm starting to get that. After we land this birdie, I won't put you on another one."

"Promise?"

If she keeps looking at me the way she is, with her big round eyes and pouty lips, I'll promise her the goddamn universe. How anyone has ever told her no, I'm not sure.

"I swear. Now, I want you to turn on a movie and focus on that for the rest of the flight. We'll be on the ground in no time."

A s planned, a swarm of security surrounds us as we deplane and load up into an SUV. The plane following us doesn't land, which I'd counted on since the airfield I chose only has space for one plane. They obviously don't want to cause a crash. Whoever is a threat to Ember doesn't want her dead. So, they're not after money, and they aren't trying to kill her. What the fuck could they possibly want?

After driving for twenty minutes, I pull over and we switch vehicles again. We'll continue changing vehicles along the way to stay under the radar.

Ember has been silent since our conversation while we were in the air, but she has complied with every instruction I've given her. That thrills me and causes my dick to ache against the zipper of my pants. I want to tell her how good she's being, but it's not my job to praise her. I'm here to keep her safe. Thankfully, the second we touched the ground, her shaking stopped, and the haunted expression she wore disappeared.

I pull out my cell and call Cassian again.

"I see you, brother," he says when he answers, his voice coming over the speakers. "Car number four is waiting for you."

"Thanks. I'm heading to safe house twelve for tonight."

"I'll let Ghost know. What's your plan after that?"

"Right now, I'm not sure. I need to talk to Ruth. Something tells me she's withholding information. Whoever the fuck was tailing us isn't some broke amateur after her father's money."

Cassian curses under his breath. "I can have another plane ready in an hour. Bring her here. This is the safest place for her."

He's right. The Ranch is the most secure place to protect her, plus my brothers would help to keep her safe as well.

Ember gasps, and without thinking, I reach over and squeeze her hand. "No planes," I tell him while keeping my eyes locked with hers.

Cassian pauses his typing in the background. "No planes? It will take days for you to drive here."

I wink at Ember. "It's not an option."

My brother stays quiet for a moment, then clears his throat. "Okay. I'll have cars ready and waiting along the way. Sending a route now. Rylan and Koda are going to fly out to meet you in Nebraska so you can get here within forty-eight hours."

I almost tell him that I don't need him to send anyone. Because, for some reason, I don't want this time with Ember to be interrupted. I want to have her to myself. Her safety comes first, though. "Yeah. Sounds good."

We end the call, and I quickly load the route he sent me onto the GPS. Cassian will continue to track us, but for the time being, it's just the two of us.

"Who are Rylan and Koda?" she asks.

"My brothers."

"Oh. How many brothers do you have?"

"A lot."

What I don't tell her is that none of us are related by blood and that we are all trained to be the deadliest men in the world. She may only be a client, but I don't want to see disgust on her face when she finds out what a monster I am.

The silence is awkward as fuck. She's been restless for the past hour, and I'm not sure what will fix that.

"Why are you wiggling so much?" I finally question.

She turns her head, and when I glance at her, she blushes. "I need to use the bathroom."

Fuck.

Swerving to the side of the road, I park. "Wait for me to come around."

When I throw open her door, her eyes widen and her mouth drops open.

"Come on." I hold out my hand to help her down, but she doesn't take it.

"There's no bathroom here."

I look around the deserted road and peer over at a bush that looks like a perfectly good peeing area for me.

"Go behind that shrub over there. I can find some tissue or a leaf for you."

She blinks, like she doesn't understand what I just said. I'm pretty sure I made it clear.

"Are you high? I am not peeing behind a tree. I need a toilet. With a door!" She crosses her arms over her chest and glares at the windshield for a second, then turns to look at me again. "And not a freaking leaf to clean myself up, thank you very much."

"Why not?"

Her cheeks turn red, and she closes her eyes. "Because girls pee on their feet when they squat behind a bush.

And with my luck, you'd give me a poison ivy leaf and I'd break out in hives down there. No, thank you. Not happening."

Tipping my head to the side, I consider that for a second. "Why would you pee on your feet? Maybe you're not doing it right. Do you need me to show you?"

She gasps and stares at me in silence for a few seconds. Then she reaches out and closes the door, leaving me to look at her through the window.

What the fuck just happened?

Why is she so upset?

I don't get it. Why can't girls just pee on the floor? Their aim can't be that bad, right? I need to do some research on this because, once again, I think I've misread the situation, and Ember is once again pissed off at me.

Shaking my head, I stride around the SUV while wishing I had a bomb to dismantle instead of having to try to figure out the little red-haired woman inside the car. Bombs are much more reasonable. They don't talk back. Or make my dick hard.

5

EMBER

I s he kidding me?

We're out in the middle of nowhere, and he expects me to squat behind a freaking tree? I have no clue what kind of predators they have out here. Rattlesnakes? Spiders? I can just imagine it: As soon as I squat down in an attempt not to pee on my feet, a deadly snake would slither right up and bite me right on my ass, and then I'd end up peeing all over myself. I think I'd rather get on another plane. Actually, no. I wouldn't. I don't care for any of these options.

Today freaking sucks.

I really need to go, though. I've needed to go since before we got off the plane. Cage has been so busy with trying to figure out a plan that I didn't want to bother him. But I think I'd rather wet myself than go out in the wild.

Cage climbs into the driver's seat and tilts his head to look at me. "It's about twenty minutes until the next restroom. Can you wait?"

"Yes," I bite out, hoping I'm telling the truth.

Every second stretches on, and every slight bump almost makes me wish I'd gone behind the bush. I've held my bladder way past its limit, and it's becoming painful.

Thankfully, he seems to realize it. As soon as we pull into a rest stop, he rushes around the car and quickly helps me get out, then leads me to the lone brick building. I squeeze my thighs together as tightly as I can as each step becomes more urgent.

I'm nearly running by the time we reach the metal door, and I don't even look back as I hustle inside, slamming the stall closed behind me. I'm mid-pee when the door opens, and heavy steps move inside.

"Are you okay?" Cage asks.

I yelp, nearly falling off the toilet at the sound of his voice. Unable to stop peeing, I screech and bring my hands up to cover my face even though he can't see me.

"Cage, get out!" I scream.

Instead of doing just that, he chuckles. "You're just peeing, Ember. It's a human function. Besides, I wanted to be here in case you needed help."

"I think I can go to the bathroom by myself."

I definitely can. What could I possibly need help with? My cheeks heat, and I look up at a spot on the ceiling. My clit does a little spasm, though, and I don't know what the heck that's all about.

"You might be able to, but sometimes Little girls need help cleaning themselves up or washing their hands."

Little girls.

Ohmygosh.

Does he know?

Did he look in my bag and find Spike?

No. He was right behind me. He wouldn't have had time to do that.

I quickly dry myself and flush, then step out of the stall. Cage is leaning against the wall directly across from me. Glaring, I stomp past him to the sinks.

"We need to talk about personal boundaries," I hiss.

He pushes off the wall and shrugs, then follows me and turns on the water before I have the chance. "Yeah, I'm not really good with those. Wash your hands."

This guy is making me dizzy. One second, he seems halfway human, and the next, he says stuff like that.

"Well, you need to learn some. Like not coming into the bathroom with me. I'm perfectly capable of." I flap my hands, hoping to make him understand what I'm trying to say. When he looks confused, I huff. "...*cleaning* myself up," I squeak.

"Don't know why it's a big deal. There's nothing wrong with needing help with some of your basic needs, firefly." He hands me a wad of paper towels. I'm trying not to think about the fact he helped me by turning on the water to wash my hands and giving me something to dry them with. And what does he mean by *basic needs*?

"I don't need help. I'm a big girl," I reply before I brush past him to leave.

Before I can touch the door, he grabs the handle and steps so close to me that my back is pressed against his front.

"Do not *ever* step out of a door before me. Do you understand?" His voice is low and stern. There isn't a drop of sarcasm in it. No, this is a new side of Cage.

My bottom clenches, and the part of me I want to keep a secret peeks out the tiniest bit. No. I don't want him to know. He probably already thinks I'm a freak.

"Sorry," I whisper shakily.

He doesn't move, and I have to fight the urge to melt into his warmth. I don't like him. He's my bodyguard. Not my friend. Not my Daddy.

"It's for your protection, Ember." His voice is softer now. "I'm lenient on a lot of things, but safety isn't one of them."

I nod and swallow hard, unable to speak with the knot in my throat. What exactly does he mean by *lenient*?

He steps in front of me, which is when I notice he has a gun pulled out as he opens the bathroom door and looks around. Using his free hand, he grabs one of mine and leads me back to the SUV.

As soon as I'm in my seat, he leans over to buckle me in, and I can't breathe again. His freshwater scent, his solid broadness, his penetrating dark eyes, all of him is so close to me. As soon as I hear the click, I expect him to pull away, but he pauses and stares at me intently for a beat before taking a step back and closing the door.

Whoa. What's happening? Why am I aroused? This kind of thing only happens when I'm reading or fantasizing in the pitch black of my bedroom at night.

We sit in silence for nearly an hour before he finally speaks.

"You need to tell me the next time you need to go to the bathroom. It's not good for you to hold it."

I peer over at him, ready to roll my eyes, but the serious look he shoots my way keeps me from doing that. I don't think he's being sarcastic.

"You were kind of busy," I reply quietly.

I learned at a young age not to interrupt my father when he was busy. I thought maybe if I left him alone as much as possible, he wouldn't keep sending me to boarding school. It never worked.

Cage sighs. "It doesn't matter how busy I am. If you need something, you tell me. If you're hungry, tell me. If you need to pee, say so. I can't take care of you if I don't know what you need."

Oh.

He has to stop saying things that speak to my Little side. The last thing I need is to slip into that headspace because once I'm there, I can't snap out of it quickly.

Thankfully, I've learned to suppress it over the years so I'm overly aware when those feelings are surfacing.

"It's not your job to take care of me. I'm a big girl."

This time, the look he gives me is anything but serious. He raises an eyebrow and smirks. A dimple appears on his cheek, and I can't keep from staring at it. How is it that Cage is both terrifying and hot at the same time? I bet he has girls crawling all over him. Hot ones. Like models. Not skinny, freckly redheads like me with no boobs and no butt. It's truly unfair just how good-looking he is. I kind of hate him for it.

"Are you?"

I blink several times, drawing my eyebrows together. "Am I what?"

What were we talking about? I got distracted by his pretty face.

"A big girl. Because from what I've seen of you, throwing a tantrum, refusing to tell me you have to pee, then having another tantrum about me following you into the bathroom, I'm starting to wonder if you actually are."

"I didn't have a tantrum." I huff as I roll my eyes.

Nice, Ember. Real good argument. I'm really showing him.

"Whatever you say," he replies, though his tone is dripping with sarcasm.

I have a feeling it's going to be a very long few days with Cage. Hopefully, his brothers aren't as annoying.

"How many brothers do you have?" I ask again. I've

lost track of how many people he's talked to on the phone since we were on the plane. He called multiple men brother.

"Fourteen."

"Fourteen?" I repeat louder than I mean to. But sheesh, that's a lot of freaking brothers.

"None of us are blood-related. We're all sort of... adopted," he adds.

I scrunch my face, confused by his statement, but as someone who grew up without any siblings or really any family, I guess he's pretty lucky to have so many people in his life.

"Are they all bodyguards too?"

He gives me a sideways glance. "None of us are bodyguards."

That makes me sit up straighter. "What?"

Oh my God. Did my father hand me off to the wrong person? Is Cage here to kill me?

"Relax, firefly. We're fully qualified to protect you. It's just not what we typically do."

Bringing my hand up to my racing heart, I let out a breath. "What do you normally do?"

Cage shrugs. "Bad shit. For the greater good. Things Little girls like you don't need to know about."

"Oh, that makes me feel better," I mutter.

He chuckles. "Just speaking the truth, firefly. You're too fucking innocent to know the details of what we do. I'm not a good man, but of all the men in the world, I'm the one who can and *will* keep you safe."

I believe him. Though I won't tell him that. His head already barely fits through a doorway. He might be a bit strange at times. Eccentric, maybe. Cocky as heck. Way too good-looking for his own good. But...

Crap.

I think I like Cage Black.

6

CAGE

Rylan and Koda are waiting for us when we arrive at our meeting spot. And just like we've already done a couple of times, I move Ember from the SUV into the one my brothers brought. One of our contracted people who arrived with them takes my vehicle and drives in a different direction to throw off anyone who might be trying to follow us.

Koda doesn't say anything, but Rylan decides to be Rylan, sending a prickle of irritation down my spine.

"You must be Ember." He flashes his bright white smile at her. "I'm Rylan. This big guy over here is Koda, but you can ignore him. You should probably ignore Cage, too. I hear we're going on a road trip. We're going to have a blast."

Ember giggles and reaches out to shake his hand.

Meanwhile, I'm shooting daggers at my brother, trying to decide whether to annihilate him now or wait until later when he's sleeping and least expecting it. Because he sure as fuck can tell it's coming based on the smirk that he gives me as Ember climbs into the back seat.

"She's cute," he mouths.

I shake my head and drag my finger across my throat as if I'm slitting it, which will happen to him if he doesn't keep his eyes and thoughts to himself.

"She's a client," I snap after I shut her into the car.

"Uh-huh. Weird, considering we're not bodyguards," Rylan replies with a shrug before he rounds the hood to the passenger side and gets in.

Almost as soon as he does, he says something that makes Ember laugh again. Fucking asshole.

I don't know why I care that he's making her smile and laugh. It doesn't matter. It's not my job to get her to like me. I'm here to protect her. To keep her alive and safe.

Normally, people find me so damn likable, and for whatever reason, she hates me. I still don't fucking know why she had such a problem with me following her into the bathroom. Maybe I should ask Rowie. She might be able to explain it to me in a way I'll understand. Although, I'm pretty sure Ember was the unreasonable one. Not me.

As soon as I get into the SUV next to her, Ember's smile falls, and she stops talking. Yeah, I don't like that.

"We need food," I tell Koda.

He nods, and twenty minutes later, we're in a drive-thru line.

"What do you want?" I ask her.

Ember glances out to the menu. "A burger with no lettuce or pickles or mustard. Fries. Oh, and a Mountain Dew."

"Koda," I murmur. "Sprite."

"Got it," he replies, then turns toward the speaker. "Need a number one with no lettuce, pickles, or mustard. And a Sprite."

"Mountain Dew," Ember hisses, tapping Koda on the shoulder.

"A small Sprite," I add.

Koda repeats my order before he pulls forward.

"I wanted Mountain Dew," Ember snaps, glaring at me.

I shrug and lean my head against the seat. "That's full of caffeine. You're having Sprite."

She scoffs and scrunches her nose.

Something settles inside me, but I'm not sure what it is. She might not realize she's a Little, though I'm almost positive she is. It's possible she doesn't even know about Age Play. Lots of Littles have no clue about it until they finally discover what it is and begin to understand their true selves. Whatever the case, it's not up to me to expose her to what she might be. Maybe being around Rowie will open her eyes.

"I don't like Sprite."

"You may have Sprite, water, or juice," I reply firmly.

The corner of Koda's mouth twitches, but he doesn't say anything. Meanwhile, my other asshole of a brother twists around to look at Ember.

"You know what's really good?" Rylan asks. "Adding some cherry flavoring to the Sprite. It's fucking delicious. You should try it."

Ember's eyes light up, and she sits a little taller. She looks Little, and something churns inside me.

"Do they do that here? Can I try it?" she asks.

Rylan nods and leans over the center console to talk past Koda to the cashier. As he does, Ember glares at me and crosses her arms over her chest.

Man, if she were mine, she'd be sitting on a red ass right now and Rylan would be roadkill.

Thank fuck she's only a client.

When the food gets handed to Koda, I grab the bag and her soda, then go about unwrapping her burger. She watches me curiously but doesn't say anything. I hold it out for her, pleased when she takes it and starts eating.

Us three guys wolf down an obscene amount of food while she eats at a snail's pace. When she's halfway through, she wraps the burger and shakes her head.

"Do you not like it?" I ask.

"My stomach hurts."

Panic rushes through me. "What's wrong? Do you need to vomit? Fuck. Koda, pull over."

Ember reaches over and puts her hand on my forearm, instantly soothing me in a way I don't expect.

"I'm fine. I think it's because of everything that's happening. I woke up this morning thinking I would go pick up my final transcripts and then take myself out for a celebratory piece of cake. Instead, my life is being threatened, I had to go on a stupid plane, and I'm now driving across the country with three men I don't even know."

Her eyes sparkle with tears. As soon as the first one falls, it guts me. I hadn't considered how she must feel about all of this. Does she know what's going on? Has her father told her anything at all? I need to do some research on the guy. I didn't get a good feeling about him when we met, and I'm rarely wrong about these things. Reading social situations isn't always the easiest for me but being able to tell if someone is trustworthy is something I excel at. And something tells me Ember's father isn't a man to put much faith into. His weak handshake was the first clue. The second was that he wouldn't look me directly in the eye. He kept his gaze on my chin the entire time. A man who can't look another man in the eye isn't to be trusted in my book.

Without whether it's the right thing to do or not, I use my thumb to swipe one of her tears away. She blinks several times as if I surprised her, but she doesn't pull away.

"I know this is scary, firefly. I promise you're safe with us. I'll never let anything happen to you."

She looks up at me like she's trying to decide if she can believe what I'm telling her. When she finally nods, I let out a deep exhale. I don't know why it feels so important that she trusts me, but it does.

"You just finished college?"

"Yes."

"What did you go to school for?"

Why the fuck do I care?

"I got a degree in English Lit."

I quirk an eyebrow. "A politician's kid, and you got a degree in Lit? Surprised your father was okay with that."

A ghost of a smile spreads on her face. "He wasn't happy about it. He wanted me to follow in his footsteps. There's no way in hell I'm stepping foot into that world, and he knew it, so he didn't try to argue with me."

"And what are you planning to do with that degree?"

Her expression sobers, and she sighs, not saying anything for several seconds. "I honestly don't know. Everyone's been asking me that for the past four years. My teachers, my father, his campaign manager, people who have no business asking, though they think they have the right since I'm a politician's daughter. I should know exactly what I'm going to do, but I don't."

"It's okay not to know."

For the first time since I dragged her from her father's car, she smiles at me. A real, genuine smile that makes my heart pound harder.

"Thanks," she says quietly.

Giving her a nod, I hand over her soda and take the wrapped-up burger from her. "We'll stop for more food in a bit. The Sprite will help settle your tummy."

"Sprite is so gross," she mumbles.

I shoot her a stern look as she takes a drink. Her head pulls back in surprise as she stares at the cup for a second. Then she starts sucking it again.

"Oh my God, this is so good."

Rylan looks back at her and winks, and my mood instantly sours. Why the fuck is he being so flirty with her? And why does she seem to enjoy it? He's a dead man.

Nothing but darkness surrounds us. We're driving in the middle of nowhere in the middle of the night.

Ember finally fell asleep an hour or so ago, and I haven't stopped watching her. Every time I try to focus on something else, my attention is drawn back to her. Yet I continue to try to fight it.

All three of our phones sound with our message tones, and when I look at mine, I chuckle.

> Lex: Why is it that when it's time for Rowie to go to bed, she's suddenly dying of thirst, needs to use the toilet half a dozen times, and wants to know the meaning of life?

Theo: You fucking idiot. She's stalling. Tell her to go to sleep or she'll lose five Good Girl Points.

Cage: I don't know. She made me feel like a real asshole this morning when I threatened to take some away.

Rylan: Get ready because there's about to be another Little in the house, and she's nearly as sassy as Row.

I silently growl at my brother. Why is he talking about Ember like he knows her? I don't like it.

Cage: Shut the fuck up, Rylan. We don't know if she's Little.

Rylan: Cage is a bit touchy about Ember. I can feel his eyes burning into the back of my head right now as he glares at me.

Ghost: Ah, shit. Does Cage have a crush? Is she actually Little?

Theo: Rowie has never been around another Little. It might be good for her.

Cage: Or it could be a fucking disaster. We don't know for sure that Ember is Little.

Cassian: Way to be positive, Cage. BTW, why the hell didn't you want another plane?

Cage: Ember is terrified of flying.

Ghost: C-R-U-S-H

Cage: Fuck off, Ghost.

"Hey," Koda murmurs quietly.

I glance up at him and then follow the direction of his gaze. My heart thuds against my sternum as I take in the sight of Ember, sound asleep with her head resting against the window and her thumb firmly lodged in her mouth.

She looks so fucking small and innocent. A surge of protectiveness washes over me.

I'm going to keep her safe.

Forever.

When I look at Koda again, Rylan is turned in the front passenger seat, staring back at her.

Leaning forward so my face is only inches from his, I give him a death stare. "Keep looking at her like that and I'll end you," I say quietly.

Rylan chuckles and winks at me before turning to face forward again and muttering something about me being a jealous bastard.

Fuck him.

I'm not jealous. I'm being protective. Maybe more than I should, but I can't help it. She brings it out in me even more than usual.

Ember is a client. That's all. It's my job to keep her safe. Not that Rylan would ever harm her. He would give his life to protect her if it came down to it. We all would.

It's the life we signed up for. Just because he wouldn't hurt her, though, doesn't mean I want him looking at her like he was. Hell, I shouldn't be looking at her like that, either. There's just something too fucking sweet about her. Every second I'm near her, it becomes harder and harder to remember why she's the last thing I need in my life.

"You need to tell me everything you know about this job because it seems you may have left some shit out."

Rylan and Koda are standing guard outside of a rest-stop bathroom while I make a call to Ruth to chew her ass out.

"What are you talking about, Cage?"

I huff and shake my head. "Don't bullshit me, Ruth. The second I left DC, there was a plane following me. Who exactly is after Ember, and what do they want with her?"

"I don't know."

"What do they think her father has?"

"I don't know."

"Jesus Christ," I snap. "Then what the fuck do you know, Ruth? I can't keep her safe and stay ahead of the threat if I don't have all the information."

"Don't be an asshole, Cage. You know I would give you

more details if I had them. We weren't even sure the threat was a credible one."

I pace, keeping my eyes on the bathroom. I'm not sure why. My brothers are there to keep lookout. If it were me, I'd be inside that restroom. I don't give a fuck if it's crossing a boundary or not. Honestly, I'm surprised Koda didn't bulldoze his way in after her. He's so goddamn over the top sometimes.

"Well, I'd say they are credible, Ruth," I grind out, barely holding on to my temper. This is fucking bullshit. Giving me a mission without the correct details can be a death sentence. She knows that—so why the fuck does she not seem concerned? "I need you to find out more information."

Ruth sighs, and I can practically picture her seething on the other end of the phone. The woman doesn't like being told what to do.

"I'll be in touch," she says before ending the call.

It doesn't matter what she finds out. As soon as we arrive at The Ranch in a few more hours, I'll get to work finding the information myself. Ruth might be CIA, but I'm Cage fucking Black, and her resources don't have shit on mine. If she hadn't sprung this job on me, I'd be a lot more prepared.

"Ready?" I ask when Ember shuffles wearily out of the bathroom. I should have followed her in there to help. She's too drained to take care of herself right now. That's what Daddies are for.

Fuck, goddammit. I'm not her Daddy, though.

She needs more sleep. I hate seeing those dark circles under her eyes. Maybe I'll put her down for a nap when we get home.

No. I won't put her down for anything. She's not my Little girl. She's a client. And for whatever fucking reason, I seem to keep forgetting that.

7

EMBER

Rows of trees line the road on both sides. Twenty minutes ago, we were passing through a small city, and now it's like we're in the middle of a dense forest. It's beautiful. So many shades of green. I've never seen so much stunning land. It's not like this in DC.

I feel like I can actually breathe here.

"Only a couple more miles until we reach the house," Cage tells me.

This is where he lives? Out in the middle of nowhere? I'm not sure what I expected, but I didn't think it would be like this. Do they have running water out here? Oh, God. Maybe he pees behind a bush on a regular basis. That's why he acted so casual about wanting me to do it. I won't survive. I'm not a roughing-it kind of girl. I don't need anything fancy, but a toilet and a shower are a minimum requirement. What if they live in tents? Or a shack with no heat and electricity.

Don't panic, don't panic, don't panic.

"You live in the woods?" I ask hesitantly.

Koda chuckles. "Not quite."

Just as he says it, the thick clusters of trees become sparser until we reach an enormous clearing. I perk up, leaning forward to try to get a better look out of the front windshield. What seemed like the middle of nowhere now resembles a neighborhood you'd see in a wealthy area in the suburbs.

Meticulous grounds, perfectly green grass in every yard. As we round the bend, another large, two-story farmhouse comes into view; only it's not like the others. I've never seen a farmhouse quite like this. The other houses are dwarfed in comparison. I can't be sure by looking at it, but it's probably twice the size of my father's mansion. Kind of odd to have it in the middle of a compound like this. Not that there's anything wrong with the other homes. They've been built with beautiful crafts-manship, however, they're on a different level than the big one.

"What is this place?"

My gaze darts around the area, taking in everything. It's like all the homes are built with the backs all facing in, so it's one huge circle with a playground and pool in the middle. In the center of it all is a garden with several benches and a stone fountain. It reminds me of a park my mom used to take me to when I was a kid. I smile, my heart squeezing at the memory.

"This is where we live." Cage points toward the homes. "The big house is where we spend most of our time. It holds our offices. Then, we each have our own individual places. We call this compound The Ranch. We own over a hundred acres all around. There are multiple lines of security surrounding the entire property. No one gets in or out of here without triggering a dozen alarms and setting off traps."

My mouth hangs open as I take it all in because this was absolutely not what I was expecting. I'm not sure how they had the ability to build something like this in the middle of the freaking Oregon forest.

"This is amazing," I murmur. "I can barely breathe. It's so beautiful."

Even though I'm looking out the window, I can feel his gaze on me. "It's our home, and for now, it's yours too, firefly."

Those damn butterflies, or maybe they are fireflies, erupt in my tummy again. Why do I like it when he calls me that? I can't remember anyone ever calling me a cute nickname.

"I guess being kidnapped by a bodyguard has its perks." I blush and dip my head. Whoops. Didn't mean to say that out loud.

Cage chuckles. "Didn't kidnap you, firefly."

He can call it what he wants. I call it kidnapping.

Although staring out at this beautiful landscape, I might not mind it so much.

Koda dropped Cage and me off in front of his house, which isn't as impressive as the larger one but still nothing to blink an eye at. Every one of the homes here is built farmhouse style with wraparound porches and shutters framing all the windows. I've never seen such a beautiful setting. My father's mansion is gorgeous, of course, but it's snooty and pretentious, just like the five Corvettes in his garage. It's clear The Ranch was built with tons of money. Each home is full of character, though.

As soon as Koda drives off, the two of us stare at each other awkwardly.

"Come on. I'll show you your room." He reaches out and takes my bag from me, then slings it over his muscular shoulder. I feel like such a shrimp compared to him. No wonder he could toss me around like I weigh nothing.

So hot.

Cringing, I scrunch my nose. Cage Black is not hot. I mean, he is, but not to me. Nope. Definitely not.

As soon as we step inside, a blanket of warmth fills me, and the smell of burning firewood lingers in the air.

"One of my brothers came by and lit a fire for us. It can still get chilly up here this time of year."

I nod, following him through the house and taking everything in. There isn't a lot of décor. The walls are painted a soft beige color that gives a calming feel to the place.

There's an awkward tension hanging between us, and I'm not sure what to make of it. Is it because we're alone again? Or is it because I'm in his home? I'm not even sure if it's sexual or just good ol' tension because of the situation.

"Sorry to be intruding on your space," I mumble. "I'll try not to be a burden."

Because that's what I've always been. A burden to my father. To my teachers. And now to Cage. The other people I don't really care about, yet for some reason, I don't like the thought of being a pain in the ass for Cage.

Without warning, he hooks a finger under my chin, lifting it so I'm forced to look up into his nearly black eyes. A small scar on his forehead catches my attention, and I want to ask about it. Did he get it as a boy while playing? Or is it job-related?

"Hey," he says softly. "You're not intruding. I want you to be comfortable here and make this place your home. There's a pool, a playground, and a sandbox in the back, and there's a movie theater and library in the main house. The rule is that I know where you are at all times. Understand me?"

When he talks like that and gets all stern and serious, it does things to me that I'm not sure I want to think too deeply about. Like why my panties are soaked.

"Yes," I murmur. "Why do you have a playground? Do you guys have kids?"

Cage rubs his thumb over my chin as he stares down at me, a small smile at the corners of his lips. "No kids, firefly."

Then he takes a step back and pulls his hand away, taking all his warmth with him. Gosh, the man smells yummy. Manly. We both need to shower, but the scent of his cologne still lingers.

"Come, I'll show you your room, then take you to the main house for introductions and rules."

What is it with this guy and rules? Is he a control freak? It seems like it. Then again, I guess most bodyguards want to be in control at all times. He said this is not his normal job. I don't actually understand what he does, but it sounds dangerous and maybe even illegal.

The bedroom he leads me to is as bare as the rest of the house, but the furniture and linens are definitely high-end and match the cream-colored walls, giving the entire room a serene feel. I can hardly wait to crawl into the bed, though I might need a step stool to get into it. Why is it so dang high?

"There's a bathroom through there and a walk-in closet here. My bedroom is the next one over. There's a trapdoor in your closet with stairs leading to a tunnel. All our houses connect down there. If anything ever goes down, you get in that tunnel and stay there until I find you. Got it?"

"Ominous much?"

He flashes me a smile. "Just prepared, firefly. This compound is the safest place on Earth for you to be. We have things in place here to keep everyone safe at all times. Every closet in every house has a door down to the tunnels. Every house also has a safe room."

The flutters I had in my tummy a few minutes ago disappear, replaced with a huge weight.

"Why do you need so much security?"

Cage studies me for a second before he sighs. "Because, with the stuff we do, people are always after us."

Yeah, that doesn't make me feel any better. He's really not the best at making things sound less scary. I want to ask what they do exactly, but I already know he won't give me a direct answer. He seems to want to protect me from whatever it is. Maybe I should stop asking questions. It's probably for the best.

"The only thing you need to concern yourself with is following the rules," he adds.

Yeah, because I've always been so good at that. Not.

A table full of men greets us when Cage leads me into an enormous dining room in the main house. And not only that, but a woman comes charging at Cage.

"You're home!" she squeals as she leaps into his arms and wraps her legs around his waist.

Something twinges inside me as I watch her hug him, grinning from ear to ear as she does.

"I'm sorry I didn't make it back the other night. You know how things go," Cage says to her softly before kissing her forehead and setting her on her feet.

I can't stop staring. She's clearly a grown woman, but her sparkly tutu and the way she's bouncing on her toes says otherwise. She reminds me of myself when I'm deep in my Little headspace.

"Rowie, I want you to meet Ember. She's staying here for a while. Ember, this is Rowena."

As if it's the first time she's noticed me, Rowena steps closer to Cage, her fingers coming up to her mouth. Cage sees and wraps his hand around her wrist, pulling it down in front of her. The way he touches her is so different than the man I've known for the past two days. He's gentle.

Is Rowena his girlfriend?

Oh my gosh, I'm so stupid. All this time, I've been getting turned on around him and thinking he's hot, and he has a girlfriend.

"Nice to meet you." I force a smile that I don't feel.

Her dark eyes study me, and when she gives me a wide

grin, I relax the tiniest bit. Does she know I was thinking dirty thoughts about her man?

"You, too. I like your necklace," she replies quietly.

This makes me smile back at her as I touch the silver compass. "Thank you."

A man clears his throat in the background, breaking the awkwardness between Rowena and me. We turn our attention to the table of men.

"Ember, these are my brothers. A few of them aren't here right now. Everyone, this is Ember."

"Cassian briefed us," one of them says, then looks at me and smiles. "I'm Elias. Nice to meet you."

Having so many sets of eyes on me, I want to step closer to Cage for protection. However, Rowena is still at his side, and I'm sure she wouldn't appreciate me using her boyfriend as a shield. Guess I need to pull up my big-girl panties.

Except I don't have any big-girl panties. And for whatever reason, my Little is creeping to the surface. I've tried to push her back into the box, but it's not working. Without meaning to, I bring my fingers up to my mouth and catch myself just in time before I slip my thumb between my lips. Instead, I stroke my chin with it, hoping it will provide the soothing effect I need.

A second later, a small, warm hand slips into mine, and Rowena is now at my side. "It's okay. They all scared me at first, too, but they're all harmless. You're safe here."

Cage watches us, a small smile playing at his lips. I

melt under his gaze, hating that he has this effect on me even though I know he belongs to Rowena.

"Thank you," I murmur.

Rowena grins and looks between me and Cage. "I've never seen my brother look at anyone the way he looks at you, by the way."

Her *what*?

"Brother?" I squeak out.

She giggles. "Yes. They're all my brothers. What did you think... Oh, ew. That's gross." Rowena scrunches her face like she's about to vomit, and all I can do is stare at her in shock.

They aren't together. She is his *sister*.

And what the heck does she mean by the way he looks at me?

"You're not his girlfriend?"

Rowena looks at me and bursts out laughing. "No. Definitely not. I think he likes you."

Shaking my head, I peer at him from under my lashes. "Not possible. I'm pretty sure it's the opposite, actually. Ever since he snatched me out of my father's car, he's been being nothing but a bossy, growly, controlling bear."

The smaller woman's smile widens. "Believe it or not, Cage is only like that when he likes someone."

She skips away, leaving me staring at her in shocked silence because there's no way Cage Black feels anything for me other than annoyance.

8

CAGE

I'm not sure what Rowie said to Ember earlier, but Ember hasn't stopped glancing at me since.

Almost as soon as Rowie greeted me, it was like Ember shut down. The light in her eyes dimmed. I didn't understand it, and I didn't like it one bit.

"What do you know about your father's business dealings?"

Ember startles and whirls around to look at me. Her hands are full of clothes. I'm pleased she's unpacking and not planning to live out of her bag. That would have driven me up the wall. I would have probably found myself in her room at some point unpacking her clothes, which she would likely think was crossing a boundary, but I don't give a fuck. I like order.

A glimmer of purple catches my eye on the bed. I look down at the stuffed dragon lying on the comforter right behind her. A toy. Cute. Ember's gaze follows mine, and as soon as it falls on the stuffie, she gasps and drops an armful of clothes on top of it.

"It's okay to have a stuffed toy, firefly. Lots of people have them."

She raises an eyebrow, her cheeks turning pink. "Do you?"

I chuckle and step into the room. "No. But you do, and you shouldn't be ashamed of it."

When I sit on the edge of the bed and uncover the dragon, she snatches it up before I can and pushes it into her bag, her entire face flushed.

"I'm not ashamed," she says quietly, a hint of sadness there.

"Then why are you hiding it?"

Her head is lowered. Shoulders slumped. I don't like it.

"Ember, tell me."

She shifts uncomfortably as I wait in silence for an answer. I'll sit here all day until she tells me. I'm pretty sure I'm not going to like whatever her reasoning is, but I still want to know.

"I used to get made fun of at school for having one. Some of the girls stole a stuffed toy that my mom gave me a few months before she died."

Jolting off the bed, I let out a string of curse words.

"Who the fuck are they? I want names. Right fucking now."

Ember turns her gaze to me, her eyes wide. "What?

Why? It doesn't matter, Cage. It was when I was in boarding school. I just, I don't want anyone to hurt Spike."

Spike. That's fucking cute. It's also cute that her toy is a dragon.

"I want names," I repeat, scowling as I pull out my phone. "Who are they?"

I don't give a fuck who they were or where it happened; what those girls did is unforgivable. It doesn't matter that they're women. Some men have morals when it comes to hurting women, but when it comes to someone hurting what's mine, I have no morals whatsoever.

Fuck. Did I seriously just think of her as mine? What the hell is wrong with me?

"I'm not giving you names."

"Why not?" I put my hands on my hips and glare at her.

She mirrors me, and it's adorable that she thinks she looks fierce. "Would you give me the names of every person who ever wronged you if I asked?"

"I can give you a list, but they're all already dead, so it wouldn't really be useful for you."

Her mouth falls open, and she stares at me like she's not sure if she should run away or report me to the cops. Good luck with either. I'd catch her in two strides, and the cops wouldn't do a goddamn thing about it.

"Calm down, firefly. I'm not going to hurt them. I just want to make them suffer a little. Maybe have their hairdresser accidentally melt off their hair or something. A waxing mishap. A fungal infection on their toenails. Nothing drastic."

She blinks. Once, twice, a third time. Then she shakes her head.

"You are truly fucking crazy, you know that?"

I smile. "It appears that way, but I'm actually not. I've been through rigorous testing."

"Cage," she whispers, curling in on herself. "Please."

Furrowing my eyebrows, I really look at her. Her bottom lip trembles.

Shit. I'm scaring her.

"Ember, I was kidding," I go to her and sit on the bed again, putting myself at eye level. "Firefly, breathe. Fuck. I was trying to joke around with you."

Mostly. I do like the idea of those women's hair melting off. It wouldn't cause permanent damage, unlike what they did to Ember, but it would definitely upset them.

"Really?" she asks.

Grabbing her wrists, I pull her down to sit beside me, then lean forward, resting my elbows on my knees.

"I'm not the best at reading social situations or people's emotions. I try, but I don't always catch on right away. I didn't mean to upset or scare you, though."

"You also have no boundaries," she murmurs.

I chuckle. "As you've mentioned."

When she doesn't say anything, I stand and point

toward her buried dragon. "You never have to hide that stuff from me or anyone else here. In fact, I'll be upset if you do. Okay?"

Just as I reach the doorway, she sighs. "Thank you. For everything. I'm sorry I haven't been easy either. I'll try to be less difficult."

I turn and face her, warmth spreading in my chest. "I won't be happy if you do that, too."

"Do what?" She turns her wide, chocolate eyes up toward me.

"Try to be less difficult. Just be yourself, Ember. That's the version of you I want to see."

She smiles and pulls her knees up to her chest before she gives a single nod.

"Dinner is at six sharp every night. Everyone who is at home is required to show. I'd like it if you came as well."

"Oh. Um." She scratches her temple and looks around nervously. "Okay. Should I dress up? I didn't bring anything nice, though."

"Firefly," I say softly, breaking her out of her panic. "Come however you're comfortable. Half the time, Rowie is already in her pajamas at dinner. We will welcome you no matter what. Connecting with family is more important to us than what we're wearing. You're part of the family... while you're here."

Adding in that last part felt like swallowing acid, but *I* need the reminder that Ember will only be here for a short amount of time. Once she's gone, I'll go back to my life doing regular missions, and she'll go back to hers doing whatever she chooses. She'll probably find some rich, sophisticated guy to marry and have kids with.

I wince at the thought. I don't fucking like the idea of that. Not one goddamn bit. Especially since the asshole won't appreciate her the way he should. He probably won't care about making her orgasm. I already hate the guy. Fuck, maybe I should go on a killing spree and get rid of any asshole her father might see as a potential son-in-law.

"Cage?" Ember asks, her brows scrunched together.

Shaking my head, I push away all the bullshit running through my mind and offer her a forced smile. "Yep, sorry. I'll see you in a bit."

And then I get the fuck out of her room before I do or say something I'll regret.

"**Y**ou're sure I look okay?"

If she asks me that one more damn time, I'm going to end up telling her in full fucking detail just how *okay* she looks. When she met me downstairs in the entryway to head over to the main house, I nearly told her to turn around and change. I don't want my brothers seeing her in those tight fucking leggings and loose crop top that shows off a sliver of her tummy. I thought about making her wear one of my hoodies that would surely reach her knees. Actually, that's a good fucking idea.

"I'll be right back." I take the stairs two at a time and return with a sweatshirt in hand. "It's chilly out. Put this on."

"It's huge."

I bite back my smart-ass response about other things that are huge and shrug. "Put it on."

She takes it from me and sniffs it, then hesitates. What the hell? It's clean. Does she not want to wear it because it's mine? Does she hate me that much?

Finally, she pulls it over her head. As soon as she does, my cock goes rigid. For fuck's sake. I'm going to dress her in my clothes every goddamn day she's here.

"Better. You'll be warmer." Because what's important is that she's warm. Not that her perfect body is hidden behind my clothes. It has nothing to do with that at all.

The main house is loud when we walk in. Someone is screaming at the TV, which is pretty typical whenever we watch sports. Rowie is curled up against Theo, sleeping with a pacifier in her mouth. It's the strangest thing. She can sleep through us yelling, but not through a rainstorm.

Fuck. I probably should have warned Ember about Rowie being Little. I didn't think about the things that make it glaringly obvious, like her using a pacifier. If Ember doesn't know anything about the lifestyle, it might come as a shock to her.

I keep my eyes focused on Ember as her gaze lands on

Rowie. No one else has noticed us yet so I get this moment to watch as a small smile pulls at the corners of her mouth. Then she sighs and glances up at me, her cheeks a soft pink hue.

"Hey," Rylan greets, interrupting the moment. "Dinner's almost done. Excited to have you here with us, Ember. I hope you like homemade pizza."

Ember's eyes light up as she bobs her head. "Sounds amazing. Do you need help?"

"Thanks, pipsqueak, but I got it." Rylan starts to walk away but pauses and turns back toward me. "Love the sweatshirt, by the way. Sure you didn't want to just make a sign?"

I glare at him while Ember looks between us trying to figure out what Rylan meant. Then he just strolls off to the kitchen, laughing like the asshole that he is.

"You glare at him a lot."

Tilting my head down to look at Ember, I shrug. "He's an asshole a lot."

"Are you sure it's just him?" a guy asks as he approaches.

Ember snorts, using the back of her hand to hide her laughter. Brat.

Theo smirks at me and then focuses his attention on her. "You must be Ember. I'm Theo."

Polite as can be, she shakes his hand and smiles. It's the kind of handshake a politician gives to people. Rigid. Forced, but with a smile. Why did she do that?

As soon as Theo lets go of her hand, which is as quickly as he could without offending her, Ember steps closer to me. Is she scared? That doesn't seem right. If she were, she wouldn't be so sassy with me. I may not be the biggest or the scariest-looking guy in the family, but I'm also no one to blink an eye at either.

Once Theo leaves us, I corner her. "What's wrong? Why were you hiding behind me? Do you need to go potty?"

Ember gasps and looks up at me like I asked if she wants to go to space. Good lord, she's touchy about her bathroom habits.

"No. I don't. I'm fine."

I lean down so we're face to face, and with every breath I take, I get the lingering smell of her vanilla body spray mixed with the scent of my sweatshirt. The two combined make my cock go rock hard as something possessive swirls inside me. Fuck, I like that. I bet she's as fucking edible as she smells.

"You're a shitty liar, firefly. Tell me what's wrong so I can fix it."

She shoots me an irritated look, but her shoulders drop. "I'm having a panic attack. Being around a lot of people who I don't know is hard for me. I'm fine. I just need to get over it."

What the fuck? Get over it? Who told her that BS? Because that's what it is, and I'm going to make it perfectly fucking clear right now.

"Go." I nudge her toward a hall that will lead to the back stairwell.

Ember lets me lead her to the second-floor landing before she stops in her tracks.

"Where are we going?" she demands.

"Into my bedroom. Come on, firefly."

She hesitates for just a second before she enters the room I use when I stay in the main house. We all take turns rotating so someone is always here with Rowie.

"Sit." I point to the bed, pleased when she follows my instructions. She's breathing heavily and looks exhausted. Maybe I should have tucked her into bed instead of bringing her over for dinner. But for some reason, I wanted her here. I'm going to keep telling myself it's because when my eyes are on her, I can ensure she's totally safe, but in reality, she's safe anywhere on The Ranch. Our land is completely secure.

I go directly into the bathroom and get a washcloth, then run cold water over it and wring it out.

"Here. It's cold and will help soothe you. Take some slower breaths, baby."

As soon as the word comes out, I freeze and stare at her, but she doesn't seem to catch it because she's staring off into the distance. Shit. I know nothing about this girl. If Ruth had given me a proper heads-up, I would have gone over her doctor's notes. I would most likely already know she has anxiety. Then maybe I wouldn't have forced her onto a goddamn plane.

I lower myself to one knee in front of her and rest my hand on her thigh, slowly moving my thumb in gentle strokes.

"Feel me touching you, firefly. Each time I stroke your leg back and forth, count it."

9
EMBER

I't's too much. This is *all* too much. The noise. The laughter. Strangers. A new place. Cage.

My breaths are coming out shallow, but my heart starts to race. Blackness clouds my vision. I blink several times to bring myself back to focus. It won't work. Every muscle in my neck stiffens, and it's getting harder to stay standing. I rub my fingers together, hating their clamminess.

Cage speaks to me, but I'm struggling to make sense of it. I say something back. What did I say? He looks unhappy. His eyebrows are drawn together, and then he nudges me.

Walls pass me by. Have I passed out? I still can't breathe, and my knees feel weak.

"Firefly, count," Cage urges. "Count each stroke of my thumb."

Blinking several times, I glance down to where he's touching me, his hand on my knee. Where am I?

He moves his thumb over my thigh, back and forth in slow motion.

"Count them, baby."

I silently count the strokes, and with each one, my breathing slows until I no longer feel like I'm having a heart attack.

"Good girl. That's good, firefly. Keep counting."

"I'm sorry," I whisper, squeezing my eyes shut.

How humiliating. Did his family notice that I was panicking? Cage is probably embarrassed to have me here.

"Look at me, baby." His voice is quiet and gentle, yet I want to obey him. To please him. Why do I want to make Cage happy?

Slowly, I lift my lids and meet his gaze. He doesn't look scary right now. Instead, his forehead is creased with concern.

"That's better," he murmurs. "That's a good girl."

My bottom lip trembles, but I fight the urge to burst into tears.

"I want you to listen to me, Ember. Are you listening?"

I nod, keeping my eyes on him.

"The next time you feel yourself getting anxious, I want you to come to me. Tell me. Touch me or give me a look. I don't care. Let me know because expecting yourself to just get over it isn't healthy. I don't want you to have to deal with it alone. Okay?"

There he goes, being so kind and sweet again.

"It was just a lot. Being around a lot of new people is hard for me. I didn't mean to ruin your night."

Cage chuckles and squeezes my knee. "If you think that could possibly ruin my night, you have a lot to learn about me, firefly. I know it's hard to believe, but having someone to take care of is where I thrive."

Ouch. When he said *someone* and not me specifically, it shouldn't hurt like it does. I'm nobody to him. That's fine. He's only my bodyguard. Nothing more. Besides, I don't want just anyone. I want a Daddy.

The memory of Rowena leaning against Theo while sucking a pacifier pops into my mind.

"How come Rowena uses a pacifier?"

There's an obvious answer to that, but that kind of stuff doesn't actually happen in real life. Not that I haven't thought about it.

"Because she has anxiety too, and it helps with that," Cage replies.

"Oh. That makes sense." I nod, a pang of disappointment in the pit of my tummy.

"She's also a Little," he adds. "Just like you are."

Every nerve in my body tenses. Oh, God. Am I that obvious? Maybe that's why I got picked on so much in school. No matter what I try to do, I can't hide that side of myself well enough.

"No, I'm not." Deny, deny, deny. Maybe if I deny it enough, it will happen.

I've tried that before, though. My Little side is part of me in a way I can't control. As badly as I wish I was normal, I know I'm not. I never have been. He'll think I'm a freak if he knows the truth.

My breathing becomes shallow as I start to panic all over again.

"Ember Elizabeth, lie to me one more time and see what happens," Cage says firmly.

My attention snaps to him, pulling me out of the dark hole I was heading down. My chin drops. "You can't threaten me."

What was he threatening me with? Was he saying he would spank me? Of course he wasn't. Duh. I'm so stupid to even think that's what he was implying.

"Baby girl, I can do whatever I want." He smirks and reaches out to tap my nose. "Lying is against the rules. So, let's try that again. Rowena is Little, just like you are. Am I wrong?"

"You can't do whatever you want."

Great. Awesome, Ember. Phenomenal response.

My answer obviously amuses him because the corners of his lips twitch.

"Stop trying to dodge my question, firefly."

I sigh, running my fingers over the hem of the sweatshirt he gave me to wear. It's so big and warm. It smells like him, too. I never want to take it off. That would probably be weird, though.

"Yes. I'm Little." My voice is so quiet that I'm not sure he hears me.

"How long have you known?"

Using my thumb, I run it over my chin, fighting the urge to suck it. I've never spoken openly about this side of me.

"Look at me, Little one."

I raise my eyes to meet his again.

"There we go." He smiles, his eyes warm and approving. "That's what I like to see. Those pretty brown eyes."

His praise makes me smile, my heart rate calming even more.

"It's okay to be yourself here. Understand me?"

I hear what he's saying, but after being bullied for years because of who I am, showing the other side of me isn't something I think I can do.

"Yeah. Okay."

"I don't like that you're agreeing just to pacify me, firefly." His tone is stern again, sending a shiver down my spine. "I can tell we're going to have to go over your rules and make sure you have a good understanding of them."

Letting out a very unladylike snort, I scrunch my nose. "You really have a thing about rules. Have you ever thought maybe there should be less of them?"

He stares at me for a second, then tips his head back

and laughs. "Spoken like a true Little girl. Come on, firefly. You ready to eat?"

Warmth spreads through me, and I stand to follow him downstairs. Before we leave the room, he reaches back and slips his index finger into my palm.

"Remember, if you feel anxious, I'm right here."

Looking down at where we're connected, I close my hand around his finger. My entire body tingles with need, and as we make our way down the stairs, I walk funny as the wetness in my panties brushes against my bare lips.

The closer we get to the first floor, the tighter I hold onto him. Like an anchor.

Several of Cage's brothers are already at the dinner table when we walk in, along with Rowena, who looks wide awake for someone who was sleeping twenty minutes ago. As soon as she sees me, her face lights up, and she waves enthusiastically.

"You're here! I'm so happy," Rowena says in a bubbly voice.

I grin back at her, all the remaining anxiety I had disappears into thin air. She seems so genuinely happy to see me, and I feel the same about her. Especially knowing she's also a Little.

Cage leads me to a chair and pulls it out for me. As soon as I sit down, he pushes me in. I look around the room, but nobody seems to notice or care.

"I don't want any broccoli. Who even eats broccoli

with pizza?" Rowena makes a face and shakes her head. "No, thanks. I'll pass.".

"You're having broccoli," three different men say at the same time.

"This is a nightly conversation," Cage tells me as he sits next to me. "Doesn't matter what vegetable it is, Rowie never wants it."

"Well, broccoli is gross," I murmur. "Who wants to eat tiny green trees? That's just silly. I'm convinced it's the devil's vegetable."

Cage shoots me a look. "Nice try, firefly. You're also eating the broccoli tonight."

My shoulders slump, and I wrinkle my nose. "No thanks."

He raises his eyebrows and leans over so his mouth is close to my ear. "You can fight me as much as you want, Little girl. I won't hesitate to put it in a blender and puree it into baby food, then spoon-feed you right here."

I gasp and glance at Rowena, who nods. "Unfortunately, he's not bluffing," she says and then sticks her tongue out at Cage.

"Do we stick our tongue out at people?" Theo demands from beside her.

Rowena shrugs. "Maybe you don't, but I do."

Several men chuckle and shake their heads as Theo pinches the bridge of his nose.

"Let's eat," Rylan announces as he brings two huge pizzas into the room.

Cassian follows him with an enormous bowl of broccoli. I automatically scrunch my face.

When I reach for my plate, Cage picks it up first and fills it with a piece of pizza and some broccoli. Then, instead of setting it in front of me, he sets it on top of his own plate and starts cutting the pizza into pieces.

"I can do it," I insist.

"Little girls don't use knives or cut up their own food," he replies without pausing.

"You're not my Daddy."

That makes him stop what he's doing and look at me. "None of us are Rowena's Daddy either, but we still look after her because she deserves to be taken care of. Just like you do."

I swallow heavily and stare at him, a swell of longing in my throat. I've never really had anyone want to take care of me before. My father certainly didn't. He didn't even give me time to grieve after my mom died before he sent me off to boarding school. I don't think he had the capacity to care for anyone after she died. He lost part of himself when he lost her.

"I want all of that gone." Cage motions toward my plate as he sets it in front of me.

My tummy does that fluttery thing as I look down at the cut-up pizza. It's silly. Stupid. I shouldn't get so much joy from something like that, but it's the first time any man has done something Daddyish for me.

"Thank you."

"Such good manners," Cage says with a wink. "Good girl."

I really hope I don't leave a pool of wetness on my seat when I get up. However, if Cage Black keeps acting like my Daddy, I can't be held responsible for the way my body responds.

But if he keeps handing out the good girls, it *might* be worth eating broccoli.

10

CAGE

"Brush your teeth before you go to bed."

She stops mid-stride and turns to look at me. "You know I've been managing myself for twenty-two years now; you don't have to remind me to brush my teeth before bed."

Maybe not, yet it feels damn good having Ember in my house to look after. She might not be my Little girl, but she's fulfilling this longing I've had for so many years. I love taking care of Rowie. She's brought so much light into our lives. She's not mine, though.

Neither is Ember.

Fuck.

I need to remember that part.

"Sorry," I mutter with a sigh.

What's wrong with me? I've known this woman for two days, and now I'm attached to her for some reason.

This has never happened before. I've played with women and let them go without blinking an eye. I haven't even touched Ember, and she's all I can fucking think about. The cute way she scrunches her freckled nose when she doesn't like something. And how fire lights up in her eyes when she's about to sass me. How she slept in the car with her thumb in her mouth. She needs a pacifier. Then there was that fucking panic attack that killed a piece of me on the inside. My poor girl. She should never have to suffer like that.

She's not *my* girl.

It's the job. That's why. I'm always obsessed with my missions, and keeping her safe is one of them.

"Night," she says softly.

"Night."

I need a drink. And some information.

Within two minutes of texting him, Cassian shows up with his laptop.

We head directly into my office. I don't bother to offer him a drink. He wouldn't take it.

"I've been looking into her father, and so far, other than some scammy business dealings, I haven't come up with anything major. He's a politician. Slimy as fuck, but his dirt is much cleaner than a lot of guys in power."

That's not what I wanted to hear. I'm glad for Ember's sake that he's not a total piece of shit, but I wish there was something on him to help us figure out who is threatening Ember.

"She said her mom died in a helicopter crash."

Cassian nods. "I reviewed all the reports. The weather turned bad quickly and before they could land, the helicopter lost control and crashed into a mountainside."

Jesus. That sounds horrific. No wonder she doesn't want to fly. I can't really blame her for that.

"So, her father has been raising her since?"

My brother shrugs. "I guess; if you can call it that. Ember has been in boarding school from the time her mom died until she graduated from high school. Even during summer breaks, he had her enrolled in camps. She did stay at his house while she attended college locally. Not sure why he allowed that or what changed?"

"Fucking asshole." I didn't like the guy the second I met him, and now, knowing he pawned Ember off during her childhood makes me hate him. No wonder she has anxiety.

"There's been threats on Griffin's life over the years, but nothing uncommon from any other politician. It kind of comes with the territory of being someone who votes on laws," Cassian says. "Ember has no clue what the threats are or what they're asking for?"

I rub at my temples. "No. Yesterday, she said she woke up with plans to go pick up her final transcripts and celebrate with a piece of cake. Before she could leave the house, her father laid the news on her. She knew nothing of it prior to that."

"Jesus Christ."

"By the way, I need to get her a cake. She may have not gotten her transcripts yet, but she still deserves a reward for all her hard work."

Cassian stares at me, his gaze penetrating. I don't care for it or the way he seems to read people so fucking easily, unlike me.

"You like her," he mutters.

Holding my glass to my lips, I pause for a second to soak in those words before I tip my head back and down the entire thing. "It doesn't matter. This is a job. We don't have time for complications."

I haven't told anyone that she's admitted to being Little. I'm not sure she would appreciate it if I did, and also, I kind of like having that secret between us.

"We've dedicated our lives to The Agency. We're allowed to have women and families. We're also allowed to start slowing down. We're at the age where you'll be recruiting a new team soon, and we'll be running it from behind the scenes," Cassian says.

My only response is a grunt. For the past two decades, I've dedicated my life to our team. To our missions. Our family. And as someone who came from a shit back-ground, I've felt on top of the world ever since I was recruited. I get to be part of something. Make the world a better place. And I have people who love me. I have Rowie.

It wasn't until recently that I started feeling like I've been missing out on something. My friends in the lifestyle have all been finding their Little girls despite having dangerous lives as mafia leaders. I'm envious of them. Seeing the way those women look at their Daddies and how they trust them completely, makes me want something more. Makes me want to capture a beautiful firefly and keep her forever.

"It's not an option. Right now, I need to focus on finding whatever the threat is so I can eliminate it. Then Ember can go back to her regular life."

Cassian runs a hand over his jaw, and I know my brother well enough to know that I'm not going to like what he's about to say.

"Her regular life where she has no family other than her neglectful father who always seems to send her away? That life? Because I think that scared yet fierce Little girl deserves more than that. She deserves a Daddy. There's no fucking doubt that she's Little, and with the way you look at her, it's pretty damn obvious you like her."

Yeah. I knew it. He was going to say something logical, and he didn't disappoint. Instead, he irritated me.

"Can you mind your fucking business and keep digging for information?"

My brother smirks as he turns back toward his computer. "Touchy, touchy."

Asshole.

"By the way, I need you to look into her school records. I need some names. I'll text you details."

I f I don't stop pacing, I'm going to wear a hole in the carpet.

Where the hell is she? It's nearly noon. She should be up by now. It's way past breakfast.

She needs to be on a schedule and have a set bedtime, naptime, and wake-up time. In fact, I'm going to make a chart. That way, there's no confusion about the rules.

Rules are another thing we need to discuss today. I never got the chance to talk to her more about them last night. She can pout all she wants about it, but too bad for her, I'm in charge.

Unable to stand it any longer, I take the stairs two at a time, not making a single noise as I move. I reach up to knock on her door, which is already open just a bit.

Slowly, I push it open, my gaze landing on her back. She's still in bed, lying on her side, facing away from me. Her gingery hair is messy and tangled, hanging behind her shoulders. Fuck, I love her hair. It's so different. The perfect shades of orange and brown, and with her freckles, she's so uniquely beautiful that it's breathtaking.

"I'm afraid to show him my Little side. What if he makes fun of me? Or what if I do something too Little? I don't want to be bullied again."

At first, I think she's talking to me, but then I realize Spike, her purple dragon, is propped up in front of her. She's talking to it while she strokes its fur.

"I don't even know if he likes me. He's probably just being nice. My father said he's paying Cage a hefty amount of money to keep me safe, so of course, that's why he's being nice to me. A guy like Cage would never want someone like me." She sniffles and lifts her arm to wipe her nose.

Oh, hell no. Does she seriously think that? Does she not see that she's way the fuck out of my league? That she could have any man in the world, and the thought of that makes me want to murder someone. No one deserves an angel like Ember. Not even me. Fuck, I wish I did because she's everything in the world I never knew I wanted.

It's wrong to eavesdrop, but getting a glimpse of her Little isn't something I can pass up. I have no doubt she'd run circles around me just like Rowie. I'd also bet all my money that she'd be the sweetest Little girl in the world.

Maybe I should convert one of my spare rooms into a playroom for her while she's here.

No.

This is temporary. I can take her to the playroom in the main house.

When she stops talking to Spike, I tap on the door, startling her. She rolls back to look at me, her face ghostly white.

"Cage, I, I—"

Fuck, the last thing I want is for her to be embarrassed.

"I just wanted to check on you. Wasn't sure if you normally slept this late. Are you feeling okay?"

She glances down at the stuffed toy then back at me and swallows. "Yes."

I lean against the doorframe and stare at her. "You know you're a terrible liar, Ember."

With a sigh, she rolls all the way over to face me, bringing Spike with her, clutched to her chest. Her pastel-green tank top suits her perfectly against her creamy skin and hair color. I can't see her wearing pink very much. She'd look adorable in any color, but she's more of a pastel girl. Soft green, light yellow, lavender. I know just the place to get her some special clothes for her Little too that would look cute as hell on her. Some ruffle-butt panties would be first on the list.

Fuck. Now I'm hard. Not that I've been soft since I laid eyes on her, but thinking about her all dressed up in cute clothes that I chose for her sends every ounce of my blood straight to my dick.

"I'm feeling physically fine. I'm not sick."

Now we're getting somewhere. Without waiting for an invitation, I stride into her room and sit on the edge of the bed, taking in every freckle I can.

"What's going through that pretty head of yours, firefly?"

She picks at Spike's fur and bites her bottom lip, and I give her a moment to figure out what she wants to tell me.

"It probably sounds ridiculous, but I don't know

what's going through my mind. So many things. It feels all jumbled up, and I'm overwhelmed. Part of me is upset with my father, and another part of me is scared something will happen to him. Then there's seeing Rowie with a pacifier last night. I've never thought there were other Littles like me, and I'm not sure what to think about it. On one hand, maybe it means I'm not a total freak. On the other, it means that I've been denying that side of me for so long because I was bullied just for having stuffed toys at my all-girls school." Her breaths are shallow, something that happened right before her panic attack yesterday.

I reach out and put a hand on her cheek. "Breathe, baby."

She does. The entire time she holds my gaze, her eyes are tortured with emotion. I want to fix it. Make everything right and perfect for her.

"Does this happen a lot? All these things in your head at once?"

"Yes," she whispers, tears filling her eyes.

My stomach twists, and I'd do just about anything to keep her from crying.

"What do you normally do when you're overwhelmed like this?"

Her mouth opens and then closes.

Leaning closer so our faces are only a few inches apart, I slide my hand down her cheek to cup her chin. "Tell me, firefly. You're safe to tell me anything."

She wets her plump lips and lets out a slow breath.

"Usually, I spend time in Little Space to clear my head for a bit. And by the time I come out of that headspace, I feel a lot better."

"How old is your Little, firefly?"

I would never press her to play at a certain age. Whatever makes her comfortable is all that matters. But fuck me, I hope she plays young so I can take care of her more intimately. She may not be mine, but she's mine for now. My job is to protect her and giving her what she needs to be happy and healthy is part of that. This is the safest place for her to be Little anyway.

"I think, like, two," she whispers, looking everywhere but at me. "Maybe sometimes younger, and sometimes a little older."

Her cheeks turn bright pink, and she uses her hands to cover her face. If only she knew I found her embarrassment to be a turn-on.

"Good. Then, for the rest of today, you are two. Now, I'm going to give you thirty minutes to go potty, brush your teeth, and get dressed, and then after that, we're going to head over to the main house."

She bolts upright, her eyes practically popping out of her skull. "Wait, what? Cage, no. I'm fine."

I rise from the bed and make my way to the door. "Your safeword is red. If at any time you want this to come to a halt, say red and it will. Otherwise, you have thirty minutes before I come back in here and start taking care of you the way I want to. Do you understand me, firefly?"

Seconds stretch by as I wait for her answer. As a man who likes control, giving her the out is hard, especially since I know she needs this more than anything right now. I won't do anything without her consent, though. But once she gives it to me, unless she safewords, all her choices go out the window. All she'll have to think about is being Little.

"Yes," she finally murmurs. "I understand."

With a nod, I disappear from the room and pull the door closed behind me. I reach down and adjust myself, inwardly groaning. Being around her is delicious yet painful torture.

That should be enough time for her to decide whether she needs to say red or not. Something tells me she needs this time in Little Space too much to use her safeword, even if she is shy about showing that side of her. She needs this, and so do I.

I can hardly fucking wait to Daddy her. I have a feeling there's going to be a lot of push and pull, but there will also be satisfaction for both of us once this is over. Because it will end. Just not today.

11

EMBER

I s this really happening? Did I seriously tell Cage how old my Little is? He didn't blink an eye, though. Oh, God. My stomach twists, and I think I might be sick. I'm not sure if it's with excitement or humiliation. Maybe both.

I'm not sure why I'm embarrassed. Rowena is clearly Little in front of all the men, and they indulge her the entire time. Maybe being Little isn't as rare as I thought? Maybe I'm not a total freak.

He gave me an out. A safeword. I've read about them before. Considering what a control freak Cage is, I'm surprised he's offered me one. Then again, consent is everything when it comes to this lifestyle. Even consensual non-consent should be consented to. And I have a feeling that even though Cage doesn't play by the rules very much in life, he would never do anything I didn't really want him to.

The opportunity to slip into my smaller headspace sounds perfect. I need it. Badly. Before Cage came into the room, I was pouring my heart out to Spike because he never judges me when I'm overwhelmed like this. Surprisingly, dragons are very good listeners.

I don't know if I can let go in front of Cage, though. I've never been Little around anyone. What if I do it wrong? What if he laughs at me?

Tears prickle my eyes, and my sinuses begin to burn again. Gosh, I'm such a mess. I feel like I could spend the entire day crying. Which is a clear indicator that I definitely need to regress. It *always* helps.

There's a quick tap on the door before Cage walks in like he owns the place, but then again, I guess he does.

As soon as his gaze lands on me and he notices my tears, he rushes over to me. Without warning, he picks me up, then sits on the edge of the bed, settling me onto his lap. My heart races but the warmth of him surrounding me soothes the panic that's been building.

"Why are you crying, baby girl?" he asks softly as he strokes my back.

Before I have the chance, he uses his thumb to wipe my cheeks. It's such a small, Daddyish thing to do, and for a second, it makes me wish he actually was my Daddy. Cage might be a bit different, but something tells me he'd be a good one.

"Everything," I say, sniffling. "I've never been Little in front of anyone, so even though I want to, I'm not sure if I can."

He tightens his arms around me so my head rests against his chest, and his steady heartbeat gives me something to focus on.

One... two... three... four...

"It's okay if you can't, but why don't we go over to the playroom and see how you feel? I can even leave you alone in there if that would help you be more comfortable."

I want to tell him I'm perfectly comfortable right here on his lap, but I keep that to myself.

"Why are you being so nice to me?" I ask.

Cage rests his chin on the top of my head. "Are you saying I'm usually an asshole? That hurts. I'm usually such a delight."

Giggling, I look up at him. "I never called you an asshole. But compared to the guy who kidnapped me, you're being super nice."

The corners of his lips twitch. "Didn't kidnap you, firefly."

I rest my head on his chest again and sigh. "I'm sorry you got dragged into babysitting me. I know this isn't your normal job. It seems like I'm always a burden."

Why am I always a burden to people? Cage didn't want me. But he got stuck with me, and now he has to deal with me being an emotional wreck who has random panic attacks. Lucky him.

Cage reaches down and cups my chin, forcing me to look at him. Our faces are only inches apart, giving me the perfect view of his strong chin and dark eyes. Would it be weird if I ran my fingers over his beard?

"I didn't get dragged into anything. I could have turned it down if I truly wanted to. And while it might not be a normal mission, I'm enjoying my time with you. You're a special Little girl, firefly. You deserve better than the life your asshole father has given you."

His words penetrate my heart. I know he's right about that.

"My father lost the love of his life when my mom died. It wasn't right that he sent me away after that, but I think he did what he thought was best. Before I left, he told me that when all of this is over, he wants to work on our relationship." I sigh. "But then he let you kidnap me, so I don't know how much weight I should put into that."

Cage laughs. "I didn't kidnap you, Little girl. I'm starting to think you have a thing about kidnapping. Is it some kind of kink of yours I should know about?"

I burst into giggles and cover my face, my cheeks hot against my palms. "No, definitely not."

And just like that, with a little teasing, the mood in the room lifts and I'm smiling instead of crying.

"Come on, firefly. You're going to be so excited when

you see the playroom." He sets me on my feet. "Do you need to go potty before we walk over?"

I open my mouth to remind him about boundaries, but that's not what comes out.

"Nope. I went potty a little bit ago."

My entire face heats, and I duck my head. Instead of making a big deal of it, he takes me by the hand and leads me out of the room.

"Wait, I'm still in my pajamas." I stop and look down at myself, horrified that I forgot I haven't gotten dressed yet.

"Baby girl, the only people who are going to see you are Rowie and my brothers. None of us cares if you're in your pajamas."

"But..."

He studies me for a second, then turns me back toward the room. "Okay, I'm picking out your clothes and helping you get dressed."

Wait, what?

"I can do it."

Ignoring me, he heads straight for the closet. "Little girls don't pick out their clothes, and they certainly don't dress themselves. That's their Daddy's job... Or their caretaker."

Right. Because he's not my Daddy, and I need to remember that. But getting me dressed? What panties do I have on? Oh yeah, I'm wearing my pink polka-dot cotton briefs. Whew. At least they aren't ratty. They're damp, though. Shoot. He'll be able to see.

As soon as he notices me breathing faster, he's right in front of me, concern etched on his face. "Firefly, breathe. I'm just going to get you dressed, okay? I'll close my eyes."

I can do this.

"Do you remember what your safeword is?"

I meet his gaze and nod. "Red."

"Good girl. You can say it at any time if you need things to stop. Otherwise, I expect you to obey me. If you're naughty or break the rules, you'll be disciplined. Okay?"

Disciplined... Like spanked? I squeeze my thighs together as those pesky butterflies erupt in my tummy again. Why does being spanked by Cage arouse me? His hands are huge. Surely it would hurt.

"Okay," I whisper.

"Lift your arms up."

I do, and when I look at him, he closes his eyes and pulls my shirt over my head. Then he fumbles with the clothes he picked out until he finds the top and lowers it over me.

"Wait. I need a bra."

"You don't need a bra, baby girl. If we leave the property, you can wear a bra. While you're here, you can go without."

As soon as my shirt is on, he opens his eyes and meets my gaze. The only time I've ever gone without a bra is in bed. Although it's not like I really need one. My boobs are small and boring. There's not much there to perk up. Probably a good thing he closed his eyes. He would have been disappointed with the view.

When I don't argue, he tucks his thumbs into my pajama shorts and pulls them down. Then he reaches for my panties, and I hold my breath. As soon as he takes them off, he's going to see the wet spot. I'm going to die of embarrassment at the age of twenty-two.

He closes his eyes once again, and I let out a relieved breath. Even without being able to see, he dresses me quickly and efficiently. As soon as he's done, he takes my dirty clothes and tosses them in the bathroom hamper, then comes out with a hairbrush.

Every movement he makes is confident and calculated. He's efficient with everything he does. Would he be like that in bed? Efficient and detailed?

My cheeks heat at the thought. Why am I thinking about Cage in bed? When did I become such a pervert? I've never fantasized about any man, but I guess Cage is the exception. And I'd bet my last stuffie he's an exceptional lover. Which is saying a lot because Spike is my best friend. I'd never take the risk of losing him.

"Do you want a ponytail, pigtails, or two braids?"

My mouth falls open as he comes to sit on the edge of the bed. "You know how to braid?"

"Of course. Been doing Rowie's hair forever. Although, she says I never get her pigtails even."

I purse my lips, fighting the smile I feel inside. "I want pigtails."

After he has me stand between his legs, he starts brushing my hair, and every so often, something hard presses into my bottom.

"Is Rowie in Little Space a lot?" I ask, wanting to distract myself from the fact that his dick is hard.

"She lives in Little Space pretty much all the time. It's how she copes best."

Scrunching my nose, I bring my thumb to my chin and start to rub it. "Copes?"

He's gentle as he works on my hair, taking the time to comb out all the tangles without pulling.

"Rowie went through hell before she came to us. If Theo and I hadn't found her when we did, she would have been killed at the hands of her foster parents."

My chest aches for her. She's so small and sweet. It's hard to imagine anyone ever wanting to hurt her.

"Rowie is close with all of us, but she's closest to me and Theo. We're the ones who found her and brought her home."

"Wow," I say sadly, shaking my head. "I'm a real asshole for thinking my life was so hard when it sounds like she had it so much worse. I'm so glad you found her."

He tightens my pigtails and reaches below my armpits, lifting me onto his powerful thighs so my feet are dangling in the air.

"Look at me, firefly."

I turn my gaze up to him, and like every other time, I'm breathless when he locks eyes with me.

"Just because your circumstances were different doesn't mean you're not allowed to have feelings about your upbringing. Abandonment is abuse, whether it's on the streets or at a school. You deserved so much more than what he gave you."

Biting my lip, I offer a small, sad smile and nod. "Thanks."

"Let's go check out the playroom, yeah?"

He wasn't kidding when he said I would like it. Who wouldn't? It's the playroom of all playrooms. A Little's dream come true.

My mouth has been hanging open since the moment we stepped in. The threshold is a wide arch with no doors. Just across the hall from it is another sitting room with another enormous TV mounted to the wall. Boring.

"This is..." I have no words.

I've imagined what a playroom would look like in my mind, but never would I have envisioned this. Someone hand-painted an intricate forest on the walls. Trees, similar to the ones I saw when we drove up to the house; birds of all kinds, and even tiny rabbits. 3D branches stretch up near the ceiling with twinkle lights hanging from them like a starry night sky. A stuffed squirrel is perched near the partial trunk that appears to be coming right out of the wall.

"A magical forest," I murmur.

Cage smiles down at me. "Go on. You can explore. We already made sure Rowie was okay with you playing in here."

Tears well up as I take a tentative step inside. Rowie doesn't know me, yet she's willing to share such a special place with me. I'll have to make sure to thank her later.

The forest theme runs all through the room, from the wooden rocking chair that looks like it was chopped up and made from small logs to the area in the opposite corner built like the opening of a tree trunk. Pillows and blankets are stacked inside it, making the perfect reading nest.

My heart flutters, and I fidget with the hem of my shirt as I take it all in. I could live in this room forever and I'd die happy.

In an opposite corner of the room, there's a stump that's varnished. As I get closer and squint to read the writing on it, my eyebrows shoot up.

Naughty Seat.

Sheesh. Even the timeout chair matches the theme. That was... thoughtful.

"I love it here."

Cage steps up behind me and squeezes my shoulders.

"I'm glad, firefly. I want you to spend some time in here playing."

"Really?"

"Yes, really. I'll stay if you want me to, or if you'd rather be alone while you play, I can go do some work."

I peer up at him, worried he might be upset. Part of me does want him to stay, but this is all so new. I'm not sure I could really get my head into it, knowing he's watching.

He smiles, and I swear, my panties are soaked all over again.

"Tell you what. I'm going to go and do some work. I'll turn on the baby monitor. If you need anything, call out for me, and I'll be here in a heartbeat. Okay?"

My shoulders relax, and I wrap my arms around his waist, listening to his heartbeat as I hug him. "Thank you."

"You're welcome, baby. Stay in this room, though. If you need to go potty, there's a button by the doorway that will call me. Understood? No leaving."

Yes, Daddy.

The words almost slip out. If I weren't so nervous right now, they probably would have. Thankfully, I catch myself before they do. "Okay."

He studies me with a slight frown but doesn't say anything. Was he hoping I'd call him Daddy?

When he releases me and steps back, I immediately miss his touch. Maybe I should ask him to stay. He wouldn't want to watch me, though, and he certainly wouldn't want to play with me.

"Oh, I almost forgot," he says as he reaches into his pocket. "I want you to use this instead of your thumb."

He sets a pastel-green pacifier on the small art table before he walks out of the room, leaving me staring at it in shock.

12

CAGE

Cage: What information do you have for me?

I drop my phone on the worn desk and turn my attention to the fixed baby monitor camera mounted on one of the tree branches. Since I've come to my office, I've gotten nothing done other than watching Ember on the security cameras and sending a text to Ruth. What I should be doing is digging for my own information instead of relying on our CIA handler, but I'm so fucking enthralled by the Little girl in the playroom.

So far, Ember has only explored the room, though she's been spending most of her time by the dolls. She's also gone over to the art table a couple of times to check out the pacifier I left her. There are so many questions I want to ask to learn about her Little. I want to get to know both the woman *and* the Little girl. I also want to keep her. I've never wanted to keep anyone in my life. Not like this. Not like I want her to belong to me in every single way possible.

She deserves so much more than me. I can't give her the city life she's used to. With me, she'd be locked down and smothered. Kept on this property ninety percent of the time because I know that's where she's safest. It's ridiculous to think she'd want that kind of life. Hell, she's only twenty-two. Ember hasn't even begun to live her life yet. As much as I'm drawn to her and have this overpowering need to Daddy her, I have to remember that this is temporary. While she's here, I'll get my Daddy fix. Once she's gone, I'll continue living my life here while she returns home to DC.

"What are you doing?"

I have one good thing going for me after Ember leaves. I'll always have this Little girl to brighten my day.

Rowie shuffles in, a bright smile on her face that warms my heart. She has on a footed bear onesie with the hood pulled up. The little ears flap about as she moves, and I can't help but laugh. Fuck, I love this girl.

"Oh no, a bear," I cry out, holding my hands up defensively.

Rowie giggles. "I'm not a real bear, silly. Sheesh. For such a badass, you sure get scared easily."

Narrowing my gaze, I fight the smile playing at my lips. "Rowena Black, no swearing."

She stops and stares at me, then rolls her eyes dramatically. My palm twitches. As it often does around her. We've never spanked Rowie, though. When my brothers and I realized she was Little, we sat down as a family and went through boundaries, rules, and limits with her. Because of her past, we didn't even present spankings as one of her punishments if she misbehaved. Doesn't mean I don't want to give her a good hard swat every now and then. Lovingly, of course. Because even when she's naughty, she knows we're going to love her no matter what. We've made sure to reassure her over the years.

"Such a buzzkill," she murmurs as she rounds my desk.

Then she throws her arms around me, and all thoughts of punishing her go out the window because I'm too busy melting for her.

"I've missed you," I whisper as I pull her onto my lap.

"I know," she says confidently.

When I shoot her a stern look, she breaks into a grin. "I missed you, too. I always miss you guys when you're gone."

Sometimes I forget how fucking lucky I am. How differently my life could have gone if Deke hadn't shown up at that shitty detention facility. I'd be dead if it hadn't been for The Agency. I was already on the fast track to being six feet under when I was recruited. I never would have known what it's like to be missed. To have people to come home to. It means everything to me.

"What are you up to today?" I ask.

She shrugs. "Mostly wandering around terrorizing you guys. Ghost took away one of my Good Girl Points, so I put slime in his boot, then got the heck out of there before he found it."

"Rowena," I scold weakly because it's actually funny as hell. I've been the victim of her sliming my shoes. While I didn't find it amusing at the time, I wish like hell I could be a fly on the wall when Ghost discovers his gift.

"Well, he was being grumpy for no good reason. Maybe he needs to get laid."

"Rowie!" I bark, pressing my fingertips to my eyes. "Jesus Christ, Little girl."

She wiggles off my lap and goes over to a chair across from me, her expression turning serious. "You seem to really like Ember. Is she going to be your Little girl?"

The cords in my neck tense, and my smile falls. "I do like her, but no, she's not going to be my Little girl."

Those words taste like poison on my tongue. Why does it piss me off that I said that?

Rowie picks at the fur on her onesie; her gaze lowered from me. "Maybe she should be. I mean, you like her, and she likes you. She needs a good Daddy, I think. Her eyes are sad a lot, but not when she looks at you."

Leave it to this Little girl to notice things that no one else does. "Just because I like her doesn't mean I should be her Daddy. She's only here because she needs protection."

"You like her more than just a client."

She's right about that. I want to do things to Ember that I haven't ever done with any other Little before. I don't want to just play with her. I want to completely own her.

"Ember is a special woman. She deserves more than what I can give her. She's from a whole different world than me."

Maybe if I say it enough times, I'll start to remember it.

Rowie pulls a face, then looks up and glares at me. "More than you can give her? You can give her everything, Cage. You're one of the most unselfish people I've ever known. And as someone who was born into a *whole different world*, I know first-hand that it doesn't mean anything. Just because it's covered with silver and gold doesn't mean it's good. In fact, it could be downright hell."

My heart cracks, and I have to blink several times as I swallow the pain swelling in my chest. I'd do anything to erase the pain Rowena went through. To make her forget all the abuse.

I get up and stride over to her, leaning down to look her in the eye. "You deserved so much more."

She searches my face with her deep brown eyes, then lets out a shaky breath. "I know," she whispers.

Taking a step back to lean against the edge of the desk,

I shake my head. "I'm not a good person, Row. I'm tainted with blood. She's so fucking pure and sweet. I'd ruin her."

"You haven't ruined me." Her voice is small and soft. "You won't know unless you take the risk."

That's the thing about me. I was trained *not* to take risks. Everything I do is calculated and planned to eliminate all danger. If I didn't do that, I'd be dead by now. We all would. The problem is, as much as I want to take a chance with Ember, if it doesn't work out, it would be my heart and soul that dies, and I think that might be even worse. Besides, with my job, I'm often gone from home, and she couldn't come with me. It would be too dangerous. And expecting her to stay at The Ranch while I'm working wouldn't be fair to her. Even if it is nearly time for me to start slowing down. There would still be jobs I'd have to leave her and travel to. As obsessed as I already am with Ember, I can't imagine how bad I'd be if she were mine.

"She's only here temporarily, Row. It's just a job." I think it is. It doesn't really feel like one.

Rowena nods, her eyes lowering to her lap. "I get it. She's just so sweet. I've never had a friend before. It's kind of nice having another girl here."

Something heavy settles in the pit of my stomach. "Rowie," I say softly. "Are you unhappy here?"

Her head snaps up to meet my gaze, and she quickly shakes her head. "Not at all. I love my life here. It's the best life I ever could have imagined."

My shoulders drop with relief.

"It's just," she adds slowly. "Sometimes, I wish I had friends. Someone to play with. Another girl to talk to. It can be lonely being the only one."

Fuck. How did I not realize?

"Does Theo know you feel this way?"

I'm pretty sure he would have said something if he knew. Rowie and Theo are even closer than I am with her, so maybe she's talked to him about it.

"No. He worries enough about me."

I reach out and cup her chin. "We all worry about you. You're our girl. We all love you."

She smiles and leans into my hand. "I know. There hasn't been a day that's gone by since I've been here that I haven't felt loved."

My phone rings, and when I pull it out of my pocket to check who it is, I wince.

Pointing at Rowie, I shoot her a stern look. "Don't move a muscle. We're not done talking about this."

Turning my back, I hit the accept button. "What do you have for me?"

"Well, hello to you too, Cage," Ruth snaps.

I smile, pleased that I've already irritated her. It's almost as fun as irritating Ember. Not quite, though.

"Have you found out anything?" I ask.

Ruth sighs, and I can already tell the answer is no. Instead of being annoyed that she's about to tell me she has nothing, I'm fucking thrilled. The longer we go without resolving this, the longer Ember stays. The Ranch is impenetrable, so she's safe as long as she's here.

"I haven't got much. I believe the threat is coming from Europe, but I haven't been able to narrow it down," she says. "I have people working on it."

Running a hand over my face, I stare out my office window at the courtyard that all our houses look over. One of the playground swings sways in the breeze. Ember would look so fucking cute playing out there, wearing an adorable outfit that I chose for her. Rowie would love it, too. As much as I hate to think it, maybe we aren't enough for Rowie. Maybe she needs some Little friends.

The overcast skies have grown more angry since Ember and I walked over from my house. Looks like it's going to storm tonight.

"See if Zeke can recall anything specific. Has he had any run-ins with someone based in Europe? And can you send me copies of the threats? I'll have Cassian examine them, too."

"Sending it over now." Almost as soon as she says it, my encrypted email inbox sends an alert. Ruth might be a pain in the ass, but the woman is efficient as hell.

"Thanks. Keep me posted," I say before I end the call.

After sliding my phone back into my pocket, I spin around to finish my conversation with Rowie. Except when I do, she's gone.

Why doesn't that surprise me?

"Hey, man." Jasper strolls in with a folder in his hand.

I glance behind him. "Did you see Rowie out there?"

Jasper looks behind his shoulder and then back at me. "No. Was she supposed to be out there?"

Rolling my eyes, I shake my head. "No. The brat was supposed to keep her ass right in this chair while I took a call."

"When has she ever stayed where she's supposed to?" Jasper asks.

True.

"When did you get home?" I'll have to corner Rowie later. If she's lonely, I need to do something to fix it.

"Late last night."

I study my brother. The circles under his eyes are darker than usual. Which means he didn't sleep last night after he got home.

"The explosion in Mexico have anything to do with you?"

The corners of Jasper's mouth twitch. "I don't know why you automatically assume it was me."

We grin at each other, both knowing full well that the explosion was all him. We've been on the trail of a sex trafficker for months, but every time we think we've got a pulse on his next move, he seems to be one step ahead. We still send him a friendly little explosive message every time. He's only down to a dozen or so more properties to hide in that we know about.

"You need to sleep. You look like shit."

My brother snorts. "Yeah, because sleep is what I excel at."

I don't argue with him because I can tell him he needs to rest until I'm blue in the face. Unfortunately, he's the one who has to deal with the demons still torturing him when he closes his eyes.

"Then go get laid. That will help you pass out."

Jasper smirks at me. "Maybe *you* need to get laid. Make you less grumpy."

Narrowing my gaze, I flip him off. Getting laid sounds great. Except the idea of fucking some random woman makes me sick to my stomach. The only woman I want touching my dick is in the other room. And I've already been away from her for too long. Every second I'm not with her, it's more difficult to breathe.

How have I let myself become so obsessed with her? I want to possess her. Hear her cry my name as I bring her to the peak of ecstasy. And yet, despite wanting all of that, I know she's off-limits. Maybe it's a good thing I've never cared much about limits.

"I'll see you at dinner," I say over my shoulder as I stride toward the doorway.

"Got it," Jasper calls out. "Good talk, bro."

13

EMBER

"Can I play with you?"

The small, hesitant voice startles me. Whoa. I was really absorbed in playing with all these adorable baby dolls. There are so many of them. Ones with curly hair, straight hair, even red hair like mine. And the clothes. There are a lot of outfits to choose from. Frilly dresses, skirts, furry coats. I'm envious of all the toys Rowie has in this room, but I'm downright jealous of her doll collection.

I turn to look at her as she stands in the doorway, nibbling on her bottom lip and peering at me shyly.

"I don't want to bother you, and it's okay if you'd rather play alone," she says, waving her hand dismissively. "I'll just leave you be."

"Wait!" I call out as she takes a step back. "You... um,

you don't have to go. It's just, um, well, I don't really know how to play. I probably won't do it right."

"Oh." Rowie shuffles over and plops onto the floor beside me, crossing her legs and tucking her feet under her knees. "There's no right or wrong way to play. You just do what makes you happy and what feels natural."

She picks up one of the dolls and a small brush and starts combing out the tangles. "Have you ever played before? Or is being Little new for you?"

I tense, my hands trembling slightly as my mind flashes to the past.

Rowie's eyes go round, and she reaches out to touch me. "I'm sorry. I shouldn't ask so many questions. I'm so awkward. Such a dummy."

My mouth drops open, and I quickly shift to face her, shaking my head as I do. "No. No, you're not a dummy or awkward. I mean, I guess we're all a little awkward. I certainly am. But no, you're totally fine." I offer the most reassuring smile I can manage.

She returns mine with a grin of her own, then starts brushing her doll's hair again. I pick up one that has no clothes on and search for an outfit.

As I dress my doll in a yellow skirt and polka-dot shirt, I bite the inside of my cheek until I taste blood. Rowie has been nothing but kind to me every time she's seen me. She's also a Little like me. She's not *them*. She won't be mean and cruel. Will she understand, though? What if she thinks I'm ridiculous because what happened in the past still affects me?

With every second that passes, it gets harder to breathe.

Just tell her.

Just be myself.

Cage said I can be myself here.

"I attended boarding school, and during eighth grade, I had a dolly. Her name was Betsy. She had the prettiest green eyes, straight black hair, and freckles like mine. I loved her so much. I always struggled to make friends because I felt out of place, so Betsy was my best friend. Some girls caught me playing with her one day and took her from me. They were so mean. They." I swallow thickly, trying to push the lump in my throat back down. "Um, they cut her to pieces and would leave them in my room, body part by body part. And every day, they would harass me for playing with toys at my age. It got so bad that I had to see a doctor because I started having regular panic attacks."

When I finish talking, I glance at Rowie. Is she going to pity me? Tell me to get over it? It's been years since it happened. I need to let it go, but for whatever reason, it's one of those memories that haunts me. The seconds pass like hours, and I hold my breath as her gaze narrows. I've probably already scared her away from being my friend.

Her eyebrows draw together, then turn into a scowl. "Those fucking bitches. How dare they!" she nearly shouts, her hands balling into fists. "Who are they? Give me their names. My brothers will destroy them. *I'll* destroy them."

She jumps to her feet, her face beet red with anger, and all I can do is stare at her in awe. This tiny spitfire of a woman, probably doesn't even weigh a hundred pounds soaking wet, is ready to go to battle for me. She barely knows me. Is this what friendship is? Being ready to bury a body at a moment's notice?

"I'm going to get Cage. Those bitches need to pay."

I leap up and grab her hand before she can take off. The last thing I need is for him to get involved.

"No, don't go," I plead. "I don't want to make a big deal of it. Maybe I shouldn't have said anything."

My bottom lip trembles. What a mess. I don't know Cage very well, but I know him enough to be certain that if he discovers all the things those girls did to me, he won't let me get away without giving up names.

Rowie frowns. "But you deserve revenge. That was a horrible thing for them to do. I want to cry just thinking about it."

Her eyes are watery, and now mine are burning with tears as I sniffle and use the back of my hand to wipe my nose.

"It was a long time ago. After that, I never tried to play again. The only toy I have is my stuffie, and I keep him hidden as much as possible."

Even though my heart aches from reliving the past, I

feel lighter than I have in a long time. I've never told anyone the entire story before. My father only knew bits and pieces because I was too ashamed to tell him everything. It was an irritation for him to have to pull me from that school and move me to another one. I barely remember my mom, but my memories were always of the three of us spending time together. After she died, it was like I was this thing he had to take care of but didn't want to.

Linking her fingers with mine, Rowie pulls me over to the tree trunk opening. Together, we crawl in and prop ourselves up against the pillows.

We don't speak for a few minutes, instead, we stare up at the twinkle lights and faux tree limbs hanging from the ceiling.

Finally, Rowie breaks the silence. "I've never had a best friend, either. I've never had *any* friends actually." She pauses and turns onto her side to face me. "Would you maybe want to be my best friend?"

Rolling my head to the side to look at her, tears fall from my eyes, and a lump forms in my throat. As I stare at the small woman beside me, part of my sad, broken heart heals right here in the middle of the playroom. I smile. "I'd like that."

"Hey, sleepyheads."

The voice is deep and smooth. Gentle. It's not his voice, though.

I furrow my eyebrows and hide my face. Whoever it is, I'm not waking up. I'm warm and cozy, and I want to stay here forever because it's just that perfect.

"Rowie," the voice persists.

"My name isn't Rowie," I mumble.

A soft chuckle and then another. The second one sounds familiar. I like that one.

"No, baby girl. Your name is Firefly."

I'm so warm and comfy, I don't want to move. Yet I can't help but peek out of one eye.

It's not just Cage who's looking back at me. Both he and Theo are squatting down just outside the tree. And Rowie is stirring beside me.

Huh. We must have dozed off after we declared we were going to be best friends.

"You two need to wake up so you can sleep tonight," Theo says, nudging Rowie's foot.

She kicks his hand away and curls up into a ball. "Go away," she mumbles.

Theo grins, then reaches in and grabs Rowie by the ankle. As he drags her out of the tree, he tickles the sole of her foot, sending her into a fit of giggles. I grin and peek at Cage again, expecting him to be watching Theo and Rowie, but he's not paying them any attention. Instead, he's focused on me, his gaze heated. A twinge of arousal shoots through me, and I quickly squeeze my thighs together.

"Hey, pretty girl." Cage smiles at me. Gosh, he's handsome.

He may be a difficult man to deal with at times, but I think that smile might make up for it. Hell, all he has to do is flash me those pearly whites and I'd probably do just about anything he wanted.

"Hey."

"It's almost dinner time," he tells me.

Oh, right. They eat together every night. Like a family. I can't remember the last time I sat down for a meal with my father. Christmas last year, maybe? I imagine it's nice knowing you have people to come together with at the end of the day to share a loud, messy, loving dinner with. These men might be a bit unusual, but they certainly love each other. And they are all practically over the moon for Rowie. It's obvious she means a lot to them, and I get the feeling they mean a lot to her, too.

Together, Rowie and I crawl out of the tree and stand. Then she looks up at Cage and shoots him a mischievous grin.

"Ember and I have decided we're going to be best friends, so I think she should stay here forever."

Something flickers in Cage's eyes. Worry, maybe? Guilt? I'm not sure. It's there and gone in a heartbeat.

"You two can be best friends, but Ember can't stay here forever," he replies tightly.

His words are like a knife to the gut. Why does it bother me that he said that? That he doesn't want me here. I don't care how he feels about me. He's my bodyguard. Just because I'm attracted to him or the fact he knows my deepest secret and gave me a pacifier doesn't mean he has any interest in dating me. Or in being my Daddy.

"Both of you go potty and wash your hands. Meet us in the dining room," Theo instructs.

I glance up at Cage, and he gives me a slight nod. "Go ahead. Unless you need help?"

My eyes go round, and I quickly shake my head before Rowie and I scurry away. I don't know why the man is so obsessed with helping me in the bathroom. I also don't understand why it intrigues me so much. It would be embarrassing. Totally humiliating. Yeah, I definitely don't want his help.

Nope. Totally not.

14

CAGE

Theo grins at me as we leave the playroom.

"What the fuck are you looking at me like that for?"

He shrugs. "I was just checking out those hearts in your pretty brown eyes."

I frown. "What are you talking about?"

"I'm talking about you having a thing for Ember. The way you look at her is... intense."

Shrugging, I shake my head. "I like her, but she's a client."

"She's a Little. An adorable and sweet Little," he replies.

"Yeah. So?"

Theo scoffs and rolls his eyes as we enter the dining room. "So, she's Little. You like her. You're a Daddy. What the fuck more do you need? A map?"

"Who's Little?" Roman asks as he sets a pile of plates on the table.

"Ember. You'll meet her at dinner," Theo answers.

Warmth settles in my chest. I've never had a woman here before. Not sure I ever intended to. The Ranch is my sacred space. My home. It's where my family is. The only place I truly ever feel safe. But having Ember here, around my brothers, at our dinner table. It feels right. Like it's supposed to be.

"Good to have you home. How'd the mission go?" I ask Roman. He must have finished since he's back earlier than expected.

Roman gives us a menacing grin. "Great. Nothing like some fresh blood to invigorate me. Everything is wrapped up, and the problem has been delivered wrapped in a bow. Or a body bag. Same thing, basically."

I grin at my brother and reach out to give him a fist bump. "Nice."

"Anyway, back to Little Ember," Roman says. "Does Cage have feelings for a woman for once?"

"No," I snap.

"Yes," both Theo and Rylan reply at the same time.

I turn around to glare at Rylan who appeared out of nowhere. Fucker.

"I do not. She's a client. Who's cooking tonight?"

"Nice, trying to change the subject." Theo chuckles. "Dom is."

Thank fuck. Dom is one of the better cooks in the

family. I try to be out of town as much as possible when Lex cooks. I love my brother, but the dude makes some weird shit.

Rylan grins, his eyes sparkling. "A client who he's told me to stay the fuck away from. He threatened my life over her."

Theo snorts and slaps me on the back. "Say what you want, bro, but we all know you better than anyone. You like her. She's more than just a client. Besides, you heard Rowie. They're going to be besties, so Ember has to stay."

I groan and press my fingers to my eyes. Jesus. When did my brothers become a bunch of gossiping hens? I love them more than I can ever express, but damn, they test my patience sometimes. Especially Rylan. He's lucky he's so goddamn loyal because otherwise, I might actually worry about him going after Ember. Then I'd have to kill him, which would be hard to explain to the rest of the family.

Before I can curse them all out, Ember walks in, her fingers twined together. I suppose coming in here can be a bit intimidating. It's a lot of men, and we aren't the average kind of guys. We're all damaged. While some of us wear our scars on the inside, many of us wear them on the outside as well, making other people a little wary. We also carry ourselves differently. Years of training have made us paranoid, on guard, always watching for danger, and on edge. Gotta be ready for anything at any time. The last thing I want is for her to be afraid of us, though. Especially me. Every one of us would give our lives to protect her. She just doesn't know it yet.

"Come here, firefly," I say gently as I pull out her chair.

A rosy blush appears on her cheeks as she glances around the room. No one blinks an eye at me using her nickname.

As soon as she sits, I push her in and then sit beside her. "That's Roman over there. And Jasper is the pale, tattooed vampire-looking dude over there."

Ember's mouth drops open as she looks down the table toward my brother. I'm not sure if it's because of my description of him or because of how fucking scary Jasper is, but then she elbows me in the ribs and glares.

"That wasn't very nice to say. He doesn't look like a vampire," she whispers. "Well, I mean, he kind of has Edward Cullen vibes, but still. That was rude."

A slow smirk spreads over my face as I watch her nose wrinkle as she scolds me. Fucking cute little thing.

Mine.

All mine.

Fuck. Nope. She's not.

Not mine.

Thankfully, Jasper interrupts my thoughts.

"Nice to meet you, Ember. Rylan has told me so many nice things about you," he says while fighting to keep from smiling.

"Jesus, are you trying to start shit, asshole?" Rylan asks, throwing his hands in the air.

"Hey, no swearing. I'm taking away one of your Good Boy Points," Rowie says.

Rylan shoots her a look. "Try me, brat. Next time I take away some of your Good Girl Points, I'm taking double."

Rowie scoffs and crosses her arms over her chest. "Rude."

Ember giggles from beside me, my entire mood lifting with the sound. Hearing that sweet sound is like therapy straight to my soul. So sweet. Angelic. Mine.

"Let's eat," Dom announces.

The room grows louder with multiple conversations while we fill our plates, and Ember leans over with a mischievous expression.

"Maybe I should start taking away your Good Boy Points when you do something irritating," she says quietly.

I raise my eyebrows and lower my face so it's level with hers. "The only one giving and taking away points here will be me, Little one. And if you don't watch your sassy self, you might find some points taken away before dinner's over."

Her pupils dilate, and she licks her lips at the same time, her tongue peeking out just slightly. My cock grows hard.

She likes the idea of that.

So. The. Fuck. Do. I.

Maybe I need to make her a chart for while she's here.

This is all temporary, so why not make the most of it?

"**W**hy do you guys always eat dinner together?"

It's been four days since I found Ember in her bed talking to her stuffed dragon. Four long days and even longer nights. I've taken so many cold showers, but it doesn't matter. My cock is constantly hard around her. My next resort will be ice baths, though I don't think it will matter how freezing the water is; being around Ember gets my blood racing right to my balls. I'm desperate for her. It's an out-of-control feeling that makes me uneasy.

Tonight, before we left the main house, I told her it was time to go home. As if it's *ours*. Because for some goddamn reason, it feels like she belongs there.

"When we all became a family, we made a rule that anyone home had to attend dinner together. It's our bonding time, and it's so we all see each other regularly and can make sure everyone is doing okay."

Ember thinks about that for a moment as we walk the paved path toward my house in the dimming evening light. She's so small beside me. The top of her head barely reaches my shoulders. For every step I take, she has to take three. Part of me wants to pick her up and carry her home on my hip.

When she looks up at me, her eyes sparkle with sadness. "I never had dinners like that. With family. Not since my mom died, but I was so young, I don't really remember them."

I stare at her, swallowing thickly. "You deserved better, firefly. You still do. Maybe it's crossing a boundary, but your father is an asshole."

Every time she tells me something about her childhood, I hate him more and more. He might have a flawless public record, but that means nothing to me. The way he treats Ember, that's what I care about and from what I can tell, he's failed miserably.

She snorts, and I'm starting to wonder if there's anything about her that I don't find cute.

"Offering to help me in the bathroom is totally normal to you, yet calling my father an asshole is possibly crossing a boundary?" she asks.

Shrugging, I pull my hands from my pockets and reach for one of hers. When I lace our fingers together, I expect her to shake me away. When she doesn't, I give a gentle squeeze as we step onto the porch.

"I don't really know what's normal or not. Don't care, either. I'm certainly not what anyone would consider normal. Pretty sure most people think I'm strange as fuck."

When I let go of her to open the door, she doesn't release me. "Fuck those people," she says casually. "Art is strange, but it's still beautiful."

I blink several times, letting her words soak in. And as she stares up at me with those deep brown eyes, I'm finding it harder and harder to remember why she shouldn't be mine.

My woman. My Little girl. *All mine.*

"No swearing," I mutter.

She sighs, a soft smile playing at her plump lips. "Yes, sir," she says sassily as she salutes me.

Arching an eyebrow, I step closer and put my face inches from hers. So close that I can feel her breath on my lips.

"The correct answer is 'Yes, Daddy,' but I'll let it slide for now. Next time, you'll lose a Good Girl Point."

We stare at each other, breathing each other's air. Everything around us fades, and all I see is her. So beautiful. So shocked by my words. So fucking mine. And as we stand here, I'd do just about anything to hear her call me Daddy once.

When she starts to open and close her mouth like a fish out of water, I give her a gentle shove inside, chuckling to myself. I guess I've shocked her.

Once she finally recovers, she peers up at me, her cheeks bright pink and her pupils blown wide. "I'm, um, I'm going to go take a shower."

My cock twitches at those simple words. Fuck. Ember naked, with water dripping down her body. That's a goddamn beautiful fantasy right there. But she's meant to be in Little Space today, and even though she was more in her adult headspace during dinner, I want her to end the night feeling Little.

"Little girls don't take showers. They take baths."

She pauses mid-step and turns toward me, nibbling her bottom lip. "Oh. Um, okay."

I stride over and take her by the hand. "Come on, firefly. I'll run you one."

"You don't have to do that. It was really nice of you to let me play these past few days, but you don't have to take care of me. I don't want to be a bother."

Oh, fuck no. What is it with her and thinking that? Did her father make her feel that way? I really fucking hate Zeke Griffin. He's going to have a lot to answer for when I speak with him again. Ember might not be mine, but I'm sure as fuck not going to let him get away with being a shitty dad. She deserves family dinners and movie nights and holidays spent doing festive activities that make her happy. Birthday parties and traditions. She deserves everything and more.

Stopping halfway down the hallway, I let go of her hand and turn to face her. She nearly collides with my chest.

"Omph! Cage, why'd you stop? I almost smacked right into you," she snaps as her palms rest against my pecs. As soon as she realizes it, she yanks them away like she's been burned.

That shouldn't irritate me. It fucking does, though. I curl my fists at my side to keep from grabbing her wrists to place them back on me. Why doesn't she want to touch me? Is it fear? Or something more? Does she feel the same explosion of electricity that I do every time we touch?

"Look at me, Little girl," I say firmly.

Her gaze snaps up to mine, and my cock twitches again. Obedient Little one. I like it. Yet she can be so damn sassy at the same time. My girl is full of fire. My little firefly.

Mine.

"I know I don't have to do anything, baby. If I didn't want to do it, I wouldn't. You being Little and me being able to take care of you fills my Daddy cup. So, don't assume this is an inconvenience for me because it's not. Do you understand?"

She swallows. "Yes."

"Good girl."

I hold out my hand and wait, hoping she won't reject it. As much as I don't give a fuck what other people think of me, it's different with Ember. Everything is different with her. I care about what she thinks of me. How she feels about me. How she sees me. Does she find me attractive? Does she like it when I go into Daddy-mode? I sure as fuck love it. It's as if my entire being comes alive when I get to Daddy her.

Only a second passes before she slides her fingers into mine, and my entire soul smiles. When she entrusts me with her care and lets me lead, it makes the side of me that I've kept buried for so long come roaring to life, and I feel like the king of the world. Even more, I feel like *her* king. I like that way more than I should, but I am who I am. Might as well embrace it while she's here.

I walk us through her bedroom into the bathroom. When I turn and lift her by the hips, she grabs my shoulders. I set her on the counter and then release her, placing my palms on either side of her thighs.

"You smell like vanilla cupcakes," I murmur, leaning in to get a better sniff.

"We had cupcakes for dessert."

Lifting my head, I meet her gaze and inwardly groan. "Yeah? Seems to me like you should be my dessert."

I stare at her, my cock throbbing. Those freckles. That cute button nose. Those wide, innocent eyes. So sweet. Too good for me. And yet, I can't find the strength to pull away. She has me under some sort of spell. One where I'm ready to throw caution to the wind and fuck her right here and now.

"I bet you taste as good as you smell, firefly."

Her breaths come out heavier, and her lips part.

Jesus Christ.

If I don't get control over this situation, I'll end up bending her over this counter and driving into her without mercy. She'd be begging for me to slow down, but there's no way I could. I already know once I have a true taste of her, I won't have an ounce of strength to stop. Her cunt would probably strangle my cock in the best fucking way. She's so damn sweet and innocent, though. Would she like it rough? I'm not sure I could be soft even if I tried. When I fuck, I fuck hard and dirty. In the past, some women haven't been able to handle it, and the last thing I ever want is to hurt Ember.

"Cage," she whispers, her fingers flexing on my shoulders.

Another scent lingers between us. Arousal.

Fuck. Me.

"Firefly," I grit out. "I'm barely hanging on by a thread."

She widens her knees, letting me get even closer. "Why are you trying to hang on?"

I huff out a frustrated breath and look at the ceiling, silently counting to ten to calm myself. She doesn't know how badly I want to claim her. Mark her. Possess her. Why is she pushing me? Does she want this, too? Maybe it's what we both need. To fuck and get it out of our system.

"Is it." She pauses to take a deep breath. "Is it because I'm a virgin?"

Her words are like a knife to the gut. A virgin? Fuck. I knew she was innocent, but she went to college. She's a virgin?

My cock grows harder. All mine. She could be *all* mine. I could own every part of her. And what's so messed up is I want that. Which is why I'm a sick bastard who doesn't deserve her. Sure, I could give her everything she would ever want or need. She'd have a family here with no questions. But despite all the years I've spent training and becoming the man I am today, I'm still fucked up in the head. I'm still the kid who came from the gutter. I'm just one of the lucky ones who got out.

"We can't do this." I take a step back, though it almost kills me to do so. "I'll run your bath, then leave you be."

I make myself busy, gathering everything she needs. Once I get the water to the correct temperature, I plug the drain and turn back to her. She won't make eye contact with me, and I hate the way her shoulders droop. I haven't done anything with her, and I've already let her down.

When she sniffs, I nearly fall to my fucking knees. Goddamn, I hate myself right now. "Look at me, baby girl."

The hurt in her eyes kills me. I did that. This is *exactly* why we can't do anything.

"It's not because you're a virgin, Ember. There's nothing wrong with that. It's because you're my client, and sex complicates things."

"Okay," she whispers, her voice shaky.

She lowers her gaze from mine again. I don't like it. I reach out and gently grasp her chin. "It's not that I don't want you, Ember, because I do. Fuck, I want you like I've never wanted anyone before. It's a bad idea, though. Okay? It's better to keep things platonic. You can still be Little, and I can still take care of you. As friends."

Even as I say it, I know it's a lie. We're already past the point of friendship. I have feelings for her. Strong ones. And it scares the hell out of me.

When she nods, I release her and lower her from the

counter so she doesn't hurt herself by jumping down. As soon as she's steady on her feet, I take one more deep inhale of her toxic scent, committing it to memory forever before I take a step back.

"Enjoy your bath, firefly," I say as I shut off the water.

Then, like a damn coward, I leave the bathroom without looking back, closing the door to create a physical barrier between us so I can try to get a grip on myself. The only problem is that I hate myself a little more with each step I take away from her.

15

EMBER

You're pathetic. Who plays with dolls at our age? What kind of sicko are you?

"Ember, baby, wake up."

Why don't you just kill yourself so we don't have to look at your ugly face anymore?

"Firefly, wake up. You're having a nightmare, baby."

Hands grab at me, pulling my hair and scratching me. Letting out a cry, I fight back, clawing away from them.

"Ouch. Fuck. Baby, it's Cage."

"No. Leave me alone. I'm not a freak," I sob. "I don't want to kill myself. No. *No!*"

I keep fighting, thrashing as hard as I can to get away.

"Ember, stop." His voice is harsh and firm. "Stop, baby. It's me. It's... Daddy."

My eyes fly open, and I gasp, my heart pounding like a jackhammer. "Daddy," I whisper.

Safe. I'm safe.

As soon as I meet his gaze, I whimper. Tears stream down my face, and suddenly, I'm being smothered. Cage is on top of me, hugging me with his entire body. I cling to him, his warm skin soothing me as I continue to tremble and gasp for air.

"Shh. I got you. I'm right here. Breathe with me. Touch me, baby. Feel me here with you." His voice is deeper than usual.

"I'm sorry," I rush out. "I'm sorry I woke you."

"Don't ever be sorry, baby. Never be sorry for needing me." He strokes my hair and continues to hold me. It takes several minutes until I'm able to take a full, deep breath. When I do, he lets out a shaky one of his own. Is he upset?

"That's my girl. I've got you."

I continue to quiver underneath him, but the weight of his broad, muscular body is therapeutic, soothing me from the inside out.

"That's my girl," he whispers. "Daddy's good girl. Slow breaths, firefly. Slow breaths."

He keeps murmuring in my ear, his words distracting me from the nightmare I just endured.

I'm not sure how long we lay like this, but the air slowly shifts and begins to crackle. My core hums, and my breasts ache for his touch. I've never felt this way about a man. Not that I've been around a ton of guys. All through school, I was surrounded by girls. Mean, catty, spoiled girls. It wasn't until I started college that I was around men on a daily basis. I was even asked out a few times. I'm sure glad I always turned them down because I never knew I could feel this way just from an innocent touch. Well, it may not be totally innocent. The long, thick shaft pressing against my thigh certainly isn't.

Ever so gently, he presses a kiss to my neck just below my ear, and I moan. Butterflies flutter wildly low in my tummy.

"Cage."

"I like Daddy better, firefly." His voice is rough and strained.

Slowly, I widen my legs even more and then wrap my ankles around his waist. He's wearing a pair of tight boxer briefs and nothing else.

"Daddy," I whimper as he flexes his hips a fraction.

He threads his fingers in my hair, closing his fist around it. The slight sting shoots a bolt of arousal through me. I discovered I like a bit of pain while pinching my nipples one night when I was touching myself. I've always wondered if I'm weird because of it. Now, I have a hard time getting myself off if I'm not either fantasizing about pain or inflicting some on myself. Maybe I'm a total freak, but at the moment, I don't really care. It feels so damn right.

"Fuck, Ember. You don't know how badly I want to fuck you. How much I want to strip your clothes off and lick you from head to toe."

A strangled sound escapes me, and now I'm breathing faster for a totally different reason.

"Do you know how many times I've stroked my cock in the shower while fantasizing about you? Then you went and told me you're a virgin and being the fucked-up bastard that I am, all I've thought about since is popping that cherry of yours. Taking away your innocence and turning you into what you really are."

My hips move against him, grinding against his length. Every so often, it rubs the perfect spot that has me seeing stars. I've never even come close to feeling this good when I've given myself orgasms.

"What am I?" I ask, trying to keep focus on his words.

Cage rises onto his elbows so he can stare down at me, his hair messy like he's been grabbing at it.

"Mine," he growls right before he slams his mouth onto mine.

From the second he captures my lips, he kisses me passionately. Deeply. Thoroughly.

He slides his free hand up my body, lingering briefly as his fingertips graze my breast. His cock throbs against me. I've never been so wet before. He doesn't stop until he reaches my neck.

A flash of fear laces my senses when he squeezes the sides of my throat. Then he lets go, and a rush of arousal soaks my panties even more.

After giving me a final nip to my bottom lip, he slowly pulls his mouth away. We stare at each other in the dimly lit room. He must have turned on a lamp when he came in here. It's just the right amount of light to see each other's features. How is a man who is so dangerous, so terrifying, also so dang beautiful? And why does he make my heart pound like it's trying to escape my chest? The way his is racing against my hand makes me think he might feel the same.

"Please don't leave," I whimper.

I can feel him hesitate. He's probably pissed that he gave in to the moment. If I know one thing about Cage, it's that he likes to be in control of everything, including his own feelings.

"Ember," he groans.

"No. I'm firefly. Or baby. Or baby girl. I don't like it when you call me Ember."

Now I sound like a pouting two-year-old, but I don't care. He can't kiss me like that and then tuck tail and run.

"Is that so?" he asks, amusement sparkling in his dark eyes.

I smile, feeling smug as hell. "Yes. *That's so.*"

Totally a two-year-old.

"Last time I checked, firefly, I make the rules in this relationship."

I stare up at him, my fingers running over the thick silver chain hanging from his neck. "We have a relationship?"

He studies me for a long moment, then sighs and lets out a curse. "I don't know what we have." Cage closes his eyes for a few seconds. When he opens them, there's something vulnerable there. Something I've never seen in him before. It's raw. "This is a bad idea, firefly. A really fucking bad idea."

Swallowing the lump in my throat, I reach up and touch his face. "I think it's a great idea."

I'm not actually sure it is, but I've never wanted something so badly. Not only does he turn me on beyond anything I've ever experienced before, he also makes my Little feel safe.

"Ember."

I narrow my eyes. "Cage."

That gets the response I'd hoped for. He scowls at me, his jaw clenched. "I don't like when you call me Cage."

"If I call you Daddy, that would mean we have a relationship, so since you think it's such a bad idea, I'll call you Cage."

I'm poking the bear. It's probably a bad idea. I've never been a brat on purpose, but he brings it out in me. The man is just so dang stubborn.

"You're testing me, Little girl."

"Maybe." I bite the inside of my cheek to keep from smiling. It's kind of fun being a brat.

"It's a bad idea, firefly."

"Maybe. But it would be temporary. Once I'm safe, you'll be able to send me on my way and never see me again."

"I'm not taking your virginity, firefly. Especially if this is a temporary thing."

Jutting out my chin, I keep my gaze pinned to his. "If it's not you, it will be some other temporary man, I'm sure."

Cage's scowl deepens, and he bares his teeth like a pissed-off animal. "Say that again and I will pull down your panties and spank your ass until you're crying and begging me to stop."

Could this man be any more confusing? He doesn't want to take my virginity, but he gets jealous when I talk about someone else doing it.

"I'm a grown woman. I get to decide who and when. You might be the Daddy, but I still get to call the shots over my body."

I'm being difficult. Yet, unlike when I'm around my father or his business associates, I don't feel the need to behave. To be quiet and invisible.

"You're right, firefly. Your body, your choice."

Oh. Well, I wasn't expecting that. I figured he'd go all caveman on me. The feminist in me is proud of him. The Little girl in me wants to kick him.

"Doesn't mean I won't kill every single man you come across before he can even try to put his dirty hands on you." His fingers, which have been resting over my pulse point, tighten around my throat again, bringing my attention back to the present. "And you see, baby girl, if I fuck you, I'm not just going to fuck your pretty pussy. I'm going to fuck that smart little mouth and your naughty little ass, too."

My ass?

A shiver works its way down my spine. Why does the thought of Cage doing those things arouse me? Why am I panting so hard? I haven't seen his dick, but I've felt it several times; it's not small. The man could split me in half, and he wants to put it in my most intimate hole?

"Jesus. That fucking turns you on, firefly," he mutters. "You're supposed to tell me to fuck off, not get even hornier."

Using my nails, I scrape lines down his chest hard enough to draw the lightest trail of blood. "I want to experience having a Daddy. I've never had one, and I may never have one after this."

His eyebrows draw together. "Why wouldn't you ever have one? You're young and beautiful. There are tons of Daddies out there."

I swallow, lowering my eyes from his. "Because it's just better to keep this side of me a secret from the world."

Cage's entire body goes rigid, and he starts to shake his head. "No. Fuck that, firefly. You are who you are. I'm not saying you need to shout it from rooftops, but you sure as fuck shouldn't keep it a secret. What are you planning to do, live an unhappy vanilla life with some guy who doesn't even make you come? Fuck, no."

And just like that, the moment we were having

vanishes. Tears burn my eyes. I try to push him off me, but he doesn't budge.

"Don't push me away. Never push me away, Ember. Understand me?" he growls. When I don't answer him, he lowers his face, so our noses are touching and I'm forced to look at him. "Do. You. Understand. Me?"

Unable to stop it, I let out a soft sob. As soon as I do, Cage rolls onto his back and pulls me on top of him. We stay silent for several minutes while he strokes my back. His cock is still hard, but we're no longer grinding against each other, though my aching pussy wishes we still were.

"Tell me what happened to you, firefly. Why are you so scared to be who you are? To really show me your Little side." His voice is soft yet unrelenting. He's not going to let me get away with not telling him. Rowie has told me multiple times I should, but Cage can be a bit scary when he's angry. And for some reason, I know if I tell him, it will set him off. Which, in a way, makes me want to tell him because I want someone else to be angry for me. My father never was. He couldn't have cared less.

I let out a shaky breath and slowly tell him everything. The whole time, he continues to rub my back as he listens in silence. The only thing that gives away his anger is how rigid his body gets underneath me the more I speak.

When I finally finish, I close my eyes, and just like it did when I told Rowie, it feels as if another weight has been lifted off me. I've never talked about what I went through to anyone else, but it seems that getting it off my chest is somewhat therapeutic.

"They're dead," he mutters.

"No." I run my hands over his ribs. "They aren't worth it."

He slides his fingers up the back of my neck into my hair and fists it again. Then he pulls, so I'm forced to lift my head and look at him. "They're not. But you are."

I bite my bottom lip, trying to keep from bursting into tears. Gosh, when did I become such a crier? Apparently, The Ranch brings it out in me. Or maybe it's because I feel so safe here. Or is it because the people here, even the ones I've barely gotten to know, seem to care about me? I don't remember ever having that before. And every time one of them shows me even a sliver of tenderness, I practically turn into an emotional ball of tears. It's nice to feel something other than loneliness.

"I can't give you forever, firefly, but if you want to know what it's like to have a Daddy while you're here, I can give you that."

The lump in my throat grows bigger, and my heart aches a bit more than it did a second ago. Why do I feel disappointed? He's giving me what I asked for. Something temporary.

Am I sad he isn't demanding to keep me for the rest of our lives? That would be silly. He's not my type. At least he's not the type my father has planned for me. Cage is the complete opposite of everything my father would choose. We come from two different worlds. Yet, some-how, this world is where I feel most at home.

Thankfully, he lets go of my hair, so I lower my head back onto his chest, listening to his steady beating heart. It's easier when I don't have to meet his gaze.

"I want to know what it's like to have a Daddy. So yes, I accept," I finally reply. "Thank you, Cage."

His dick throbs beneath me. Does this mean he will have sex with me?

"Starting now, it's always Daddy. The only time it would ever be acceptable for you to use my name is if we were in a public setting, but we won't be going anywhere, so that doesn't apply. If you use my name here on The Ranch, I'll take away a Good Girl Point."

My nipples bud against him. "But what about in front of your family? What should I call you then?"

"Daddy. My brothers are all Daddies, too. They won't even bat an eye. Consider them your platonic uncles while you're here. Although, if you're naughty when I'm not around, they will be allowed to discipline you."

I snap my head up to look at him. "What? They'll spank me?"

Cage reaches up and cups my chin in his palm. "No. Not unless that's something you and I agree on. I'm not opposed to them spanking you if you deserve it. You get to decide whether that's a hard limit or not. Otherwise, they may put you in timeout, take away Good Girl Points, or make you write lines."

My tummy flutters, and my clit tingles, but my heart is racing. What have I gotten myself into? I'm not sure what I expected if Cage became my Daddy, but this wasn't it. I should have known it would be intense. Everything about the man is. All he has to do is look at me a certain way to get me panting. What's troubling me the most, though, is I don't hate it. Would I want one of his brothers to spank me? Cage hasn't even spanked me yet, so I don't know how I'll feel about it when the time comes.

"What are Good Girl Points?"

He grins. "They are points you can earn or have taken away. If you collect five points in one day, you get a reward. If you lose five points in one day, you get punished. However, there are some things you would be punished for right away that don't apply to your points. Safety things. Or if you're really naughty."

I frown and pinch my eyebrows together. "I'm not naughty."

The way he bites his lip makes me think he's trying not to laugh. How dare he. I'm the goodest girl in the world.

"In the morning, we need to go over your rules. I also have a journal for you. It will give you a place to put thoughts and feelings that you might be too nervous to tell me. We'll also discuss your limits. For right now, though, you need sleep."

Does he seriously think I'm going to be able to sleep? He's my Daddy. I have a Daddy. There's no way I'm going to be able to doze off. I have questions. And I want to know what my rules are. The thought of having someone set rules for me has always made me squirmy.

"I'm not tired," I murmur.

Cage lets out a sigh. "I can already tell you're going to be sitting on a red bottom quite often, firefly. Quit arguing and close your eyes."

The corners of my lips twitch as I obey his command. He shifts slightly, as if he's reaching for something. A second later, he taps my lips.

"Open, baby girl."

As soon as I do, he slides something soft into my mouth. A pacifier. The same one he left for me in the playroom that I was too nervous to use. I'd thought about it. Practically non-stop while I was in that room until Rowie came in.

I blink several times, chewing on the silicone to get a feel for it.

"Just relax and let yourself experience it. You're safe to be Little here."

His words soothe me. It doesn't take long before I find myself gently sucking on the nipple, my eyes getting so heavy I can't keep them open for another moment.

16

CAGE

Fuck.

What did I do?

I did exactly what I wanted to. But it's not what I should have done. For a man with so much control, I don't seem to have any around Ember.

As I glance down at her sleeping form, a pacifier lodged in her mouth, I replay our conversation. I should spank her for goading me. She knew what she was doing. Pushing my buttons. Talking about losing her virginity to another man. The thought of it enrages me. If another man so much as touches her, I'll fucking destroy him. Maybe I'll just have to do that. Kill any guy who so much as looks her way. I'm not above stalking her once she goes back to DC.

I care for her. As much as I want to deny it, I'm lying to myself. In the short time she's invaded my life, she's somehow wiggled her way under my skin. It's uncomfortable yet comforting at the same time. It's also the scariest fucking thing I've ever experienced.

When she told me what those girls did to her in school, I could barely keep myself in check. I wanted to jump up and punch something. The only reason I didn't is because she was on top of me, spilling her fucking heart out and breaking mine with her story. It might have been a long time ago that it happened, but those women will pay for hurting my firefly. For still hurting her now. The evident pain in her eyes last night nearly killed me. I don't need Ember to give me names. I'll find them myself and ruin their lives. I hate bullies. I dealt with them until I was recruited to The Agency. Like hell will I allow bullies to continue to haunt my girl.

As happy thoughts of how I'm going to destroy those women run through my head, I let myself relax under the warmth of my girl's body. I start to drift to sleep, for the first time in a long time, feeling whole.

She belongs here. At The Ranch. Where she can be herself. Where she's cared about. Maybe even loved.

I stare at the list before me and go over each line again. I've been working on it since dawn while Ember continues to snooze beside me, her pacifier still in her mouth. She hardly moved all night. After her nightmare, I was worried about getting her back to sleep.

When I heard her crying out last night, it broke my heart. She sounded so sad and scared. My poor girl. Her father is now on my list of people to destroy. The only reason he's been spared so far is because, even though he's a shitty parent, I can tell Ember still loves him. She wants him to love her so badly, and the asshole doesn't seem to see it or care. Whatever the case, I've hit my limit.

She stirs beside me. I glance over and watch as she stretches, a soft sigh escaping her. My cock jumps at the innocent sound. I don't know how the hell I expect to control myself around her. It's torture. Taking her virginity when I can't promise her anything isn't right, though. She deserves *everything*. Not just a broken man like me who struggles to be gentle with her.

"Morning."

Her eyes fly open, and she meets my gaze. I reach out and brush her hair away from her face then give a tug on the pacifier. She opens her mouth and lets me pull it free.

"Hi," she murmurs.

"You slept like a baby once you dozed off."

The pink hue on her cheeks deepens as she moves her gaze around, as if trying to avoid my stare.

"You have eighty-seven freckles on the bridge of your nose," I tell her.

She freezes and snaps her eyes up to meet mine. "What?"

"I counted. Three times to make sure I wasn't off. Eighty-seven."

I'm not sure why, but I couldn't stop myself this morning. I want to know every single thing about her all the way down to something as simple as her adorable freckles.

"You counted," she repeats. "While I was sleeping."

I nod and hold up the pad of paper. "Yes. I also made a list of rules for you."

Her eyebrows draw together, and she sits up, resting her back against the headboard. "You like rules."

"I like *you* having rules."

"Maybe you should have rules, too."

I chuckle. "Believe me, firefly. I have rules. Ones I set for myself. When I fuck up, I punish myself harsher than anyone else could."

Her messy hair sticks up in places, only adding to her sleepy cuteness. I could get used to this. Waking up beside her every morning. Her pink sleep shirt has a sparkly rainbow printed on the front and it just adds to how adorable she is. I wonder what kind of panties she has on. I didn't get a glimpse last night. Once I start dressing her, I'll be putting her in the most innocent cotton panties possible to make her feel so Little. Maybe I'll even make her wear some training panties.

The past few days with her have been some of the best I've had in a long time. So much that I've been all but ignoring the issue at hand. Instead of trying to figure out the threat, I've been obsessing over her. Because the sooner I eliminate the threat, the sooner she leaves, and that makes my chest burn. She's safe here. Not a single fucking soul can get to her here unless I allow it.

"You're really hard on yourself, you know?"

If only she knew.

"Baby, I didn't get to where I am by taking it easy on myself."

"What is it you do exactly? And how did you end up here with all these men and Rowie? You said you were adopted, but I get the feeling it's not the type of adoption I pictured."

I knew at some point I'd have to tell her my story. The longer she's here, the more she'll learn. Then she'll decide for the both of us that she belongs in DC. As much as I hate that thought, I won't hide who I am, even if she hates me for it. I didn't want to start this morning out with this conversation, though. Guess we may as well get it out of the way so she can decide if she still wants me to be her temporary Daddy.

"I never knew my real parents. I was dropped off at a church when I was a baby. From there, I went to seventeen foster homes throughout my childhood. Most of the families were abusive in one way or another, so I ran away often. Got into trouble. Did some really bad shit. I went to juvie nearly a dozen times from the time I was nine until I was thirteen."

Ember's bottom lip trembles, but she doesn't say

anything. Instead, she reaches out and takes my hand in hers. My throat goes tight. She's comforting me. This precious Little girl, who had a nightmare in the middle of the night because of the shit she went through, is trying to comfort me. Fuck me. I don't deserve something so damn precious.

"I'm smart. Like genius smart," I say, smirking down at her. "You knew that already, though."

That gives me the reaction I'd hoped for as she smiles widely and rolls her eyes.

"So humble, too," she says.

I nod. "The humblest."

She snorts and shakes her head.

"Anyway, I didn't know it, but someone had been tracking me for a few years. A company called The Agency."

"The Agency? I've never heard of them."

"It's not the type of organization known by the public."

Ember squints, her nose scrunching in confusion. If only she knew what that does to me. At least I have blankets over me to cover my forming erection.

"Why had they been tracking you? I'm confused."

"One particular person in The Agency was tracking me. Deke Black. He showed up at the juvenile detention center I was in and told me that because of my genius and psychopath tendencies he had an offer for me."

"Psychopath?" she squeaks.

"Yeah, baby. Pretty sure you already knew that, though."

The pink flush returns to her cheeks as she ducks her head. "Well, I mean, I might have called you that a few times, but I was joking. Mostly."

My chest warms, and fuck, if only things were different. She'd have my last name already—on paper and tattooed on her.

"Good thing for you, I'm not actually one. They tested me. I just have *some* of the tendencies."

She laughs softly. "That makes me feel so much better."

Reaching under the blankets, I gently pinch her thigh, although instead of letting out a yelp, she whimpers and squirms. What the fuck? My girl likes some pain.

"Watch it, brat. I'll have you face-down over my lap in a heartbeat if you keep being sassy."

She nibbles her bottom lip, her eyes sparkling, and my heart starts to pound harder as I stare at her. I'm utterly and completely fucked when it comes to Ember Elizabeth Adams.

"So, what happened? How did you end up here?" she finally asks.

"Deke made me an offer. Family, money, and freedom to do things that quiet the monster inside of me without spending the rest of my life in prison."

Seconds pass, and I wait for her to pull her hand away from mine. To decide she's heard enough and kick me out of her room. I wouldn't blame her. Nothing about my life is ordinary.

Ever so slowly, she lets go of me, and a pain blooms in my chest that is nearly intolerable. I've been rejected by a lot of people in my life, but this will be by far the most painful.

Then she reaches up and smooths her hand over my cheek. "People are always afraid of monsters, but I think they're misunderstood. If they were just given a chance, I think the world would see that we need monsters in our lives to keep us safe from our own demons."

If I wasn't already in love with Ember, I think I am now. Fuck, I know I am. And when I lose her, it will destroy me.

"Thanks, firefly," I say softly. "You know you're safe with me, right? That no matter what I am or what I do, I will never hurt you. I will always protect you."

She smiles and leans into me, letting out a soft sigh. "I know, Daddy."

Those three words render me speechless, and all I can manage is to wrap my arms around her and kiss the top of her head.

"Are your brothers the same as you?" she finally asks.

"Yeah, baby. We were all teenagers when Deke recruited us. Some of us were in juvie, some lived on the streets, and some were in abusive homes. We're all fucked up from our pasts. The Ranch is our solitude from the world when we're not working."

Ember nods. "So, what is it exactly that *you* do for work? Since you made it pretty clear to me that you're not a bodyguard."

I chuckle and give her hair a playful tug. "You really want some of your Good Girl Points taken away already, don't you? Does my girl want her bottom spanked? Is that what it is? You don't have to be a sassy brat to get one; you can just ask for a spanking."

She tips her head back to look up at me, the tips of her ears bright red. "Sassing you is so fun, though."

"Okay, baby girl. As long as you know, you'll have to pay the price of that sass at some point."

"You're avoiding my question." She raises her eyebrows at me and waits.

Letting out a sigh, I lean my head back against the wall. "We do a lot of things. We're like a special-ops team but times a thousand. We all have things we excel in, and we use our skills to make the world a better place. Sometimes, that means stopping terrorist attacks, and sometimes, that means helping the mafia stop human trafficking rings. We work for every letter agency there is plus several of the syndicate families. Organizations contract us when something needs to be done without the public knowing. In exchange, we have the freedom to handle situations our way without any repercussions."

When I finish, I glance down at her, expecting to see disgust. A lot of what we do doesn't seem like it's right. Teaming up with the mob? Working under the radar for the CIA? It sounds like fictional shit. But what people don't realize is the world needs men like us to do things no one else can.

"Do you..." Ember stops and shakes her head, diverting her eyes. "Never mind."

I cup her chin and force her to look at me. "No. You have a question, you ask. Don't ever censor yourself around me."

As I firmly squeeze her cheeks, her pupils dilate.

"I was just going to ask if you kill people," she says softly. "But it doesn't matter. It's not my business."

Leaning down, I glare at her. "That's where you're wrong, firefly. If I'm your Daddy, my business is yours, and yours is mine. I don't do secrets or lies. It's a rule. I also don't believe in giving space. I'm an obsessive motherfucker, and I'll probably suffocate you. Everything in my life is your business."

She opens her mouth to speak, but nothing comes out, so I go on.

"The answer is yes, firefly. I kill people. Brutally. Always for good reason. Never just for fun. I also torture people when needed. I'm not a good man, Ember. My first kill was when I was thirteen. I have more blood on my hands than any person ever should."

Now she's really going to push me away. My stomach coils at the thought, and I think I might be sick. It's one of the reasons I've never really sought out a relationship. The chance of finding someone, specifically someone in this lifestyle, willing to be with someone like me is laughable. It's something my brothers and I have accepted over the years. I think having Rowie in our lives has made it easier for us. We may not be her Daddy, but we still get to be around a Little and take care of her as if we are.

Ember runs her fingers over the fur of her stuffed dragon. It's cute and it's her favorite, but all I can think about is wanting to get her a dozen more. I want to fill an entire fucking room with every toy I can find. She deserves that.

Her eyes are wide and searching when she turns them to look at me. There's no disgust or hatred in her gaze. Just pure curiosity. "Do you like what you do?"

I won't lie to her. I can't. She deserves the truth. Even if it is the final nail in the coffin.

"Yeah, firefly. I do. Maybe that makes me a sick bastard, but I've seen so much ugly in the world over my lifetime that when I can watch someone's horrible life drain from their eyes, it makes me happy. It heals something inside me."

Ember doesn't say anything for a long time. I'm going to be sick. I've never felt for anyone like this, and I've just destroyed it. I guess that's what I'm good at. Destroying things.

Then she wiggles closer to me and nudges her way under my arm, so she's snuggled into the crook of my armpit, and just like that, my world feels right again. "The Agency made a good choice in you. It makes me feel better about the world knowing you're one of the men helping to keep it safer."

Nothing surprises me anymore. I've seen and done too much for that. But this Little girl just knocked the fucking wind out of me.

"You don't hate me?" I ask softly.

She turns and looks up at me, her eyebrows pinched. "Why would I hate you? You were given a shit hand in life, and you've made the best of it. You have an amazing family, a job that means something, and a beautiful home where you can be yourself. I'm proud of you."

I don't remember the last time I cried. Maybe when I was a baby. But those words, *I'm proud of you*, coming from her, bring me to my knees, and I blink back tears.

Leaning down, I kiss her forehead. "Thanks, firefly," I say tightly. "Swearing is against the rules."

She smirks and rolls her eyes. "Yes, Daddy."

And for the first time, I realize I'm not going to be able to let her go. Physically, maybe, but Ember has a permanent place in my heart. She's carved out a spot right in the center and has burrowed herself in deep. When she leaves, that hole will be massive and painful. Probably the most painful thing I've ever endured. Yet, for her, I'd fucking burn if she asked me to walk through fire.

I might not be able to keep her, but it doesn't mean I won't watch over her for the rest of her life. Even if it kills me when she finds the man of her dreams. And it just might. If I don't kill him first, of course.

17

EMBER

I'm still trying to wrap my mind around everything Cage shared. I want to cry for the little boy who was abandoned. Who had to fight just to survive for so long. I don't even want to imagine what would have happened if Deke hadn't shown up. I have no idea who the man is, but I kind of want to hug him.

Every time Cage told me what a bad man he was, I wanted to shake him. He has no idea how amazing he is. But I do. Even if I do give him a hard time. It's not hard to see that Cage is bright. He's smart in that Sheldon Cooper kind of way. All of the men here are. It's why they struggle with emotions. They function on logic and facts.

I quirk an eyebrow. "What about Rowie? She's not like you guys."

Rowie is smart, there's no doubt about that, but she's different than the men. She wears her heart on her sleeve.

"Rowie doesn't do what we do. She came into this family by accident. We couldn't leave her where she was. Deke let us keep her and made Theo and me her guardians since we're the ones who found her."

"Found her?" I ask hesitantly. I'm not sure I want to know, but at the same time, I do.

"Yeah. Behind a dumpster. She was beaten and bruised and starving. We couldn't leave her."

I sniffle and swipe at my eyes. "Poor Rowie. Oh my God. She's so bubbly and happy."

Cage stares off into the distance, his gaze unfocused. "She still has her demons. We all do. She's come a long way, though."

Needing to be closer to him, I push the covers back and crawl onto his lap. He doesn't hesitate to wrap his arms around me and snuggle me into him.

"My problems seem so stupid in comparison," I whisper.

His grip on me tightens, and then he pulls back, gives me a sharp swat on the butt, and glares at me.

I yelp and reach back to rub the sting away. "Ouchie. You spanked me!"

"That wasn't a spanking, firefly. It was a warning. If I ever hear you belittling your own demons, I'll take my belt to your bottom. Do you understand me?"

There isn't an ounce of give in his stern voice. I shiver and quickly nod, though my core flutters at his scolding. Why do I like it when he talks to me in that tone? Like I'm a naughty Little girl. It shouldn't turn me on, but my damp panties are proof it does.

"I'm sorry."

He leans forward until our lips are nearly touching. Heat pools between my legs. When I shift to try and find some kind of relief, the hard length of his cock presses against my bottom. I wiggle again, and his hands flex on my hips, holding me still.

"You really need a spanking," he growls.

I shrug, a smile pulling at the corners of my mouth. "But I'm such a good girl."

"Jesus." He huffs. "Yeah, you're a good girl. You're also really fucking naughty sometimes. Which probably means this is a good time to go over your rules."

My nipples tingle and bud under the thin material of my sleep shirt. There is seriously something wrong with me if I'm getting turned on by the topic of him giving me rules. Maybe I need therapy. Or an orgasm. I like that idea better.

"This is what I've written down so far. Read them aloud, and we can discuss them if needed," he says, handing me a pad of paper that is full of his writing.

I glance at him and bite my lip, suddenly nervous. He's taking this Daddy thing seriously.

"Number one, no lying or hiding things from Daddy. Number two, bedtime is ten o'clock sharp and daily naptime from one to two." I screw up my face. "I don't take naps."

"You do now. Keep reading, firefly."

Well, isn't he bossy? Bossy McBosserton.

I inwardly smile at that. I like that nickname for him.

A sharp pinch on my bottom makes me jump. "I don't know what thought you just had, but I'm almost positive it was naughty."

Well. That's just great. Now he can read my mind.

"Read, baby."

"Number three, Daddy will choose Ember's clothes and pajamas every day. He will also dress her." Heat creeps over my cheeks. I kind of like that one. "Number four, Daddy will give Ember baths. She will no longer take showers or bathe alone."

I'm going to need to change my panties by the time I'm done with this.

"Number five, Ember will not touch her pussy without Daddy's permission." I scoff. "What? Why?"

Cage raises his eyebrows. "Because it's a rule. Daddy is in charge of your pleasure now."

"But you said you won't have sex with me."

"I said I wouldn't take your virginity, firefly. I never said we couldn't do other things."

"Oh," I murmur. "Huh. Okay. Although I'm not so sure I like that rule."

He chuckles. "Most Little girls don't. Keep reading."

"Number six, safety rules, no wearing socks without traction grips in the house. No running in the house. Ember must hold the railing when going up and down stairs. No playing outside without SPF 70 sunblock on. No going in the pool without a caregiver present and Ember must wear arm floaties. No playing on the playground without a caregiver present. No using knives. No cooking. No walking around with a lollipop in mouth." I pause and look at him, trying to fight a grin. "Maybe you should just wrap me in bubble wrap and call it a day."

He narrows his eyes and points to the list. "Read the next rule."

I sigh. "Rule seven, no sassing Daddy, especially about the safety rules. Seriously?" I roll my eyes. "You're over the top."

"Oh, baby girl, you have no fucking idea just how over the top I am. Keep going."

"Rule eight, when Daddy is home, he will feed Ember her meals. Rule nine, Ember will write in her journal every day." I frown. "But I don't have a journal."

Cage reaches over to the nightstand and hands me a book with *My Little Journal* printed on the front. I run my fingers over the fluffy clouds and pastel sky on the cover. Just looking at it makes me happy. "When Rowie first came to us, she didn't speak. She was too afraid. Theo got the idea to give her a journal so she could at least get her thoughts and feelings out in a way she felt safe. We only read the pages she allows."

"Will you read mine?"

"Do you want me to?"

I think about it. It might be easier to share things with

him that I otherwise might not say out loud. "I think I'm okay with it."

He nods. "Good. If there's ever a page you don't want me to read, you can mark it and I will skip it. Just remember, no secrets, though."

"'Kay." My voice is small, and with each rule I read, I find myself slipping deeper and deeper into that headspace. I've always heard the saying rules are made for breaking, but all I can think is that with each one I read, the safer and happier I feel. "Rule nine, no swearing. Rule ten, Daddy will help Ember in the bathroom. This means brushing her teeth, wiping her bottom, and doing her hair."

Whipping my gaze from the paper to him, I shake my head. "You're not helping me in the bathroom. No. That's *not* happening."

Ever so calmly, he reaches out and strokes my heated cheek. "Why not, firefly? What's so bad about it?"

My mouth falls open. Does he really not understand? The man is basically a genius; he should know why I don't want him in the bathroom with me. Did he not get the picture when I screamed at him in a rest-stop bathroom? The man sure is dense sometimes.

"Because that's... It's..."

"It's what, baby? It's embarrassing?"

"Yes!"

He chuckles and continues to run his thumb over my cheek. "You do know that a lot of Daddies take care of their Little girls in the most intimate ways, don't you? Some Littles wear diapers or pull-ups. Some even use them."

If I could burst into a ball of flames right now, I would. Does he expect me to do that? Cage likes to be in control, but does that include having a say on using the toilet?

"Look at me, firefly."

I do, my bottom lip lodged between my teeth. If I bite down any harder, I'm going to make myself bleed. As if he knows it, he tugs it free and gently rubs the tip of his finger over it.

"I want you to answer something, and I want the truth."

Shoot. I'm not sure if I like where this is going. "Okay."

He nods. "When I walked in on you at the rest stop, you were embarrassed?"

"Yes," I answer quietly.

"Were you also turned on because I was there while you were doing one of the most intimate things possible? Have you gotten turned on whenever I've talked about helping you in the bathroom?"

Crap.

I should lie. Deny it. But he'll know. Cage seems to understand me more than I'd like to admit. If I tell him the truth, though, what does that say about me? Why are my wants and needs so unusual?

"The truth, baby girl."

"Yes. Okay, yes." I bring my hands to my face, covering it so I don't have to look at him. "I got turned on."

A few seconds pass before he wraps his large hands around my wrists and lowers them.

"So why are you so against me doing it?"

I narrow my eyes. "You know why. It's embarrassing, and... what if I toot? Or have to do the other thing?"

The corners of his lips twitch like he's trying to keep from smiling. "Do you think I'm going to change my mind about you being the cutest Little girl ever if you pass gas? Going potty is a normal human function. It's a Daddy's job to make sure his girl is cleaned up properly. After doing either."

My eyes widen, and I might die of humiliation. Cause of death, mortification.

"I would never do anything if you decided it's a hard limit, but I'd like you to at least try it before you shut the idea down. I'm a hands-on Daddy. I'm also the type to smother you with my attention. You'll probably hate me for it at some point, but you'll get over it because of how much you love it, too. I'll want to be involved in everything to do with you. I'll even want to help you during your period. Part of it is because taking care of you makes me happy, and part of it is because the embarrassment and arousal are part of this dynamic and what makes it so special."

I'm touched that he wants to be so involved. But the bathroom? My period? Is it a hard limit for me? My mind screams yes, but the flutter of butterflies in my tummy and the dampness of my panties say something different.

"Think of it this way," he says, his voice tight like it's hard for him to speak. "I'm only your temporary Daddy, so even if it is embarrassing, once you leave, you'll never have to face me again. I'd be willing to bet, though, that you find that level of submission to be addicting."

Why does my chest ache from his words? I'm the one who asked for this. I pretty much begged him to be my Daddy for the short time that I'm here. So, why does it make me want to throw up when I think about having to leave him?

"Okay. But I can decide it's a hard limit at any time?"

He nods. "Yeah, firefly. Ultimately, you call the shots in this dynamic. You draw the lines, and I stay within them. That doesn't mean I won't push you, though. I'm going to test every single one of your boundaries, but all you have to do is say red and everything stops."

Huh. I never thought of it like that.

"The last few rules are basic things, like telling me if something is wrong, coming to me with any problem you have, making sure you ask questions if you have them. We'll add more as we go. I'm sure I'll think of plenty more."

I giggle because, of course, he will. Cage loves rules and structure. It's how he functions.

"I need to know your limits. On the next page, I wrote down a list of things I want you to check yes, no, or CNC on. If you check no, it's a hard limit and we won't do it. If you check yes, it means you're okay with it. CNC means you're giving me consent to do it even if you tell me no. The only thing that will stop me from doing it to you is your safeword, which is red. Once you're done with that, we will begin our dynamic full-time."

My clit tingles as I turn the page. He hands me a pen and silently waits while I go over the list.

Spanking: Yes

Timeout: Yes

Pacifiers: Yes

Bottles: Yes

Butt Plugs: Yes

I stare at the next few lines, biting my lip as I squeeze my thighs together. Wow, he went really in-depth with this. A lot of the things on here I've thought about but never even considered would ever happen in real life. Then again, I didn't think I'd ever have a Daddy.

Diapers and/or Pull-ups: CNC

Enemas: CNC

Using the toilet in front of Daddy: CNC

Being punished by Daddy's brothers: CNC

My face is flaming as I circle my answers, yet my pussy is tingling. What is wrong with me? I want to say, "hell no" to it, but also, I kind of want it forced on me.

As I go down each line, I get more squirmy by the second. When I finally finish and hand the paper back to him, I'm practically panting. And his smug smile tells me he can tell just how turned on I am, too.

"Do you have any questions?"

So many. I could probably fill up that entire notebook with all the things I want to ask. But something tells me I just need to trust him and let myself experience everything as it comes. After all, I can always use my safeword.

"I'm good."

He studies me for a moment before he nods. "I will let my brothers know what we are doing so they have a heads-up. They're all experienced Daddies, so nothing we do around them will shock them. Being the kind of men they are, you need to expect them to be a bit over-the-top protective of you, just like they are with Rowie. I expect you to obey them if they tell you to do something. That's also a rule. I'll write it down later. Are we clear?"

"Yes."

He cups my chin and gives it a firm squeeze. "From now on, it's 'yes, Daddy.'"

I swallow thickly, my nipples aching from his light scolding. "Yes, Daddy."

He smiles and leans down to kiss the tip of my nose. "Good."

My tummy flutters and my core is so needy it's almost painful.

"When is your next period? Is it usually heavy or light? I think a diaper would be best when you're on it. Do you get bad cramps?"

Letting out a small squeak, I cover my flaming face. "Daddyyyy."

Cage chuckles. "I love it when you get all embarrassed. It's fucking adorable. Now, we're going to go potty, and I'm going to get you ready for the day while you answer *all* my period questions. Then I have to leave for a few hours. You'll be able to hang out with Rowie today. Theo and Jasper will be here to keep an eye on you two."

My heart comes to a skidding halt. "Wait, what?"

Cage gets out of bed, the outline of his erection temporarily distracting me. He leans over and pulls me to the edge before he picks me up and carries me on his hip like he would a small child. I instinctively wrap my legs around his waist and snuggle into his chest.

"It's only for a few hours."

I start to rub my thumb over my chin. Why is he leaving? Does he need a break from me already? Maybe I'm being too needy. No, Cage has told me he likes needy.

As soon as he sets me on my feet in front of the toilet, he notices my fidgeting. Of course he does. Cage sees *everything*.

"Why are you worried, baby?" he asks as he hooks his thumbs in the waistband of my panties and pulls them to my knees.

"I'm not worried," I scoff, then look up at him with pleading eyes. "Can I go with you?"

When the heck did I become so attached to this man that I didn't want him to leave me for a few hours?

I'm so distracted I barely realize it as he pushes me to sit on the toilet, and I start peeing without thought. It's not until I'm nearly done that I squeal and bring my hands to my face.

Cage chuckles and reaches for the toilet paper. He's actually going to clean me up. Which means he's going to touch me down there. Not directly, but he will still see everything. A shiver runs down my spine at that thought. Can I be that submissive? Despite how embarrassing it is, it's also a turn-on that he wants to do something so intimate. I never imagined that being Little would include stuff like this. Not in real life, anyway.

Without warning, he leans over my shoulder and pulls me into him, then quickly reaches down to dry me. As his touch brushes over my bare pussy, I nearly moan.

"It's not safe to take you anywhere at the moment. This will be no different than the last few days that you've played with Rowie and I've been in my office. I'll have my phone on me the whole time, and you'll be able to reach me any time you want. You have the burner phone I gave you, and my brothers will call me at the drop of a hat if you ask them to. Okay?"

I sigh and nod as he pulls my panties up and over my waist, then leads me to the sink to wash his hands and brush my teeth, which, of course, he does for me, too. And the entire time, all I can think about is how I've never felt so seen and understood in my entire life.

18

CAGE

> Cage: Two things. Ember is my temporary Little until she can go back to DC. And you guys have her CNC to punish her if she misbehaves.

> Cage: Also, her next period is expected in two weeks. Add it to your calendars.

We've all made it a habit to track Rowie's periods, so it's probably a good idea to track Ember's. That way, as it gets closer, we can make sure to stock up on pads and chocolate and be more available in case they need extra snuggles.

> Rylan: I fucking knew it. Dom, you owe me five grand.

> Dom: Fuck.

Cage: What the hell? What were you betting on?

Rylan: Whether or not you would make Ember your Little girl.

Cage: You bastards. What is wrong with you?

Rylan: A lot.

Gunner: Congrats, bro.

Lex: We're going to have two Little brats running around now?

Cage: Don't call her a brat, asshole.

Theo: Rowie isn't a brat.

Koda: I'll bet all of you fifty grand that the temporary part turns permanent.

Cyrus: I'll get in on that.

Cassian: Let's make it a hundred grand.

I glare at my phone screen and try to remember why I claimed these assholes as my brothers. They're really fucking annoying.

Cage: Fuck off. All of you.

Rylan: I think the only one getting fucked in this family right now is you, bro.

A low growl escapes. Both from possessiveness and

frustration. I don't like that Rylan is thinking about Ember having sex. Even if it is with me. Add on the fact that it's not actually happening and I'm a little irritable.

I pocket my phone and climb out of my SUV. Almost as soon as I ring the doorbell, the enormous front door swings wide-open.

"Cage!" Cali squeals as she practically jumps on me for a hug.

Warmth fills me, and I grin as her husband walks up behind her, scowling at me, probably because I'm touching his girl. Possessive bastard. Not that I blame him. Cali's a doll. She's not Ember, though. I hadn't planned to settle down, though, if I had, that would be out the window now. She may only be in my life temporarily, but Ember will be in my heart for the rest of my life. She's carved a spot there, and I don't think there's a woman on this Earth who can compare.

"What the fuck are you doing here?" Declan demands as he pulls his wife away from me and tucks her behind him.

"What? No warm welcome? I'm hurt, Declan, I really am." I place my hand over my heart and smirk while the Irish mafia boss continues to glare at me.

"You showed up here unannounced," he snaps.

I turn and look down his driveway toward the wrought-iron gates where six security guards are currently posted. "They called and told you I was here. That's an announcement."

Declan mutters something under his breath about me being a psycho, but I choose to ignore it. Whether he wants to admit it or not, he likes me.

"Daddy, be nice. Let Cage in," Cali insists, tugging on Declan's suit jacket.

He looks down at her and sighs before he takes a step back. I wink at Cali and get another growl from Declan in response.

"Where's the rest of the fam?" I ask.

Cali skips alongside us as we make our way through the house. To my surprise, Declan doesn't lead us into his office. Instead, we enter a small living room, which the girls always seem to be watching movies in. Sure enough, Paisley is sitting on Kieran's lap while Beauty and the Beast plays in the background. I don't know what it is with this movie, but the girls in this family all seem to love it. Maybe Ember understands and can explain it to me.

Paisley's eyes light up as soon as she sees me, but Kieran studies me as he protectively pulls his girl tighter to him. Jesus, it's like these guys don't trust me. Don't they know I don't kill friends?

"What the fuck is he doing here?" Kieran demands.

I guess he's still a bit pissy about me goading him when he was sprung over Paisley but not ready to admit it. I let the guy punch me, so he really should get the hell over it.

Declan shrugs and sits down, pulling Cali onto his lap

as he does. "No fucking clue. He showed up without calling, so whatever it is, it must be serious."

As I take a seat at the other end of the couch that Kieran and Paisley are on, Kieran bares his teeth at me. I give him a smug look before I wink at Paisley. She giggles, then yelps when her husband pinches her thigh.

"Ouchie. Daddy, that wasn't nice."

Kieran scowls at her. "Blushing and laughing because another man winks at you isn't nice."

Paisley scoffs and glares back at him, clearly not intimidated by the hulk of a man. "So basically, I can't have fun, is that right?"

"That's not what I said and you know it," Kieran says.

All he gets in return is an eye-roll before Paisley turns her attention toward me and beams. "Don't mind him, Cage. He's grumpy today."

"Just today?" I lean back on the couch and smile at Kieran, who flips me off.

Good times.

"Can you just get to the point as to why you're here? In Seattle. Don't you live in another state?" Declan asks.

I shrug and ignore his question. Maybe that's one of the reasons they don't trust me. They know nothing about me, yet I know everything about them. It's the life of a dark-ops agent. Nothing but secrets.

"I have a problem." I quickly check my phone to make sure I haven't missed anything from my girl, then slide it back into my pocket.

"No shit," Kieran mutters.

Paisley playfully hits him on the chest.

"What's going on?" Declan asks, suddenly all business.

They may not trust me personally, but professionally, they do. If this had anything to do with a job, I know they'd lend their assistance without question. Then again, I guess it sort of has something to do with a job.

"I'm protecting a woman from a threat. She's staying at my home," I tell them.

Declan and Kieran stare at me like they don't know what I'm getting at. No wonder they need my help sometimes. They all might be a bunch of good-looking, rich mafia bosses, but I'm starting to wonder if the brains aren't all there. Hopefully, they know how to make their women orgasm.

I glance from Cali to Paisley, observing the smitten expressions when they look at their men. Okay, at least they know how to keep their women happy.

"You like her," Paisley finally says.

"I do," I answer slowly. "She's Little. I'm her Daddy. Temporarily."

"And does she know this? Or is this against her will?" Declan asks.

When I flip him off, he shoots me a smug smile. Fucker.

"So, what's the problem? Does she like you? Oh, can we meet her?" Cali perks up, her attention no longer on the movie.

The back of my neck tingles as a wave of possessiveness washes over me. There's no fucking way I'm bringing my girl around these men. I don't give a fuck if they have wives. I don't want Ember around any men other than my family. She would adore Cali and Paisley, though, so I might have to make a compromise at some point.

I run my hand over my eyebrows, trying to soothe the headache I'm fighting. "Settling down has never been my plan. It wouldn't be fair to her. The way she would have to live if she was mine permanently. She wouldn't have a normal life."

Cali raises her eyebrows. "Who does have a normal life? Besides, what is normal anyway? There's no right or wrong way to live as long as you're happy."

Declan stares lovingly at his wife and then presses a kiss to her temple. It's a sweet gesture that, a few years ago, I never would have thought I'd see the man do. But here we are, the leader of the entire North American Irish mafia, gently kissing his wife and watching Beauty and the Beast.

"Why don't you ask her what *she* wants?" Paisley asks.

Probably because I'm afraid of what her answer might be. I don't want to think about the end until I truly have to. If she confirms that it's all just a temporary game for her, I don't know how I'll feel.

"What if I can't keep her safe?" I hate how vulnerable I feel as the words come out.

I'm not an insecure man. I have abilities that most

people can't even fathom. But the tiny sliver at the corner of my brain that keeps asking that is what's stopping me from diving headfirst because I'd give up Ember forever as long as it keeps her safe.

"We all worried about the same thing when we met our girls," Declan answers, his gaze pinned on Cali with a tortured expression. "And while we do everything possible to keep them safe, there's always a chance that something could happen."

I stare at him. "Exactly. I'm not willing to take that risk. Risks aren't part of my life. Calculated plans are what I do. Sure things. Leaving nothing to chance. I'd never be able to live with myself if something happened to Ember."

Kieran clears his throat. "You have at least a dozen brothers who are trained the same as you. The risk of anything happening to her is pretty much non-existent."

"I guess that's true," I mutter. "We've kept Rowie safe all these years."

Declan's eyebrows draw together. "Who is Rowie?"

I glance up and take a second to process his question.

"Rowie is our sister. I thought I'd told you." That's a lie. Now that I think about it, I know I never told them. Damn. I guess I really haven't let these men into my life at all. Maybe I need to start. At least then, they might trust me more.

"You have a sister? Oh, how old is she?" Cali asks.

"She's around your age; she's Little too. We found her

when she was a kid. Long story, but she's in Little Space most of the time. It's therapeutic for her."

Paisley and Cali exchange a look before Paisley grins at me. "Okay, we need to have a playdate with Ember and Rowie. We could do something fun like a tea party with real tea and snacks. Would that be Little enough for them?"

For the second time since I've arrived here, my chest warms. These girls aren't even age players, yet they still want to make friends with my sister and my girl.

"We'll see," Declan says before I can answer. "So you're here because you want advice or...?"

I nod. "I didn't come here to talk sports, so yeah. Some advice would be great."

"Why didn't you ask your brothers?" Kieran asks.

Paisley smacks him on the chest again, but Kieran just shrugs.

My mind goes back to the text conversation I had with them right before I got here. "Because those bastards are taking bets on this to see whether it will actually be temporary or not."

"I'll get in on that," Declan says, holding up his index finger. "There's no way it's temporary. You wouldn't be here if it were going to be. Whatever they're waging, I'll double it."

Kieran snorts. "I'm in, too."

I glare at both of them and then shake my head. These guys are just as bad as my brothers. Fuck them.

As I start to stand, Declan lifts his hand, a grin on his lips. "Relax, Cage. We're fucking with you. Jesus. Who knew you were so touchy?"

"Look." Declan sets Cali next to him and leans forward, resting his elbows on his knees. "You're obviously in love with this girl. If she feels the same, why fight it? Why not keep her close where she's safest?"

I tap my pointer fingers together and consider that. "She's from a different world to me. Hell, she's a city girl. I can't up and leave my family. My commitment."

Paisley reaches over and puts her delicate hand on my wrist. When I look up to meet her eyes, she offers a warm smile. "If she cares about you as much as you do her, she wouldn't put you in a position to choose. Besides, just because she grew up in the city doesn't mean she likes it. I love being out here, on the outskirts of Seattle, and not having to leave the estate unless I truly want to. I have everything I need here. So, maybe you should ask her what she wants instead of assuming."

I'm glad the girls are here. Obviously, they are much wiser than their Daddies. I won't say that out loud, though. No reason to go home with a bullet wound.

"Thanks, Little one," I reply, winking at her.

Kieran grabs her arm and pulls her away from me while shooting daggers my way. Touchy.

"And maybe instead of locking her up in your base-ment, you could bring her here where she could make some friends," Declan offers with a smug grin. "We'd love to meet her, and we can tolerate you, too."

"Ohhh, maybe we could do a Christmas vacation together!" Cali squeals and rubs her hands together.

I grin. I knew they liked me.

Both Declan and Kieran glare at her.

"I have another thing I want to run by you guys. Ember is with me because her father has received threats to her life. He's a politician in DC. Anyway, I have Cass looking into it, but something isn't sitting right with me about it."

Declan narrows his gaze. "Like what?"

I shrug. "I don't know. Nothing about it makes sense. Her father doesn't know who is making the threat. My CIA handler doesn't have much more information to give. And, other than a plane tailing us when we first left DC, we haven't found any other evidence of a threat."

Kieran raises his eyebrows. "What kind of father is he?"

Irritation prickles at the back of my neck. "A joke of one. Once this is over, he's going to have to deal with me after everything I've learned."

Declan rubs his jaw, his eyebrows pinched as he considers what I said. "If there's one thing I've learned over the years, it's that my gut is rarely wrong. If something doesn't seem right, it's not right."

My mind races at that. It's time to get to the bottom of this threat. I've been putting it on the back burner because

I've been buying more time with Ember. It needs to end. She needs to know she's safe. She also needs to know that she still has a home with me once the threat is eliminated. Then I have to hope she chooses to stay.

"Thanks for the advice. I better go. There are a couple of stores I need to go to. I also need to stop by a Style Envy before I go. I ordered some Little frilly dresses from Knox's wife that I need to pick up."

Declan rises and leads me toward the door, with the others following. "I'll text Knox and warn him you're on your way. You know, since you can't be bothered to give a heads-up."

I smirk. "People tend to go into hiding when they know I'm coming. The boogeyman never announces himself. That's just poor technique."

Cali bursts out laughing and throws her arms around my waist, catching me by surprise. When I meet Declan's gaze, expecting for him to look murderous, I'm surprised as he nods at me, giving me permission to hug his wife.

As soon as she lets go, Paisley steps in and gives me a quick hug before Kieran can pull her back. After shaking both men's hands, I climb into my SUV and head into downtown.

By the time I'm done shopping, I'm surprised my credit card hasn't dissolved into dust and the pilot hasn't told me I can't bring all this shit on board. It's worth it, though. I'd spend every last dollar to make Ember's desires come true. She's never had the chance to be truly Little, and I'm going to change that.

My thoughts have been non-stop since I left Declan's. Would it be so bad if I kept Ember for myself? From what I know, she has no real ties to DC other than her piece-of-shit father. If I had it my way, she'd never see the bastard again.

She also doesn't know what she wants to do with her future yet, so it's not like she has a path already laid out ahead. With me, she can do whatever she wants. Hell, she can be my baby twenty-four-seven if she wants. It would make me the happiest man alive. It would ultimately be her choice, though. If she wants a career, I would support her in that.

Am I really considering this?

Fuck. I am.

I'm strong, but I don't have it in me to let Ember go. They say every man has a weakness, and mine is my Little firefly.

First things first, I need to figure out who the hell this threat is and eliminate them. If I'm going to offer Ember the chance to stay in my life, I want it to be by choice and not because she needs protection.

My phone buzzes, and I snatch it from my pocket as the plane starts down the runway.

> Declan: Seriously, though, how much to get in on your brother's bet?

I shake my head and send him back a middle finger emoji; he returns it with a laughing one. Maybe letting these men into my life wouldn't be the worst thing in the world. I trust them, which is saying a lot since the only people who have ever had my trust have been my brothers and Rowie.

As I go to slide my phone back into my pocket, it goes off again with a text from Jasper.

> Jasper: No need to panic, but do you know if Ember is allergic to bee stings?

Fuck. My Little girl. And I'm not there to comfort her. Some fucking Daddy I am.

"I don't care what you have to do, but make this jet go faster," I yell out as I press Jasper's name on my contacts.

I'm going to kill my brother. How could he let her get stung? Fucking Christ.

My entire body shakes with both fear and anger. Ultimately, I know it's not Jasper's fault, but it's easiest to go after him. I just hope my Little firefly will forgive me for leaving her. Even if she does, I'm not sure I'll ever forgive myself.

19

EMBER

When Cage brought me to the main house and left me with Jasper and Theo, I had to work really hard to keep from begging to go with him. It's not that I don't like his brothers. I do. And I love Rowie. But there's just something about my Daddy leaving that makes me want to cry.

Which is a huge problem. One day soon, he's going to send me away, and I'm never going to see him again. Yet I'm sad that he's going to be gone for only a few hours. I was the one who asked him to be my temporary Daddy. It seems like, instead, I've set myself up for heartbreak.

I don't want to focus on that now, though. Otherwise, I'll be a blubbering mess in front of Rowie, Theo, and Jasper, and that would be horrifying. I'm already worried about what Theo and Jasper must think of me, coming into their lives and turning their brother into my Daddy.

Rowie, on the other hand, has made her feelings about it quite clear. Not only did she jump up and down, clapping her hands when she found out, but she started making plans for us for things to do in the future as best friends. The thought of leaving her, too, makes my heart ache even more.

"Do you want to go outside and play on the playground?" Rowie asks as we color at the art table.

Jasper and Theo have mostly left us alone other than occasionally peeking in to check on us. For the most part, Rowie seems to do whatever she wants throughout the day, and the men just keep tabs on her while also making her take an afternoon nap. From what I've gathered, the guys all rotate who stays in the main house to look after her. It's sweet how they are all so involved in her life. It's like every time she sees one of them, she lights up, and so do they. It's the same way Cage lights up when I enter the room. It's an addictive feeling to be the center of someone's attention.

"Oh, that sounds so fun. I've been wanting to go on the swings."

She tosses her crayons into a container and closes her coloring book. "The slide is my favorite. We have to ask Theo or Jasper. I'm not allowed to go on the playground without someone supervising."

I follow her through the house until we find Jasper, who is rubbing his eyebrows as he stares at a computer screen. He looks tired.

"Will you come outside with us so we can go on the playground?"

Jasper looks up, his jaw immediately relaxing as though he's happy for the break. "What's the magic word?"

Rowie grins. "Pretty please with cherries and pink sprinkles on top?"

I giggle, and Jasper turns his attention to me. "And what's your magic word?"

My eyes widen like a deer in the headlights. "Um, please, with whipped cream and chocolate on top?"

He snorts and winks at me. "Perfect. Just the right amount of sugar from two sweet girls. Go potty and wash your hands first, then we can go outside."

Heat spreads over me. These men say things like that so nonchalantly, yet my cheeks burn up over being told to go potty. It's wild how those words and the way he says it makes me feel so Little.

Rowie lets me go potty first. As I pull down my leggings and cotton panties, which go up to my belly button and have tiny dragons on them, I wonder what it would be like to live like this all the time. It's wishful thinking. I know that. But what if I never had to leave this perfect ranch? Or see a stupid big city again? Or my father?

That last thought doesn't make me as sad as I would have thought. He said things would be different when I return home, but will they really? Will he sit down for meals with me, celebrate holidays like most people do, or teach me something that a dad knows how to do? Cage would do all of that for me. I'm not so sure about my father, though. He hasn't exactly given me many reasons to have much faith in him over the years.

I touch the cool metal of the necklace he gave me and sigh. Another problem to deal with at another time. For now, I get to go play with my new best friend.

When I come out, Rowie goes in as Jasper approaches. "Did you wash your hands?"

I nod. "Yes."

"With soap?"

Of course I did. And I'm sure he knows it. But that follow-up question in the Daddyish tone he's using has me feeling so dang small.

"Uh-huh. Wanna smell?" I hold my hand up for him, and without hesitating, Jasper grabs it and sniffs.

"Good girl. I'm so proud of you."

And just like that, I'm goo for Jasper. The man is scary-looking. And most people probably tremble when he even glances in their direction. Most people are idiots. I can see the man underneath the terrifying exterior. At least, I think I can. There's kindness in those tired eyes of his.

As soon as Rowie exits and sticks her hands in Jasper's face for him to sniff as well, we all go outside. Rowie and I skip happily toward the playground while Jasper follows.

"Be careful!" he calls. "No running."

I giggle because I'm starting to believe Cage when he says his brothers are just as overprotective as he is.

"Don't worry. We won't have any fun," I reply sassily.

Jasper blinks several times. I think I've stunned him. Heck, I've sort of surprised myself. It's one thing to be sassy with Cage, but I don't know his brothers well yet. I don't want to piss them off.

Then, the slightest smile spreads on his lips as he narrows his gaze. "Watch it, brat. I have a text from Cage saying I can punish you if you're naughty. I'd hate to start taking away Good Girl Points."

My mouth drops open. I turn around to face him, planting my hands on my hips. I'm not sure what's gotten into me, but it's a lot of fun.

"That is so mean." I huff. "I can't believe you would do that. I've been so nice to you."

He chuckles and shakes his head. "Better believe it, Little girl. Now, go have fun."

I grin and stick my tongue out at him, then join Rowie on the play structure, where she's already about to take her first ride down the slide.

The warm breeze is perfect for this today. All around us is nothing but brilliant green trees that line the mountain and make it the beautiful forest it is. What would it be like to be here in the winter? I bet it snows a lot. The pretty kind of snow. Not the kind in DC that immediately turns to gray slush and soaks my feet.

Rowie and I take turns going down the slide, giggling

the entire time. I can't remember going to a park when I was growing up. Yet these guys built one for her right in her backyard. I guess it's true when they say if they wanted to, they would. I guess that even goes for parents. And obviously, my father didn't want to. Or he just doesn't care.

Shaking my head, I push those thoughts aside. Nope. Not letting him ruin this time for me. This is my time to be me. To be Little. I clap for Rowie when she does a flip on one of the bars, at the same time, Jasper yells for her to be careful. Sheesh. A little overprotective. It's sweet, though.

After we've climbed and slid for nearly an hour, I eye the swings. As though Rowie already knows, she grabs my hand, and together, like best friends, we both climb onto one and start kicking our feet. Jasper is close by talking to another one of Cage's brothers. Creed, I think. There's just so many of them. I don't know if I'll ever get all their names straight.

"I need to get something to drink," Rowie announces as she jumps from the swing. "Be right back. I'll bring you some juice, too."

Wrapping my fingers around the chain on either side of me, I glide through the air with my braids, which Cage did this morning for me, swinging along with me. If my smile gets any bigger, it might split my face in half, but I don't care. I feel so free. So happy.

Almost as soon as that thought comes, it leaves as something pinches me.

"Ouch!" I cry out, jumping from the swing.

It happens again, the stinging pain radiating through me. Jasper is on his feet and in front of me almost immediately.

"Owwie," I whimper as a big fat tear rolls down my cheek. "I think I got stung on my ankle."

Before I know what's happening, Jasper swoops me in his arms and carries me effortlessly into the house. Tears continue to fall, and I'm not sure if it's because it hurts or if it's because I want my Daddy. Maybe a little of both.

He sets me on the counter and leans down to inspect my ankle, where two red welts are already appearing.

"Have you been stung before?" he asks as he starts moving through the kitchen while tapping his phone with one hand.

I sniffle and shake my head. "No. It's burning."

The skin around the spots has turned blotchy red, and it's getting harder to breathe. Jasper puts a cold, wet cloth on my ankle just as his phone rings.

"She's okay. I just need to know if she's been tested for allergies. She says she's never been stung before." He listens to Cage, who even I can hear as he yells at his brother.

Is he blaming Jasper? It's not his fault. My heart races and my breaths continue to come out shaky.

"She's breathing hard," Jasper says. "I need to get her to a hospital."

More tears fall, and I start shaking my head. The only thing I need is my Daddy right now. "I'm okay. I just... I need to catch my breath."

Jasper listens to something that Cage says and then looks at me. "Are you panicking, baby? Is that why you're having a hard time breathing?"

As soon as I nod, Jasper is in front of me. He sets his phone on the counter and hits the speaker function, then grabs my hands.

"Count my stars, Ember," he says, holding up his forearm.

Sure enough, small stars are tattooed all over his skin in between more intricate art.

"Listen to him, firefly. Count them. With each one, take a breath, baby girl. Slow and steady," Cage croons through the phone.

As my eyes travel over his arm, counting as I go along, my heartbeat steadies, and my breathing evens. The bee stings are throbbing, though.

"Take me off speaker and give her the phone," Cage says.

"I'm okay," I tell Cage in a small, shaky voice.

"That's a good girl," Jasper murmurs. "Keep breathing."

Rowie comes barreling in with Theo right behind her.

"What happened?" she demands. "Oh my God, are you okay?"

"Creed said she got stung. He's grabbing the first aid kit," Theo says.

Within seconds, five men are surrounding me while Rowie stands to the side, watching in horror as if I'm dying. The only thing I can focus on, though, is Cage whispering soft, reassuring words to me that only I can hear.

Theo, Creed, Cassian, Jasper, and—I think—Elias all dig into the first aid kit, pulling out various items from princess bandages to something that could wrap around my entire ankle. It's actually kind of comical watching these big, hulking men trying to figure out what to do to help me. It also sends a wave of emotions through my tummy. Every single one of them stopped what they were doing to fuss over me. To care for me. And they barely know me. My father never would have taken the time to comfort me over a bee sting.

"Thank you," I whisper, though I'm not sure if anyone hears me.

Cassian meets my gaze and gives me a kind smile. "You're part of us now, Little one. We got you."

That's all it takes for me to burst out sobbing. Cassian's eyes go big for a brief second before he springs into action, grabbing tissues and wiping my face.

"Shh. It's okay. Blow," he says, holding a tissue to my nose.

I scrunch my face. "Eww. No."

"Listen to him, Little girl," Cage says warningly in that stern, don't-disobey-me voice that makes my panties damp. "Let them take care of you."

Cassian raises a stern eyebrow and waits with the tissue held up to my nose. He doesn't flinch when I blow, and then he quickly wipes my face with a clean one. "Good girl."

"I'm so fucking sorry I left you." Cage's voice is rough, and I hate how upset he sounds. Is he blaming himself?

"I'm okay, Daddy," I reply quietly. "It's just bee stings. It barely even hurts."

"Do you really think lying to Daddy is a good idea, firefly?"

I smile. How is it that he's not here, and yet he knows I'm fibbing?

"Probably not," I murmur.

"Yeah, probably not, baby. You don't want to also have a stinging bottom, do you?"

My core clenches at the threat as heat spreads over my body. Cage's brothers continue to hover while I squirm on the counter. What the heck is wrong with me? Is it normal to get turned on by being scolded? Maybe I should talk to Rowie about this.

"No, Daddy. Sorry."

Calling him Daddy comes out so naturally. Every time I say it, a calmness washes over me. Cage has become my safe place. My home. My love.

The realization stuns me. I love him. I'm in love with him. I think I fell for him the first time he talked me down from a panic attack. Heck, maybe it happened before then.

"I'll be home in an hour. Let my brothers take care of you. Understand?"

I glance around the kitchen and let out a breath. My Daddy may not be here, but I know I'm just as safe around these men. "Okay, Daddy."

After the men decided I wasn't going to die from being stung, Jasper made me and Rowie snuggle up on the couch to watch a movie while he iced my ankle on and off. Who knew a big, scary, tattooed guy could be such a worrier? He hasn't left my side either, so I can't have the conversation I want to have with Rowie.

We're halfway through *Despicable Me* when Cage walks in. I leap up from the couch and run to him. As soon as I jump into his arms, he catches me. I have a feeling he always will.

"My baby," he murmurs in my ear. "You okay?"

I nod. "Yes. I missed you."

He lets out a long breath. "I missed you too, firefly."

When he sets me on my feet, I cling to him, nuzzling my face into his ribcage. I'm not sure why I'm so needy for him right now. It's an unusual feeling. My father's lack of care and attention over the years taught me never to need anyone. It seems like, in the short amount of time I've been here, Cage has turned that around completely. I almost feel as though I couldn't take a full breath today while he was gone. It's good to be able to breathe again.

"I'm so fucking sorry, Cage." Jasper comes up to us. When I tilt my head back to look at Cage, he's glaring at his brother.

"Daddy, it's not his fault." I tug on Cage's shirt until he lowers his gaze to mine.

He glances back at his brother and nods. "I know. Thanks for taking care of her."

Jasper offers me a smile and then runs a hand over his face. "I think it took about ten years off my life. Fuck, I hate seeing Little girls get hurt."

I giggle and slowly step away from Cage to wrap my arms around Jasper's middle. He seems like he needs a good hug. I must be right because he hugs me back so tightly I can barely breathe.

"I'm taking her home. I need to spend some alone time with my Little girl," Cage announces as he gently pulls me toward him, tucking me under his arm possessively.

A shiver works its way down my spine at that. I'm not sure why, but something in his words feels like a promise. What it is he's promising, I don't know. I can't wait to find out, though.

"I missed you so fucking much, firefly."

As soon as we get to Cage's house, he sweeps me off my feet and carries me to the kitchen, where he sets me on the counter and kisses me like his next breath depends on it.

We press our foreheads together, our hands roaming over each other.

"When Jasper texted me, I was so fucking scared. I don't ever want to leave you again."

His words make me still. "I don't want you to leave me either."

Ever.

I'm not brave enough to say that part out loud. Cage deserves so much more than me. He deserves someone strong. Not me. Not the scared mouse who has no idea what I'm doing in life. After being here and feeling so alive, I'm starting to realize I've just been in survival mode all these years.

Cage nips at the sensitive skin on my neck. I moan and spread my knees wider, letting him get as close as the counter will allow. He doesn't want to take my virginity, but I might actually die if he stops touching me.

The ridge of his cock brushes against the inside of my thigh. At least he's having the same reaction.

"Daddy," I murmur. "Please."

I'm not sure what I'm asking for. Anything. *Everything.* Whatever he's willing to give me. I just need him.

"Fuck," he mutters.

When he meets my gaze, his dark eyes are practically black, and his jaw is tight as though he's clenching it to restrain himself.

"Please, Daddy. I know what I want, and I want this. Please don't make me beg." Because I will. I will get down on my hands and knees and crawl to this man, begging him to make me feel good.

He groans and slides his hand over one of my breasts, giving a gentle stroke to my nipple before he continues to trail up until his fingers are wrapped around my throat. When he squeezes the sides of my neck, I nearly come apart.

"You're going to be the death of me, you know that?" he growls.

The corners of my mouth twitch as I fight a grin. I love that he feels so out of control around me. "Will it be worth it?"

In an instant, he has me laid back on the cool counter, his free hand cupping the back of my head as he does. His nostrils flare, and his grip on my throat tightens a little more, putting pressure on that perfect spot that has my pussy soaked.

"Yeah, firefly. It will be so fucking worth it. Put your palms flat on either side of you, and don't move. Understand?"

I bob my head, then yelp as he gives me a light swat between my legs.

Holy fuck.

"When I ask you a question, I want a verbal answer. Unless my cock is stuffed down your throat or you're deep in non-verbal Little Space, I want words."

Then he reaches between my thighs and rubs the spot he just smacked, right over my clit. Even my leggings and panties aren't enough barrier to block the electricity his fingers send through me.

Cage leans over the counter, hovering over me. "I asked if you understand, firefly. Would you rather I spank you for not answering me, or do you want me to make you scream?"

I slam my hands to the counter. "I understand, Daddy."

He chuckles and winks at me, then takes a step back and pulls my leggings and panties down, being careful not to brush them against my beestings as he removes them.

My skin heats as I start to tremble. I have no idea what I'm doing. Am I supposed to touch him?

No. He said to keep my hands flat. Okay, I can do this. I just need to listen to him. Daddy won't let me fail.

Knowing that gives me the comfort I need to calm myself. Daddy's got me.

"Such a pretty pussy," he croons as he bends my legs and sets my feet on the edge of the counter. "So pink and swollen for me. Do you need something to take the edge off, baby?"

I nod, then remember his warning. "Yes, Daddy."

There's something so sexy about being exposed to him while he still has on all his clothes.

When he pushes my knees apart, I whimper as the cool air touches my wet lips. He brushes the pad of his thumb over my clit, and I jolt in surprise, one of my hands flying up to my mouth to quiet my moan.

Almost as soon as I realize it, he has my ankles up in the air while he peppers my bottom with six hard swats.

"Owwie!"

Once he's done, he puts me back in position and stands over me. "Next time you move your hands, I'm grabbing a wooden spoon and using that on your ass."

My eyes widen. That isn't a threat. That is Cage making a promise. One I don't think I want to experience. My bottom already burns from his hand.

With my palms facing down, I slide my fingers under my lower back, hoping my weight will keep me from accidentally disobeying.

Cage sees me do it and chuckles. "Good girl. You're my good baby, aren't you? Always making Daddy so fucking proud."

Both my clit and my heart ache for him. God, how could this man go from being a total annoyance in my life to the best thing that's ever happened to me?

Without warning, he leans down and licks along my center from ass to clit, groaning as he does.

"You taste even better than I imagined, baby. You know why?"

I shake my head. "No. Why?"

He pins me with his stern gaze. "Because now you taste like *mine*."

Oh God.

Wrapping his arms around the underside of my thighs, he dips his head again and latches onto my clit, sucking hard and fast. I scream and fight to keep my hands under me as every nerve in my body lights up with the need to explode.

"Daddy," I cry out, breathless already.

He hums but doesn't lift his head as he continues to pleasure me with that talented tongue of his. Who knew oral sex was so hot?

Every so often, my body starts to tense, but each time it does, he slows down until I'm a ball of frustration.

"Please."

"What, baby girl? Please, do you need to come?"

I let out a pathetic whine, but I don't care. I'm desperate, and from the way Cage's eyes just darkened, he likes it when I'm a mess like this. "Yes! I need to, oh God, come, yes!"

His mouth works magic. I'm pretty sure he's putting me under some kind of spell because I don't feel like I'm in my own body. I'm floating, with nothing but rainbows and big fluffy clouds surrounding me.

Slowly, Cage presses the tip of his finger to my opening and gently thrusts. The entire time, he continues to tease my clit with his filthy mouth. Gosh, I don't know where or how he learned female anatomy, but he's passing with flying colors right now.

"You're going to come for me, firefly. Then I'm going to make you do it again." He pins me with his stare. I'm not sure I believe him, but I nod anyway. I've never climaxed twice in a row. I didn't even think it was possible.

Using his free arm, he presses it low over my stomach, giving just the right amount of pressure. My ass sticks to the counter as sweat coats my body.

"I want to touch you," I cry out, jerking as he rubs circles around my clit.

"No, baby. That's not happening today."

I peer down at him and stick my bottom lip out. He doesn't fall for it. Instead, he raises his eyebrows. "If you want to keep pouting, I can stop what I'm doing and give you a red bottom."

My heart leaps in my chest as I shake my head enthusiastically. "I'll be good. Please don't stop. I'll die."

He smirks, his lips shining with my arousal. "Well, I can't have my baby dying on me."

Then he lowers his head once more. He sucks my clit while fingering me at the same time until my legs are shaking so hard that I accidentally kick him in the shoulder while my entire body spasms.

"Oh, fuck! Sorry! Oh, oh, yes, right there!"

Noises I've never made come out of me, and I'm sure I sound like a dying goat, but holy fucking balls. Are orgasms usually like that? I've certainly never given myself pleasure to that degree. I think I might have died for about thirty seconds and went to heaven, then became half-conscious again. Scratch that, I'm still in freaking heaven.

When I quiet, he eases up slightly but doesn't stop touching me with his skilled hands. He stands, his thumb on my clit and his fingers inside me, and lazily watches me.

"You're such a good girl. Jesus Christ, that was hot," he mutters.

I can barely keep my eyes open, so I grin at him. "Thank you."

He chuckles and leans down again. "Oh, you're welcome, firefly. We're not done, though. Not even close."

"Open."

When I lift my heavy eyelids, Cage is holding something up to show me.

A bottle? No, the spout isn't like a bottle.

"Is that a sippy cup?"

He leans against the counter next to me and brings it to my lips. "Yeah, baby. Drink some water."

Wrinkling my nose, I shake my head. "I don't like water."

"Too bad for you, you're going to drink it. We're adding water to your daily rules. You're going to have at least three of these a day."

My mouth drops open as I stare at the large bottle. "I'll be peeing constantly."

Cage grins. "Which is a good thing. If running to the bathroom so much bothers you, Daddy can always put you in a diaper."

I quickly shake my head, and he chuckles. "We'll table that for when the time comes, then," he says.

Pulling my bottom lip between my teeth, I consider that. What would a diaper feel like? I've wondered but never considered wearing one. Seems like I might not get the choice with Cage as my Daddy

He nudges the spout into my mouth and holds it there while we stare at each other. This feels intimate; I suppose it is. He's taking care of me, and I'm letting him.

"While I was out today, I got you some stuff."

That catches my attention, and I turn my head away from the sippy cup. "Why did you get me stuff?"

As if the question confuses him, his eyebrows pinch together. "Why not? You're my baby girl. I'm always going to get you stuff."

I want to ask if he means only while I'm here or if he's

indicating something different, but I can't work up the nerve. If he doesn't feel the same way about me as I do him, I'm not ready to face that reality.

When I don't answer, his confusion turns into a frown and then a scowl. "Your father is a bastard who is going to answer to me very fucking soon."

Cage's tone is dark and deadly. He wouldn't hurt my father, would he? Would I care if he did? I'm not so sure. I've tried to get my father to love me for so long and it's never worked. Why do I keep trying?

"Can I see what you got?" A change of subject is good. The last thing I want to think about is going back to the man who has all but abandoned me these past twenty years. Besides, whatever Cage got me, the Little girl inside me can't wait another second to see it.

Thankfully, he lets me get away with it and grabs my discarded panties from the kitchen floor. I scoot to the edge to get down, blushing over the fact that we just did some filthy stuff. I should probably sanitize the granite.

"Uh-uh, stay up there. You stay where Daddy puts you. If I want you down, I'll get you down."

I pause and meet his stern gaze while he slides my panties up my legs. When he can't go any farther, he picks me up by my armpits and sets me on my feet. Once he's done, he holds out his hand.

"I need my pants." I look around for them, inwardly giggling when I spot them hanging over the toaster.

"You don't need your pants. Little girls can walk around in their panties at home."

My clit starts to tingle again. How is that possible? Cage just had me spread out on the kitchen counter, screaming his name with how hard he made me come. I shouldn't be getting aroused already. Then again, it seems like all he has to do is be close for me to get turned on.

He leads me into his office. I've only been in here a couple of times. Most of the time, he works in the main house. The entire room is so Cage. Clean and orderly. A pristine, minimalist desk is the focal point of the room, with a wall of bookshelves behind it. I wouldn't have taken Cage as a reader, but the one time I looked in here, I found a collection of famous novels that are way beyond the level I like to read.

We barely walk three steps into the room before we have to stop because there are piles and piles of shopping bags with all kinds of colorful things sticking out. It looks like there are clothes and toys.

"Daddy," I murmur as I look over it all. "This isn't just *some* stuff. This is an entire shopping mall."

He nudges me and points to the overly-stuffed leather chair situated near the bookcases. "Go sit. I'll bring you bags to open."

I turn to look at him, blinking several times. Is he for real? When he gives my bottom a firm swat, I get moving and let out a hiss as my thighs touch the cold leather. Note to self: put a blanket down next time.

One by one, he sets the bags by my feet. "Open the pink bags first."

As I pull out the first dress, I gasp. "This is the most beautiful thing I've ever seen."

Gliding my fingers over the soft yellow fabric, a flutter starts low in my belly. This isn't a dress he would have found at a regular store. I'm not sure where he went, this must have come from a specialty shop of some kind. It's sized for an adult, but it screams Little. Frills and ribbon with buttons on the back and a big bow. When I hold it up, I'm certain it won't cover my bottom when I wear it. I guess it's a good thing there's a pair of matching bloomers in the bag next.

There are half a dozen more dresses just like that, along with a bunch of leggings and oversized pastel sweaters. After those, I start pulling out panties, similar to the ones I'm wearing. Some of them have cartoon characters on them, while others have hearts or stars or polka dots on them. When I pull out another pair that feel different, I hold them up. There's padding in the crotch area, and my cheeks immediately catch fire.

"Those are training panties. There may be times I make you wear them. I also got disposable pull-ups and diapers. They're cute as hell. All sorts of designs. I bought six different kinds." He holds up a large package in one hand. Through the clear plastic material, a bear design is showing. They are pretty cute.

"I've only ever worn cute panties in Little Space," I tell him for no reason in particular.

He smirks. "I gathered because your cheeks turn red every single time I mention taking care of you so intimately. Don't worry, baby, we'll change that soon."

Then, he distracts me by pulling a baby doll from a bag. She has black hair, green eyes, and freckles. Just like Betsy. It only takes one look at her for me to burst into blubbering tears.

20

CAGE

S hit. Why the fuck is she crying? Did I get her the wrong doll? Fuck, did I hurt her bee sting when I was feasting on her perfect pussy? I should have been more careful. I couldn't stop myself, though.

I pick her up and plop onto where she was just sitting. As soon as she's on my lap, I grab hold of her ankle to inspect it.

"Did I hurt you? Shit, I'm a horrible Daddy."

Ember sniffles. "What? No. I'm fine."

When she pushes my hands away from her leg, I look at her face and wince. I hate seeing her cry. It kills me inside. Ember has already had enough fucking sadness in her life. I shouldn't be causing more.

"You don't like the doll. I got the one that Rowie told me to get. Is it the wrong sort? I'll take it back and get a different one."

Two fresh tears roll down her cheeks as I try to take the doll from her. She tightens her grip on it and shakes her head. "I love the doll. It's the exact same one that I had when I was young. I'm not upset. I'm crying because I'm so happy."

What. The. Fuck?

I'll never understand the "crying when happy" thing. Rowie's done it a few times, and it baffles all of us. Then again, my heart died a long time ago, so I struggle to understand most emotions.

Suddenly, it strikes me. Maybe my heart didn't die. Maybe it just stopped working until Ember showed up in my life. Since she's been here, I've never felt more alive. I've also experienced emotions I never thought someone like me could feel. True love.

"You're happy?" I ask, still not fully convinced.

Ember huffs out a half-laugh. "Yes, Daddy. I'm happy. This is the sweetest, most thoughtful thing anyone has ever done for me."

Talk about feeling like the king of the universe. While also feeling like I want to kill her father again.

"Baby, I want to make you happy. You've flipped my fucking world upside down. I don't deserve you, but I don't think I can ever let you go."

I blink several times, trying to work up the courage to look her in the eye. If she rejects me, I'm not sure what I'll do.

She reaches up and cups my face between her warm hands, searching my face. "Please don't ever let me go," she whispers.

We stare at each other, our gazes promising each other something. I'm just not sure what exactly. She asked me not to let her go. Does she mean it? Because now that she's said it, I'm never letting her leave me. Not now, not ever. She just sealed her fate. All it took was that one request. Ember has my whole heart in her grasp for the rest of our lives. I'll burn the entire universe just for her to give me a piece of hers.

"What are you going to name your baby?"

Ember stares at the doll, considering my question. "Piper Rowie Adams."

Fucking adorable. Although once I marry this Little girl, it will be Piper Rowie Black. I'll keep that little piece of information to myself for now, though. I still need to figure out what the fuck is going on with her dad and this threat.

"I think you and Piper need to lie down for naptime while I get some work done."

Her shoulders drop, and she looks around the disastrous office. It really does look like a pastel bomb went off in here. I guess that means I need to get to work on a playroom for my Little girl. Maybe I'm getting ahead of myself, but there's no way I'm allowing her to return to DC. If it's up to me, she'll never even see her asshole father again.

"Naps suck."

The corners of my lips twitch. "Don't say suck. That's a naughty word."

She shrugs. "It's better than saying 'fuck naps.'"

Narrowing my gaze, I clench my jaw to keep from laughing. "Ember Elizabeth. Do we need to go into the bathroom and have you taste the soap?"

Her mouth drops open, and she stares at me like she can't believe what I just said. "Daddy, that's so mean. Do you really think you should let me taste soap? If you do that, I might toot bubbles, and then what? There will just be tootie bubbles all around the room. Nobody wants that."

Jesus Christ. She's been spending far too much time with Rowie. I'm going to have to put a cap on that. Otherwise, I'm going to have two Little girls running circles around me.

"Up," I growl as I nudge her down from my lap. "Bed. Now. Before you *really* talk yourself into trouble."

As we leave the office, I grab a pair of training panties and a nightgown. Time to start pushing her boundaries.

I follow Ember into her room, frowning as we step through the doorway. No. Not happening. This isn't where she belongs. "You're sleeping in my room from now on."

She turns and looks up at me, rubbing her thumb over her chin. "But this is my room."

"Not anymore, firefly. I'll move your things into my

room later. Let's go." I take her by the hand and lead her into my ensuite bathroom. "Time to go potty."

Ember hesitates, glancing at the toilet and then back at me. "Can you go out?"

"No. We've already established that I will help you in the bathroom whenever we're together."

"So I don't get any privacy?" She puts her hands on her hips, and it's fucking cute. My sassy Little firefly.

"That is correct. No privacy, no space, no secrets."

She raises an eyebrow. "Does that mean *I* get to be in the bathroom when *you* use the toilet?"

I smirk and wink at her. "Yeah, baby, if that's what you want. I'll even let you hold it for me."

Her eyes practically pop out of her head. I don't know why she's so surprised. I'm pretty sure she already knows that boundaries don't exist for me. If my girl wants to follow me into the bathroom, I'm certainly not going to tell her no.

Ember lets out a huff and shakes her head, muttering under her breath about me being a stubborn donkey. Then she pulls down her panties and sits on the toilet while I lean against the counter and wait. When she doesn't immediately pee, I turn on the faucet, letting the water run.

"Kick your panties off," I instruct as I finish cleaning her up.

"Why?"

As I wash my hands, I look at her in the mirror. "Because I'm going to change you for naptime."

When I kneel in front of her and hold the training panties to her feet, she sucks in a breath. I tilt my head back to look at her.

"You don't have to use them, firefly. It's just in case you have an accident. Little girls sometimes do."

With her hands on my shoulders, she steps into them. When I pull them up and settle them over her hips, she shifts. "They're kind of comfy."

I nod. "Yeah, and I bet they make you feel super Little, too."

"Yes," she answers in a tiny voice.

Yeah, my girl is getting deeper into her headspace by the second, which is exactly what I'd hoped would happen.

"That's because you are Little. And so fucking precious too."

Her cheeks turn rosy. I lift her T-shirt up and over her head, and she moves her arms to cover herself.

"Uh-uh, arms at your sides, baby. Don't hide from Daddy. I want to see you."

She quickly obeys, and I finish getting her ready for her nap. The nightgown I chose has a dragon on the front, which thrills her.

"I need Spike."

"I'll get him. Crawl into bed and get under the covers."

By the time I return with her stuffie, she's tucked in.

It's hard not to climb in next to her. I want to be with her every single second I can. Maybe that's wrong, but I don't care.

"I'm going to be in my office. You stay in bed. You're not allowed to get up unless I'm here. If you wake up, call out for me. I have a baby monitor plugged in by the bed."

Her eyes are already closing when she nods and brings her thumb to her chin. Before she has a chance to slide it between her lips, I grab one of the brand-new pacifiers I bought and push it into her mouth. I'm pretty sure she's sound asleep before I even leave the room. I guess an orgasm or two really tires her out.

"There's got to be something."

Cassian steeples his fingers under his chin as he stares at his laptop screen. "I'm looking for whatever I can. So far, the only thing I found that was remotely off was her mom's helicopter crash."

I sit up straighter. "What do you mean?"

"There was speculation that it wasn't an accident even though the final reports ruled it as one," Cassian replies.

"Did you look into it more?" I stand and round my desk to look at the computer as if there will be some useful information on it.

Cass shakes his head. "It was ruled an accident nearly twenty years ago."

Something prickles at the back of my neck. It happens every time my intuition kicks in. I learned to trust it a long time ago.

"Pull up the reports. I want to see them." I grab a chair and move it to sit beside my brother. "I can't fucking believe you didn't tell me this already."

He gives me a sideways glance and then looks around the room at all the bags. "You've been a bit busy. I'm glad I bet on you keeping her."

I glare at Cass, who, from the neck up, looks like a total fucking square with his black-rimmed glasses. From the chin down, though, his tattoos and the way he carries himself intimidates the hell out of people. Not me, though. I'm two months older than him, and I never let the asshole forget it. "Listen, asshole. First of all, I'm not letting her go. And second of all, fuck you for betting against me."

Raising his eyebrows, he shrugs. "Was I betting against you, or was I betting *for* you? Seems to me that I was on your side since I bet on you ending up happy and all."

I might be older and wiser than Cassian, but that dickhead has always been able to talk circles around me. I think Rowie gives him lessons. Or maybe it's the other way around. Either way, fuck him.

"In all realness, Cage." Cassian pats my shoulder. "I'm so fucking happy for you."

Swallowing the lump forming in my throat, I stare at my brother, unsure if I want to have a heart-to-heart right now. Out of everyone in the family, Cass is one of the best to talk to, though. He always seems to have the right advice.

"If she doesn't want to stay, I have to let her go," I tell him roughly.

He sits back in his chair and sighs. "She looks at you like you hung the fucking moon, Cage. And she is attached to Rowie at the hip already. Plus, she seems to adore the fuck out of Rylan."

I let out a low growl that makes Cassian smirk. "I'm fucking with you. Obviously, she likes me the most. That's beside the point, though. She's in love with you. And you're in love with her. I think you're the only two on The Ranch that aren't aware of it yet."

Does she love me? Is it possible for that to happen so quickly? She's barely been here a week. Then again, I'm obsessed with her in a way that is probably considered unhealthy.

"She's not going to leave. From what I've seen and heard, she has nothing worth going back to in DC. Hell, I'm pretty sure her father won't be alive after you confront him about all the bullshit he's put her through." Cassian shrugs.

He's not wrong about that. I don't want to upset her by killing her dad, but I also can't allow the man to continue breathing for all the hurt he's caused her. I just can't fathom how a father can be so cruel to his only daughter. I'll never understand it.

"Well, I can't make anything permanent until I figure out what the fuck is going on with this threat. I want to see every single news report and document about the helicopter crash."

Cassian nods and immediately starts printing off everything he can find. While he does that, I scan everything for any tidbit of information that might be useful. Newspaper reports, online forums, and a bunch of official reports. It was a huge headline when it happened. The wife of a congressman dying in a helicopter crash.

I've gone through nearly everything twice by the time the printer stops spitting out useless information. There's nothing to be found anywhere. Fuck. I don't know why I was so sure I'd find something.

"Holy shit," Cassian mutters.

My attention snaps to him. "What? What did you find?"

He looks at me, his gaze dark. "She look familiar?"

When he turns his laptop toward me, I nearly drop the papers in my hand. "What the fuck?"

"Where and when was this?" I ask.

"This was a month after the crash at a press conference."

I stare at the photo. What does this mean? What does she have to do with Ember? There has to be a connection between this and what's happening now. But why did she lie to me? And what the fuck am I going to say to my girl?

"She know the location here?" Cassian asks.

"Yes. Of course she does. She's been one of our handlers for over ten years." I can't fucking believe this. She's played me. And that pisses me off more than anything because I don't get played.

"There was a plane tailing us from DC, though," I say mostly to myself as I try to fit the puzzle pieces together in my head. "Which is why I brought her here. And Ruth knew that's exactly what I'd fucking do."

"I think you need to talk to Ember to see if she knows anything about this new information," Cass replies. "You scanned her for bugs before you put her on the plane?"

The memory of throwing Ember over my shoulder and hauling her onto the plane runs through my mind. My lips twitch as I fight a smile. From the second my firefly insulted my plane, I was entranced by her. And obviously fucking distracted because I did not scan her for bugs.

Shit.

Without saying anything, Cassian and I rise and move to one of my bookcases, where I lower my gaze to a stack of books. As soon as the device scans my retina, the entire shelf unlocks, and we step into one of the many secure rooms in my house.

As soon as I close us in, I turn to my brother. "Why would Ruth be spying on us?"

Both of us stare at each other. Ruth is only privy to certain information. She's one of the agents we've worked closely with over the years. There's stuff that we don't speak about to anyone but each other, and only when we are here on The Ranch. Hell, there are some things we don't even talk about out loud. Instead, we use special codes we learned when we were recruited by The Agency. Things that could be used for or against the country as well as certain politicians.

"What information do we have that would benefit her?" Cass asks.

"Better yet." I start to pace around the small space. "What information do we have that will benefit *Zeke*? Elections are coming up. Is he planning to run for office?"

Cassian types ferociously on his keyboard. "According to some news outlets, there has been talk in the past about him running one day."

"And we have information that might be damning for another political leader who might want to run," I add.

"Don't kill me for asking this," Cass says cautiously.

"Ember isn't helping them," I snap, already knowing what he was going to ask. "She's a fucking victim in this. Once again, her father is doing what is best for him, even though it will hurt her."

Cassian nods. "I just had to ask."

I glare at my brother, barely refraining from punching him right in the nose. "You didn't have to do fucking anything. You know Ember well enough to know she's not part of whatever the fuck this is."

"You're right. I'm sorry. That was my bad." At least he

looks like he's actually sorry. "What do you want to do now?"

Kill Zeke. And Ruth. I've only killed a handful of women in my life. I have very few morals, but murdering women is typically one of them. Unless they deserve it. Rowie's mom deserved it. Every painful second of it. And even though I don't have the whole picture yet, I already know Ruth is going to deserve what's coming to her.

Ruth knows I'm a Daddy. It's possible she knows Ember is Little, which means she counted on me being distracted. This is exactly why I never planned on getting involved with a woman. Being distracted causes careless-ness. Which can be catastrophic in our world. Too bad I'm already too far fucking gone for Ember. There's no coming back from that.

"We do what we do best," I mutter. "We play the game and show them that the house always wins."

Cassian grins and tips his head. "After you, brother. Whatever you need."

What I need is my Little girl in my arms. Right fucking now.

Before I even approach my bedroom door, I know she's not in there. It's like I have a sixth sense for my girl. Obviously, she doesn't share that because she has no idea how much trouble she's in right now. Otherwise, she'd be where I told her to stay. She must have snuck out of bed while Cassian and I were in the secure room. I didn't have my camera screens on in there. Rookie fucking mistake.

As soon as I finish sweeping my room, bathroom, and closet, I grab one of my bug detectors and start walking through the entire upstairs. I mostly focus on the room she's been staying in since her belongings are there. Then I double back to my room and check Spike. By the time I'm done, I've come up empty. Shit. Maybe I'm wrong about this. That prickle at the back of my neck tells me I'm not, though.

I put the device away and head downstairs to find my naughty Little girl. Part of me hopes she's doing this on purpose to see how I'll react. To see if I'll actually punish her. My girl is about to learn that her Daddy doesn't make empty promises. She's not used to people in her life keeping their word. That's about to change.

"Little girl, Little girl, where are you?" I call out.

Just as I turn the corner to go into the kitchen, she yelps and jumps away from where she's wiping down the counter.

"Daddy, you scared me!" She puts her hand over her heart.

I stalk toward her, eyebrows raised. "I scared you, huh? Don't you think Daddy was scared when I checked on you and you weren't where I told you to stay?"

She opens her mouth to speak and then closes it,

shifting from foot to foot. "I, um, I woke up, and I remembered we didn't clean the counter after, um, well, you know. And then I got hungry."

My gaze moves to the tub of ice cream sitting to the side with a spoon in it. "You got hungry and decided eating ice cream out of the container was a good idea? When we're going to have dinner in about an hour?"

"Um." She takes a step back, but I don't let her create any space between us, so I move right along with her.

"And cleaning up after us isn't your job, Little girl. That's my job. I take care of you. Not the other way around."

Her eyes shift around nervously as I tower over her. When she lifts her hand to bring her thumb to her chin, I capture her wrist and hold it against my chest. "Look at me, firefly."

As soon as she does, my cock stirs. She's testing me. I see it in her gaze. Whether she'll ever admit it or not, she did this because she wants to know if I'll actually let her get away with things.

"What did I say just before I left the bedroom?"

She rolls her lips in, then squares her shoulders. "I'm not sure, Daddy. I'm pretty sure I fell asleep while you were still in there."

I bite back the urge to laugh. Smart little mouth.

"Ember Elizabeth," I mutter sternly. "This is not the right time to be sarcastic with Daddy. Your bottom is already in trouble, I don't think you want to add other punishments to that either."

Her cheeks turn pink, and she lifts her other hand like she's going to rub her chin. I follow its path, my eyes locking in on her throat as something silver sparkles in the light.

Reaching out, I grab the charm of her necklace between my thumb and index finger. "Who gave you this?"

As I turn it over, that prickling feeling hits so hard it nearly startles me.

Ember peers down at it. "My dad. He gave it to me the day he sent me with you."

Fuck. It's been on her all this time.

Leaning in close, I put my mouth near her ear and work on breaking the clasp at the same time. "Don't say a word. I'll explain everything in a minute."

When I pull the necklace away from her, she gasps and looks from it to me, confused. I hold up my finger, signaling for one moment before I disappear from the kitchen to put this fucking thing in a secure spot. Once I confirm with a sensor that there is some sort of bug inside the charm, I put it in one of my safes that blocks any and all signals. Then I go back out to find Ember.

She's still in the same spot, her eyebrows drawn together like she doesn't know what to do.

"Baby, we need to talk."

"What's wrong?" she asks frantically. "What happened? Why did you take my necklace?"

I reach out and pick her up, then set her on the counter, bracketing her thighs with my hands. "I think we might have found the threat, and it's not what we were expecting. Has your father talked about running for office lately?"

Ember goes stiff and stares at me, her eyes sparkling with so much fear that I want to put my fist through a fucking brick wall. "He was talking to someone on the phone about it recently. He didn't know I overheard him. I don't know who he was talking to."

"Do you know a woman by the name of Ruth Boyle?"

"What? Why are you asking me this stuff, Cage? What's going on?" She tries to push me away and slide off the counter, but I don't let her. I'm not letting her go anywhere. She stays right here with me.

"Is your dad in a relationship with Ruth?"

I stare at her, waiting for any answer she'll give me. I don't really need confirmation, but the fact that Ruth fucking played me is making me question myself.

"I don't know. I mean, it's never been something that's been said outright. I know they work together. What does Ruth have to do with this? How do you know her?"

This time, I step back and run a hand through my hair. "Ruth is one of our handlers at the CIA. I've worked with her for years. She's the one who asked me to take you on as a client as a favor to her."

Ember nods. "That makes sense. My father probably asked her for help when he got the threat. She's probably one of the few people he trusts."

"Baby," I say, almost pleading. Fuck. I'm about to break my Little girl's heart. "I think your father and Ruth sent you here to spy on us to get information to sway the upcoming election in his favor. The necklace your father gave you is bugged."

21

EMBER

The room is spinning.

Nope. No, it's not.

That's not what's happening at all.

It's my world that's spinning, and I'm pretty sure it's about to implode.

"What are you saying? Are you saying my father used me as a pawn?"

Cage moves toward me again, but I hold up my hands, not wanting him to touch me right now. The only thing I want is answers.

"I can't say that for certain. It's what it appears to be, firefly," he replies quietly. "I'm so fucking sorry, baby. I wish I had different information, but something wasn't sitting right with me, so I had Cassian looking into it."

"Can I see what he found?"

He stills for a second before letting out a sigh. "Baby..."

"I have a right to see it. If my... if my father used me to spy on you, I have a right to see everything." My bottom lip trembles. I'm barely keeping it together. He's got to have it wrong. My dad said we were going to have a fresh start. That we would be a family. He wouldn't have said it if he didn't mean it, right? "Please, Daddy. I need to see it."

Cage clenches his jaw but nods and pulls me off the counter, then carries me on his hip through the house. "I'll get you dressed. After that, we'll go to the main house. I want to give Cass the necklace so he can figure out what kind of device it is."

My grip on Cage is so tight that it's probably hurting him, but he doesn't say anything. Instead, he takes me into his room and sets me on the bed, then goes about finding clothes for me.

"You're still in trouble for getting out of bed," he mutters. "We'll be finishing that conversation later."

His reminder makes me smile. Of course he won't forget that I disobeyed. Because he's a good Daddy. Actually, he's the best Daddy.

Then, a sudden thought pops into my head. "Do you blame me for this?"

Cage stops before me and roughly grabs my chin, pinching my cheeks together so my lips open like a fish. "Not for one fucking second, firefly. You're the victim in this. The two of them and anyone else involved in this will pay dearly."

The churning in my tummy settles slightly. I'm not sure what I'd do if he thought I was part of this. It would probably kill me if Cage didn't trust me. Especially since I trust him more than all the people in the world.

As he undresses me and changes my clothes, I sit limply, letting him do whatever he wants. My body is numb, but my mind is racing. How could he do this to me? Use me to get elected? I don't even know why I'm in shock. Of course he would do something like this. It's always been about my father and his career. Everything has always been him.

I have very few memories of my mother. A core one that sticks out to this day is them fighting. My father walked out while my mom was crying because she wanted him to spend the day with us. When he slammed the door behind him, she collapsed into a heap on the floor. Even as young as I was, I went and sat on her lap to comfort her because she was so sad. It wasn't long after then that she died.

"Baby girl," Cage says gently. "Look at me."

Tipping my head back, I gaze into his nearly black eyes and try to swallow the lump in my throat.

"No matter what, it's going to be okay. *You're* going to be okay."

All I do is nod because I'm not so sure he's right about that. Am I going to be okay? My father used me for his own political gain. I can't overlook that. What am I going to do? Where will I live? And now that Cage has figured out that there's no real threat, I have no reason to stay here. He hasn't even been my Daddy for a full day and it's already ending.

That's not true. He's been my Daddy since the day he threw me over his shoulder and carried me onto that plane, then drove the rest of the way across the country because he found out how terrified I was. I think I fell in love with him that very same day. Saying goodbye is going to be the hardest thing I've ever done. The thought of it is more painful than thinking about my father's actions.

"Baby, you don't have to do this. I can take care of everything," Cage says darkly.

I have no doubt that my father has signed his death warrant with Cage. Ruth, too. The bitch. I never liked her. I'm pretty sure she's never liked me either, even though we've only met a few times. She always came across as someone who thinks she's smarter than everyone around her and that she's better than them.

Maybe I should be trying to talk Cage out of whatever he's going to do to them. I just can't seem to find it in me to do so right now. Perhaps once the numbness wears off, I'll feel more emotional about it.

"I want to see it with my own two eyes. I want to look my father in the eyes while he tells me that he used me. I've been the good, quiet daughter for so long."

And I have Cage to thank for that. The man might be

overbearing and a pain in the ass, but he has never wanted me to be silent and not bother him with my wants or needs. He has only encouraged me, even when he knew I wouldn't make things easy on him by doing that.

Cage studies me for several seconds before he nods. "Okay, firefly. Just know I'm right here to be your support in whatever way necessary."

He holds out his hand, the warmth of his palm calming my soul as soon as I take it. We're both silent as we walk along the paved path from his house to the main house. While my mind should be on my father, all I can think about as I look around this beautiful land is how much I'll miss it here. I've never seen so many trees in my life, and while the Cherry Blossom trees in DC are beautiful, they are nothing compared to The Ranch.

Cassian, Theo, Jasper, Rylan, Ghost, and Koda are already in the large conference room near all the offices when we arrive.

"Gunner, Dom, and Luca are coming, too. The rest of the guys aren't here but will be listening in to the conversation remotely," Cassian tells us.

Cage nods, and I look at him, suddenly feeling unsure. I hadn't expected everyone to be here.

As if he understands what I'm thinking, he leans down to my ear. "Breathe, firefly. They're all here because they care about you and want to help however they can."

That stupid lump forms in my throat again, making it too difficult to reply. Instead, I do what my Daddy said, and I take deep and slow breaths as Cage pulls out a chair for me to sit in.

A moment later, the rest of the men coming with us file into the room, closing the door behind them. Before anyone speaks, Cassian and Ghost walk around the room, both with some kind of device in their hands.

"They're scanning the room for bugs. Just a safety precaution we always take before we start a meeting in here," Cage whispers.

As soon as they're finished, Cassian sits at the end of the table in front of his computer. There's a projection screen at the other end of the room, so we can all see his screen, too.

"Can you bring up the last photo we found and the crash report?" Cage asks him.

Cassian nods and opens two different photos. The first one my eyes land on is a grainy newspaper photo of my dad and Ruth from what looks like a long time ago. He didn't have as much gray hair then. And as my gaze roams down the picture, I stop midway where Ruth's hand is connected with my father's.

"When was this?" I ask as I stare at it.

Cage clears his throat. "This was dated a month after your mother died."

My stomach coils. I glance at the photo next to it. It's some kind of report. A crash report. The final result of the crash was marked as an accident.

"I don't..." I gasp for air, the walls around me closing in. "I don't understand."

"We don't know anything for a fact," Cassian says. "We're only going off our own intuition here."

I turn my head to look at Cassian. "But you don't believe the helicopter crash was an accident?"

He turns his attention to Cage for the briefest second, then back to me. "Based on the fact that you got sent here with a bug on you—one that your father gave you—I believe we need to consider it."

Bringing my thumb to my chin, I stroke it. Without even rising from his chair beside me, Cage lifts me up and settles me on his lap, enveloping me in his arms. I wish I could stay right here, just like this, for the rest of my life. Safe. Happy. Cared about.

I close my eyes and mentally go through the possibilities. They could all be completely wrong about this. It could somehow be just one big misunderstanding. My father could be innocent. Ruth could be innocent. This could all be one big, horrible nightmare.

"I'd like you to take me to see my father," I finally say.

The entire room falls silent for a moment before Cage speaks. "I don't think that's a good idea. He could be dangerous."

"He's not."

Cage raises an eyebrow.

"He might not be innocent, but my father isn't dangerous. I want to see him. To ask him face to face if he used me for his own political gain. I deserve to know."

Gunner shifts in his seat. "I can have a plane ready in an hour."

"She doesn't like planes," Cage snaps.

I turn toward him, trembling slightly from how dark his expression is. When I touch his cheek, he meets my gaze and shakes his head. "I don't like the idea of you going to see him."

"He won't hurt me, Daddy," I murmur. "Besides, you'll be there. There's no way you'll ever let anything happen to me."

We may only be in a temporary dynamic, but that's where the temporary ends. Once this is all over, I know without a single doubt that if I were ever in danger, Cage would be there in a heartbeat to protect me. That's who he is. A protector.

While his chest rises and falls harshly, his face softens. "You'll obey every single thing I say."

It's a question and a statement because he won't go along with this unless I agree to whatever rules he puts into place. As he told me before, he's lenient with a lot of things, but safety isn't one of them.

"I will."

"It will take five days if we go by car," Cassian says.

I shake my head. "No. I need to see him today. Can't you tranquilize me or something?"

The corners of Rylan's mouth twitch. "She's into that dark shit. I knew I liked her."

Cage snorts and throws a pen at his brother at the same time as I scold him.

"Rylan!" I gasp. "Are you trying to get yourself killed? Have you not seen how protective your brother is of me?"

Rylan smirks. "Oh, I've seen it, Little one. How protective... How obsessed he is. I'm starting to wonder if you've seen it."

I frown, trying to make sense of what he means.

"The plane will be ready in an hour. Let's gear up," Gunner announces, breaking me out of my thoughts.

Just the idea of getting on that tuna-can death trap has me trembling.

"Dom, can you help me get her ready to fly?" Cage asks.

Dom nods and jumps up from his seat. "Of course."

Before I can ask what that means, Cage stands with me in his arms and follows Dom out of the room.

I cling to him. "Where are we going?"

"To get you in a better state of mind for traveling, baby."

Dom snorts.

Cage smirks.

I shiver.

"**M**y tongue is numb."

Cage smiles and buckles my safety belt. "That's nice, baby."

I glare at him. "You don't even care that it's numb."

He uses his hand to cover his mouth, like he's trying to keep from laughing. What's so funny?

"I do care, baby. It's just that you've told me fourteen times since we left The Ranch that your tongue is numb."

Squinting, I look around the room. Why are the windows so small in here?

Jasper appears in front of me and holds out a juice box. "Both hands, Little one."

"You smell nice." I smile at him and take the drink he's offering.

"He *what*?" Cage barks. "Get away from her."

Sheesh. Daddy sounds upset. He's all growly. It's so sexy when he does that.

"Daddy, you're sexy."

Several men around me chuckle while Cage pinches the bridge of his nose. "Drugging her was a bad idea."

I shrug and take several sips of the juice. "Mm, grape."

Jasper winks at me, so I do the same to him. He frowns and squats down. "You okay? Dom, should her eyes be doing that?"

Dom strides over to us, looking concerned. "What are her eyes doing?"

"Dude, I think she's trying to wink," Theo says.

I bob my head, and both Dom and Jasper exchange

glances, then burst out laughing. I giggle and shrug before taking another drink. Boy, this is fun.

"We're ready for takeoff," someone announces over a loudspeaker.

Cage shoves his brothers out of the way and then sits in the seat beside me, taking my hand in his. "Ready, baby?"

"Ready, Freddie," I reply.

He leans over, his warm breath on my ear. "If you ever call me Freddie or any other man's name again, I'll put you across my knee."

I laugh, thinking he's joking, then I look at him and the stern look on his face, and my smile drops. Shoot. Daddy's really mad.

Just as I'm about to apologize, his entire face relaxes, and he grins. "Teasing you, baby girl. Why don't you close your eyes for a bit and nap?"

At first, I open my mouth to argue with him. I am kind of sleepy, though. And everything feels heavy, including my eyelids.

He takes the juice box from me and slides something soft and furry into my arms.

Spike.

He remembered to bring my dragon.

I want to thank him. To tell him I love him and ask if we can make this not temporary. To ask him to love me and be my Daddy forever. Maybe when I wake up, I will. Right now, I'm too tired.

A s soon as I open my eyes, I sit up straight. This isn't The Ranch. As I look around, my stomach gets so tight I think I might throw up. I'm on a plane. Oh, God. I *really* got on a plane.

"She's awake."

I look to my left to find Dom next to me, holding an IV bag in the air.

"Hey, sunshine," he says gently. "Breathe. We're on the ground. We landed about thirty minutes ago. This is flushing the tranquilizer out of your system, so you'll be good to go in no time."

Cage comes over and sits across from me. "How's your tongue?"

Tilting my head, I squint in confusion. "That's a strange question."

He smirks then reaches over and cups my cheek. "Do you remember why we're on a plane?"

Because my father is a backstabbing asshole who has failed me all my life. Instead of saying that, though, I just nod. No point in talking about it. Right now, I just need to focus on what I'm going to say to him.

"He's at home. I've sent a few of my brothers ahead of us to do a quick survey of the place to see who is with him," Cage explains.

Part of me wants to tell Cage to turn the plane around

and take me back to Bend. Another part of me wants to vomit. The biggest part, though, wants answers.

Was my mom's death a true accident? I can believe that my father would use me to further his career, but killing my mother? I don't think he would do that. Even if he was having some sort of affair.

Once Dom removes the IV from my arm, he and Cage lead me off the tuna-can death trap to a waiting SUV.

Cage holds my hand the entire ride to my father's house. He helps me out of the car and keeps a supportive hand on my lower back as we make our way to the front door. They seem like small things, but if he only knew how much it means to me to have him at my side, helping me, backing me, reassuring me. His brothers, too. They don't have to be here. Yet, here they are, one flanking me on the other side to Cage; two in front of me and two behind, as if I'm someone special to protect.

I was already briefed in the car that if I want to leave during the conversation at any point, Cage will get me out immediately. He's also reminded me about two dozen times to obey him or his brothers if they give me a command.

Gunner and Koda part at the front door, giving me space to knock. When I hold my arm up to do so, I pause. No. Fuck this shit. This is supposed to be my home, too. I quickly put the code in the automatic locking door then open it and step inside.

The only place I expect him to be is in his office. That's

where he always is. Even though I'm pretty sure he just spends most of his time drinking instead of working in there.

As soon as I walk through the open threshold, my father bolts up, his gaze taking in the group of men with me.

"Ember," he says almost breathlessly, his gaze darting around. "I'm surprised to see you."

Not surprising, considering he probably has GPS on that bug we purposely left in Bend.

"Father." My voice is shaky. Like a frightened little mouse. I hate it. I have an army of men behind me.

"What are you doing here? It's not safe." My father shifts uncomfortably, moving his hands to his keyboard.

"Don't touch that. Don't touch a fucking thing, Griffin," Cage growls from behind me.

Then he puts his hands on my shoulders and leans down to my ear. "Say what you want to, firefly. I'm right here to back you up. I've got you, baby."

My tummy flutters, and the scared mouse disappears, replaced with something much more pissed off. I take a step forward, crossing my arms over my chest.

"You used me," I snap at my father.

He rises from his chair and holds his hands up as if to stop me. "Ember—"

I shake my head. "No. Shut up. Just shut up. You gave me a necklace with a bug in it so you could spy on these men to gain top-secret information that might sway the election."

His face goes ghostly white, and it takes every bit of me not to break down into a puddle on the floor and bawl.

"Did you get what you wanted, *Dad*?"

My father runs a hand over his face and sighs. "Ember, you're making this out to be more than it is."

Is he freaking serious right now? Is he really making it seem like I'm overreacting?

"No, I'm not!" I shout, stomping toward him. "I'm really not. On the day I was supposed to get my final college transcripts, you decided to devise a plan to scare the hell out of me. You sent me away with a stranger to spy for you. He could have been a cold-blooded killer. He could have raped me. He could have done anything he wanted to me. You didn't care about that, though. All you thought about was your own personal gain."

"Now you're *really* being dramatic, Ember. Do you really think I would send you with someone who would hurt you?"

I laugh. It's more of a cackle because this is so fucking unbelievable. There isn't a single humorous thing about it.

"Where does Ruth come in to play on this, Dad? How long have you been fucking her? What's in it for her if you take office?" I demand.

Cage's body heat warms me, but he says nothing. He's letting me take the lead because he knows I *need* to. It says a hell of a lot about him. A man as dominant as him letting a woman take the lead.

"Now, let's just calm down and talk about this. There's no need to shout and act crazy," my father says as he rounds the desk and gets within a few feet of me.

I throw my hands in the air and practically explode. "Are you kidding me? Crazy? Me? Yeah, I'm sure you think I am after putting me in secret therapy because, God forbid, the public finds out your daughter needs a doctor for the shit she's been through."

"I did everything for you, Ember. Whatever you needed, you had. Quit being an ungrateful brat."

This time, Cage steps in front of me, his broad body blocking my view entirely. "You call her a name again and I'll break both your fucking legs right here, right now."

"Oh, that's rich. I'm paying you, and you're turning against me." My father huffs

I move to the side so I can face the asshole who was supposed to love and support me through my life. "Did you kill my mother?"

He glares at me. "She died in a helicopter crash, Ember."

I might as well have been slapped. That isn't a direct answer. It's what he does when he's lying. He's always done it. How can he even keep a straight face? No emotion. No regret. Meanwhile, I might be sick because my own father caused my mom's death. I was so young when it happened, but there are still bits and pieces I remember. How much I loved her. How much she loved me. Why did he take her away from me?

"You did," I murmur. "You had something to do with that crash."

My father takes a step forward, and almost instantly, Cage has a gun pointed in his direction. It should scare me. I should tell him not to shoot my dad. Yet, it's strangely satisfying seeing the black handgun pointed at his head.

"Do not take another step toward her," Cage warns.

My bottom lips trembles. I thought if I came here and confronted him he would deny it and have a perfectly good explanation. Maybe it was more of a wish that my own flesh and blood wouldn't have done something so awful to me. To my mom.

"You make me sick," I whisper as a tear slips from my eye.

"I could say the same about you, sweetheart," my father sneers. "The disgusting shit you're into. That you're doing with this piece of scum. I raised you better."

Grabbing a paperweight from the end table close to me, I throw it at him. "You didn't raise me at all!" I shriek.

The glass object hits him in the chest, and he staggers back slightly, letting out a grunt of pain.

A couple of the guys behind me chuckle.

"You're dead to me." I turn to leave the room, but my father's next words stop me in my tracks.

"You were supposed to be dead a long time ago, right

along with your mother, sweetheart. *You* were supposed to be in that fucking helicopter, but you were with your nanny. Instead, I was stuck with you for years. I couldn't get rid of you after questions were raised about the crash. You should have been with her!" he shouts, jabbing his finger toward me.

My entire body turns ice-cold as I process that. He wanted to kill me, too. His own daughter. My mom didn't die in an accident. She was murdered. By *him*.

A red haze starts to cloud my vision. That bastard. How could he? For her? For Ruth? Was that why? It doesn't matter. None of the reasons are relevant. Only the facts.

I scream and run toward him, my arms flailing as I beat on him with every ounce of strength I have. He tries to push me away, though, my determination wins as I hit and kick him, my fingernails clawing at his face. Blood trickles from his skin, but I still don't stop. I can't. I hate him with every fiber of my being.

"I hope you rot in hell, you bastard," I screech. "I hate you! I hate you!"

I'm not sure how long I attack him for. It isn't until Cage pulls me away that I see just how much blood there is. It's deeply satisfying to watch it seep from his ugly face.

Cage sets me on my feet. As soon as he does, I grab a lamp from the same end table and chuck it at my father, getting so much pleasure from the sound of breaking glass.

Then, with my head held high, I stride out of the office. The last thing I see when I turn to walk down the hall is Cage grabbing my father by his suit jacket. I might enjoy seeing him bleed, but I don't want his filth on me for another second. Just as I cross the foyer to go into the kitchen to wash my hands, the front door opens.

Ruth steps in and closes the door behind her before she sees me and freezes. She does a quick once-over of me.

"You bitch," I mutter as I take slow steps toward her. "You killed my mother."

Just as I'm about to move toward her again, she reaches into her purse and pulls out a gun and points it at me.

Maybe my father is right. Maybe I am crazy. Or maybe I just don't give a shit anymore because I don't let the end of that barrel sway me from approaching her.

"Your mother was a money-hungry, needy bitch." Ruth squares her shoulders. "She was a roadblock that neither Zeke nor I needed or wanted."

"A roadblock for what?" I demand. "All she wanted was her family together. For my father to spend time with us. How was that being a roadblock?"

"Your father could have been elected a long time ago, but she didn't want that. She wanted to have a family life out of the spotlight. Stupid woman, if you ask me."

"She was a good woman. A better woman than you'll ever be or ever have been." I glance at the gun she's still holding with a steady hand. Why do I get the feeling this isn't the first time she's held someone at gunpoint?

"I guess that's up for debate, my dear."

I shake my head, tears burning my eyes. "What was in it for you?"

Ruth tips her head back and laughs. "The president chooses the head of the CIA. With him in office and me as head of the organization, we could have taken over the world. The modern fairytale, I suppose."

If my jaw could hit the floor, it would. What the fuck? Is this bitch serious right now? Rule the world?

Footsteps approach from behind me.

"Put the gun down now," Jasper commands loudly.

22

CAGE

White-hot rage seethes through me as I take slow steps toward Ember with my gun aimed at Ruth's head. My eyes are trained on her trigger finger, looking for any sign of movement. She's a dead woman, but Ember being in the crossfire isn't something I'm willing to risk. And pointing a weapon at my Little girl is the worst possible thing Ruth could have done. Torturing her before killing her wasn't on my agenda. Until now.

"Put the gun down, Ruth," I growl.

"She killed my mom," Ember grits out.

My heart aches for my girl. I don't know how all of this got so out of hand. I shouldn't have brought her here. I should have kept her in Bend where she belongs. With me. As soon as this is over, that's exactly where she's going. Home. *Her* home.

"You fucking asshole," Ruth shouts as she moves her gun from pointing at Ember to me. Thank fuck. She can shoot me as much as she wants, but she's not hurting my Little girl. "You had one job. To take her to your place, so I could get the information I needed."

I narrow my gaze. "You sent a plane after us. You knew I would take her there. You had this all planned out. Thought you had a brilliant idea, huh?"

Ruth licks her lips. "It *was* brilliant. No one was going to get hurt. All we needed was some intelligence."

Out of the corner of my eye, I watch Ghost come in from another direction, being the silent monster he is. I just hope to God that Ember doesn't notice him yet. As long as Ruth's gun is pointed at me, I can breathe.

As soon as Ghost is close enough, he leaps, grabbing Ember and bringing her to the ground while I bolt forward and disarm Ruth. It only takes seconds before I have her hands zip-tied in front of her.

"You made a big mistake," I whisper in her ear. "Did you really think you'd be able to pull one over on me, *Ruthie*?"

She tries to elbow me as I lead her back to the office, where Zeke is restrained to his chair. Dom sits casually on one of the couches, a drink in one hand, his gun in another.

I shove the older woman forward and watch with pleasure as she stumbles to the floor and struggles to get into a sitting position without the use of her hands.

"You won't get away with this," Zeke tells me.

Dom and I look at each other and smirk.

"I don't think Ruth told you exactly who we are." I tuck my gun into my waistband holster, then rub my chin like I'm thinking hard. "You see, there's no record of us. Anywhere. In any database. To the world, we don't exist. We're ghosts. To our enemies, we're the worst thing that could ever happen. I actually thought Ruth was brighter than this. She knows *exactly* what happens to people who cross us."

Ruth shakes her head. "You piece of shit, we didn't cross you. We were getting intel on things the CIA should be privy to in the first place."

Sitting next to Dom, I cross an ankle over my knee. "You think I give a flying fuck about you wanting intel? You should have just asked for it, Ruthie. I probably would have given you what you wanted."

"Then what the hell is the problem?" she shouts, looking completely exasperated.

"The problem is, you used my girl as your pawn. You murdered her mother, the one parent who actually loved her, and you pointed a fucking gun at her head."

I rise and make my way to the bar and pour myself a drink. As soon as I down the expensive liquid, I throw the glass against the wall, causing it to explode into a million pieces.

"You're both dead. I hope it was worth it," I say as I stride toward the door.

There's no doubt that Ember is safe with my brothers right now, but I need to touch her. To hold her. Comfort her. Love her.

"I'm her father. If you care about her at all, you won't kill me," Zeke calls out desperately.

Pausing mid-step, I spin around and stomp across the office to where he is, grabbing him by his hair with painful force. I lean down so he's forced to look me directly in the eye.

"Let's be clear on one thing. You might be her father, but I'm her Daddy. I'm going to do whatever it takes to protect her, even if it's from her own flesh and blood."

Using his hair as leverage, I shove him backward. His chair crashes to the floor, leaving him stuck without any way to move because his wrists and ankles are tied.

Dom stands and follows me, both of us grinning as we walk outside, only to find my girl arguing with Rylan, of all people.

"I'm about to spank your ass right here and now. You're not going anywhere," Rylan barks.

Ember tries to shove him, but he doesn't budge. When he laughs at her attempt, it pisses her off more.

"What's going on?" I yell.

Rylan turns his attention to me, but Ember takes off, walking toward a set of garages at the end of the house. Before she can get out of arm's reach, he grabs her by the wrist and swats her ass three times.

"Owwie!" she yelps, rubbing her bottom.

She scowls at him and tries to pull away from him, but he won't let go.

"Your Little girl here thinks she's going to go get in her car and drive away from here to find a place to live," Rylan tells me. "I explained that she's coming with us. She doesn't believe me."

I narrow my gaze at Ember, who is as red as a tomato now. "That so? You were just going to leave, firefly?"

Her bottom lip quivers as I approach. When she peers up at me, my heart cracks a little.

"Your job is over. You don't..." She sniffles. "You don't have to take care of me anymore. You can go home and leave me here. I'll figure something out. I have my degree and a small amount of savings."

Rylan and I exchange smirks before I force my face to look serious.

"I should pull down your pants and panties and spank you right here, in this driveway, if you think I'm leaving you here," I say calmly. "The job might be over, but my love for you isn't. It's just starting, firefly. And if you think for one fucking second that you're leaving me, you're wrong. I'll chain you to my bed if I have to until you decide you love me, too. You're mine. The only home I'm going to is the one I'll share with you for the rest of our lives."

Ember's head snaps up, tears dripping down her cheeks. "You love me?"

Letting out a huff, I reach out and cup her chin. "Never loved anyone more, Ember. You're my Little girl."

"You're part of this family," Rylan adds firmly. "Forever."

My chest swells, and though I might give Rylan a lot of shit, he's a damn good brother. I'll never tell him that, though. The bastard already thinks too much of himself.

"I hope to hell one day you'll love me too, firefly. It doesn't matter how long it takes because you're still mine, and I'm not letting you go."

She lets out a sob and pulls herself away from Rylan to throw herself at me. I catch her. I'll always catch her.

"I love you, too. I thought you only wanted it to be temporary, so I didn't want to make it any harder."

Lifting her, I squeeze her tightly, burying my face in the crook of her neck. "You're not temporary, baby. You never were, and you never will be."

When her sobs quiet, I set her feet on the ground and use the pads of my thumbs to wipe her tears away. "What do you want to grab from the house before we go? You're never coming back here, so whatever you want to keep, you need to get it now."

She glances toward the front doors. "The only thing I want is my mother's charm bracelet. It's in my jewelry box in my room."

I nod. "I can get it for you. Anything else? Do you want to go to your room and take one last look around?"

"No."

There isn't an ounce of hesitation in that answer, so I don't push it. Mostly because I'm glad she doesn't want anything. I'll give her everything she could ever want or need.

"Okay, baby. I want you to go with Gunner, Koda, and Dom. Dom will get you ready for the flight home. I'll be right behind you."

Her eyes flash with uncertainty for just a second. I don't know what I'll do if she asks me not to do anything to her father. I'm not sure I'd be able to keep a promise like that.

"Are you going to kill them?" she asks in a small voice.

I stare down at her. Will her love for me change if I'm honest? I won't lie to her, though. She deserves more than that. Even though the truth can be ugly, she always deserves it.

"Yeah. I am."

She looks toward the house again, then up at me, her eyebrows drawn together with worry. "Please be careful."

The breath I've been holding releases, and I nod. Thank fuck.

"I'll be careful, baby. I'll be right behind you."

Dom offers his hand out for her to take, and the growly side of me wants to cut that hand off, but the Daddy side of me nudges her to him.

"I love you, firefly," I tell her again as Dom leads her toward one of the SUVs.

She's going to get tired of me saying that, but I don't care. Besides, she deserves to hear it as much as possible.

Rylan, Jasper, Theo, Cassian, Ghost, and I watch as the rest of our brothers drive away with my precious cargo. I hate that I'm not going with her. She needs me right now. Which means I'm going to make this quick and impactful so I can get back to her as soon as possible.

As soon as the taillights disappear, the six of us move in unison, grabbing equipment out of the back of our SUV.

Time to get vengeance.

"I'm going to go grab her mother's bracelet. Start planting the explosives, I'll be right back," I instruct as I start up the stairs.

Both Zeke and Ruth are screaming from the office. I'm not sure who they think is going to hear them and come to their rescue. This house isn't close to any neighbors. There are at least three acres of property surrounding it.

One glance around Ember's bedroom has me fighting the urge to go put a bullet in Griffin's head right now. There are touches of my girl throughout the space, but barely. She never made this her home. Never settled in here. Because he kept sending her away. Fucking bastard.

I pocket the bracelet, noting that there are only two charms on it. It's the only one like it in the jewelry box, so it must be the right one.

Rylan is wiring some explosives at the bottom of the stairs when I get there. "Thank you," I say.

He glances up at me and then back at what he's doing. "For what?"

"For taking care of my girl out there."

"She's family, Cage. Since the day she arrived, Ember's been family. And even with as much shit as I give you, I'm so fucking happy you found her."

My heart beats faster while I stare at my brother, almost speechless. After we were recruited to The Elite Team, we all bonded and became the tightest group of brothers. We had to because we needed to trust each other when we were working. Then Rowie came into our lives and turned our world upside down. She taught us about more than just trust. She taught us love. We don't show our emotions to each other very often, but I hope my brothers know how much they all mean to me.

"I love you, Ry."

He rises to his full height and eyes me. "I love you too, bro. Now, let's go avenge our girl."

I glare at him. "She's my girl. Not ours. *Mine.*"

The fucker laughs and heads toward the office. "Whatever you say, asshole. I'm pretty sure she likes me more than she likes you."

If looks could kill, Rylan would be a dead man. I swear to God, he's going to send me to an early grave with his smart-ass comments. One of these days, I'm going to snap and he'll have a broken nose. Or worse. Yet, I know he'll continue to push my buttons because that's what family does.

Zeke Griffin has made it into a sitting position since we left him in here. Ruth is leaning against a wall, trying to use her feet to break the zip-tie around her wrists.

"You've proven your point, Cage. Cut this off, now," Ruth snaps at me.

Going over to her, I squat down and smile. "I really don't think I have proven my point, Ruthie. You see, if you paid attention to me or my brothers, you would know that loyalty means everything to us. You could have been straight with me and probably gotten what you wanted, but you were sneaky. And you put Ember in danger. You also helped to kill her mother, the one person in her life who loved her... Until now."

Ruth shakes her head, her lips curling down with anger. "Cage, I'm a fucking CIA agent. You won't get away with this."

I reach out and cup her chin. "I already have, Ruthie. You see, while I was flying here, I made a call to the head of your organization. He's in full support of what I'm about to do. Seems you've been doing quite a bit of shady shit throughout your career, and it's all starting to catch up with you. And you know what happens to CIA agents who become traitors."

Her face goes ghostly white as her eyes bulge. She tries to kick me away but ends up falling sideways to the carpeted floor. I laugh and take a step back, then turn to Zeke.

"You hurt my world. I live and breathe for your daughter, and you hurt her."

"I didn't mean to!" he shouts desperately. "I'm her father. I love her."

Striding over to him, I kick him in the face, a loud, crunching noise filling the room as my steel-toe boot meets his jaw. He howls as blood gushes from his nose and mouth.

"No, you are her sperm donor. I'm her Daddy. You don't get to hold any title for her. You never protected her. That's my job now, though. And I take that very fucking seriously. Just ask Ruthie. I *never* leave a job unfinished."

Zeke continues screaming in pain. As much as I'd love to spend more time torturing the fuck out of him, I don't want to spend another second away from my firefly.

"Cuff their wrists and ankles. Then blow this fucking place up and set it alight," I tell Rylan, who gives me that sadistic grin he's known for when he gets to blow something up.

"Happy to, brother."

"Don't leave until it's done and burned to ashes." I turn back toward Ruth and Zeke. "I hope you both burn in hell."

Then I stride out and climb into one of the SUVs, smiling the entire drive back to the airfield.

23

EMBER

"My tongue is numb."

Ghost grins at me, his normally terrifying face looking less scary than normal.

"You don't say."

"Jesus, Dom. You couldn't give her something else that doesn't make her tongue numb?" Cage asks.

I frown and look at my Daddy. "Be nice to Uncle Dom. He gave me a sucker for being so good."

Cage stares at me like I have three heads, but it kind of feels like I do. "A sucker that I had to take away because you couldn't control your drool."

Giggling, I bob my head. Yeah. Oopsie.

"Close your eyes, firefly. We'll be home in no time."

Home.

My Daddy is taking me home.

I would tell him that he doesn't have to take me

anywhere because he is my home, but my mouth is tired, and my eyes are heavy. Maybe I'll tell him another time.

I f sleeping on a cloud was a real thing, I swear, I'd be doing it right now. Wherever I am, it's the best bed I've ever laid in. I should probably open my eyes. I'm too comfortable, though.

Sighing, I roll over to my side and pause when my hand slaps on bare skin. Warm and a little fuzzy. I know this chest.

Cage.

Daddy.

Home.

"Daddy," I whisper.

His breathing hitches, and he tightens his arms around me. "Yeah, baby. I'm right here."

I smile and snuggle into him, letting out a relieved breath. Having him here is all I need.

Slowly, I glide my hand over his chest, feeling every vein and muscle as I explore his hard body. His heart pounds against my palm, and as I move my fingers lower, he stops breathing.

"Firefly," he says quietly.

Ignoring him, I continue wandering my fingers down his abs until I reach the waistband of his underwear.

Finally opening my eyes, I nearly gasp. He's rock hard, and I can't resist cupping it through his boxer briefs.

"Fuck." He groans and fists his hand in my hair.

My nipples ache, and my pussy clenches as I squeeze him gently. God, he's practically chiseled in stone. The man is so perfect. And he's mine.

"Please," I whisper. "I need you."

"Baby, it's going to hurt the first time I fuck you. I don't want to cause you any pain. We should work you up to it."

I shake my head and slowly stroke along his shaft. "I don't want to wait. I need you. Please, Daddy. Make me yours completely. In every way possible. I want to give you everything."

That last sentence pulls a low growl from him, and he flexes his fist in my hair. "You're going to be my good girl and tell me if I hurt you too much?"

"I promise. Scout's honor, Daddy."

He glares at me. "Pretty sure you were never a scout, firefly."

Grinning, I shrug and pull the elastic of his underwear back, letting his cock spring free. "No, but I promise to tell you."

"Do you remember your safeword, baby?"

Rising slightly, I move my head down, my mouth hovering over his cock. It's so thick. I shouldn't have expected anything less. Cage is a large man. *Everywhere.*

"It's red, Daddy. That can be your safeword, too," I say right before I lower my lips to the tip of his cock.

He smirks down at me. "Think I might need a safe-word with you, huh, baby? You gonna be rough with me?"

I giggle and peer up at him from under my lashes. "I guess you'll have to wait and see."

Then I take the head of his cock into my mouth and swirl my tongue around it, loving the salty taste of his pre-release.

"Fuck!" He sucks in a gulp of air and lifts his head to watch me.

Keeping eye contact with him, I dip my head down, testing to see how far I can go before I gag. It will be impossible to take him all the way, but I want to try because this is hot. It might even be hotter than what he did to me on the kitchen counter.

"Easy, firefly. Watch your teeth, baby."

My panties are soaked, and he hasn't touched me yet. Sucking his cock seems so filthy, but so damn right. I wonder if I could suck on it in place of a pacifier sometimes? Not really sure if that would work with how excited he is right now.

He drops his head to the pillow and rubs his forehead, his breathing erratic. "Fuck. Your mouth is so good. So damn good."

Using my free hand, I cup his balls and gently roll them in my fingers, enjoying the sensation. Who knew men's genitalia could be so soothing? Maybe it's just a Little thing.

"Move your hips over here, baby." He pats the bed next

to him. I shuffle over on my knees while continuing to suck his cock.

As soon as his hand touches my bare thigh, I moan and take him deeper into my mouth. I need him touching me like I need my next breath.

"Keep sucking Daddy's cock while I touch you, baby. Don't stop, or I'll punish you."

Right. Because that's not tempting or anything. Maybe I should stop. It's just so damn hot.

He runs his fingers over the crotch of my panties, and I jolt forward. Holy crap.

"So sensitive, baby." He strokes again, this time giving a bit of pressure on my clit. Even through my underwear, his touch lights up my entire body.

I close my eyes and take him in deep until I gag. Cage groans and yanks my panties to the side at the same time. As I take him in again, he slowly thrusts one of his thick fingers into my pussy.

"Such a good fucking girl, firefly. I want you to ride my hand, baby."

He doesn't have to tell me twice. My hips are already moving, searching for every bit of pleasure he's offering.

I moan and whimper, sucking him harder and faster until I'm nearly blind with pleasure.

"You're dripping down my wrist, baby. So needy. You're so close to coming, aren't you?"

"Mm-hmm."

So close that it's almost painful as I try to hold off.

Cage adds a second finger, stretching me almost to the point of pain. I keep my head down, not wanting him to see me wince. Knowing him, he'll keep me a virgin forever if it means not hurting me.

"You're going to come for me while you keep sucking my dick. Come all over me, baby. Soak this bed with your honey."

As if that's what my body was waiting for, every muscle tenses before a rush of pure ecstasy rushes through me.

"Oh!" I cry out around his cock.

I try to keep sucking, I really do. But then he curls his fingers inside me, and I scream. Sitting up on his hand, my hips move, and my head falls back while I ride him just like he told me to.

"Such a good girl. Jesus Christ, Ember. You're so beautiful when you come like this," he growls.

My moans grow quieter, and my breathing grows heavier until I'm folded forward with my head resting on his stomach while I slowly stroke his cock.

"I assume you're not on birth control?" His voice is strained, and I feel a bit guilty that he's had to hold off so long.

"I am. I have an implant. It helps with my period cramps."

He flips me onto my back so quickly that my head spins as he hovers over me, his dark eyes staring at me with so much intensity that I shiver.

"I want to fuck you bare. I want nothing between us. Not now, not ever. You're it for me, Ember. There will never be another woman in my life. And I'll kill any man who tries to take you away from me."

Reaching up, I cup his beautiful face. My heart is practically beating out of my chest. "I don't want anyone else but you, Daddy. Fuck me. Make me yours. No barriers."

The head of his cock nudges my entrance, and a million butterflies explode in my tummy. I've never been so glad I waited to lose my virginity. This, our connection, is everything I've always wanted.

"I love you, Ember Elizabeth Black."

I furrow my eyebrows. "My last name is Adams."

He shakes his head. "Not anymore. Legal or not, it's Black now."

Then he slowly thrusts into me, pausing for a second when I bite my lip in pain.

"Ouchie," I whisper.

His entire face grows dark, and he shakes his head. "I'm so fucking sorry, my love. It will only hurt this one time, then I'll take such good care of you."

"I know, Daddy." Tears drip from my eyes, and I quickly dash them away. "I know you will. Keep going."

Inch by inch, he stretches me so wide I think I might need surgery when we're done. It's worth it, though. Everything I've been through in my life has been worth it for this moment.

"You're doing so good, baby," he tells me as he slowly

pulls out and thrusts in again. "It will start feeling good in a second."

I nod and hold on to his shoulders while he stares into my eyes and fucks me. The pain quickly morphs into pleasure, and my whimpers turn into moans as I beg for more.

"Oh my God. This feels so amazing."

Cage chuckles. "Yeah, baby. It does. It's everything. Just like you."

We watch each other while kissing, exploring, feeling. There's no music, but it feels like there is. I try to think about what song would be playing right now. Something sweet and sexy. Maybe a John Legend song.

Everything around me disappears. The only thing I can truly focus on is Cage. He pushes my shirt up over my breasts, and when he latches on to one of my needy nipples, I arch up for more.

Soon, our calm movements become more urgent. He continues to praise me for being his good girl, and fuck, I love it.

My hands roam his chest, and then I run my fingernails over his back, scratching him and marking him as mine. Maybe he's not the only possessive one in this relationship. When he bites one of my nipples, pleasure shoots right down to my core. I'm breathing heavily, my heart ready to explode, and on the verge of orgasm again.

"You're so close, baby. You're going to fucking kill me.

I'm not going to last. Your pussy was made for me," he growls as he thrusts harder and faster.

"Yes, Daddy! Only you," I reply breathlessly.

"Only you, firefly. Only you."

His movements become erratic, and he tucks a hand between us, his fingers finding my clit. As soon as he circles the sensitive nub, I'm wrecked. I scream and thrash. My entire body shakes while my pussy spasms, but Cage continues to fuck me wildly.

All of a sudden, he stills, and his cock throbs inside me, filling me. When my orgasm subsides, I let out a long, satisfied hum. Bliss.

"Jesus," he mutters, staring down at me, worried. "Are you okay? I'm so sorry. I got too rough for your first time."

Shaking my head, I grin. "I'm perfect, Daddy. Never been better."

He hovers over me for a bit longer, his cock still seated inside me. "I'm glad you feel that way, baby. Because in a while, we're going to deal with the punishment you're owed. I probably shouldn't have fucked you since naughty girls don't get orgasms."

My mouth falls open. "That's mean, Daddy."

"Get used to it, firefly. You thought I was strict before, but I've been taking it easy on you."

Well... That just sucks.

"Daddy, I really don't think you need to punish me. I've definitely learned my lesson. Besides, it's in the past. We shouldn't dredge up the past, right? It's bad for our health."

Cage smirks and points to the ottoman in front of where he's sitting. He looks mouthwatering in his jeans and no shirt. I really think there are better things we could do with our time than a silly spanking. Like sex. Yes, I definitely want to do that again. The aftercare was amazing, too. Not only did he hand-feed me cheese and crackers, but he brought up my sippy cup. This was after he cleaned up my most intimate areas, then covered me in a warm blanket and snuggled me. He's perfect. Maybe not to anyone else; to me, he is.

"Oh, I really think you need to be punished, firefly. Besides, what kind of Daddy would I be if I didn't follow through? Now, come here because if I have to come get you, I'll choose an implement to use on your cute bottom as well."

Yikes. He means serious business.

Setting my coloring book aside, I crawl out of bed and go to him, pulling at the bottom of my sleep shirt to cover myself. He didn't put panties on me after we had sex, and suddenly, I'm feeling very exposed.

When I come to his side, he grabs my hands and moves me between his legs to sit opposite from him.

"Before I spank your cute bottom, I want to add a couple more rules to our relationship."

The corners of my lips twitch, but I keep my lips sealed. It's probably a bad idea to make a sassy comment right now.

"First, a lot has happened in the past day. It's going to take time for you to process. You might end up having some big feelings about it. You need to talk to me immediately if you do. I can have a therapist come here for you to work with. Whatever you feel over this, I want to know. It's my job as your Daddy to make sure you're happy and healthy, and that goes for your mental well-being, too. Understand?"

My tummy does a fluttery thing. I didn't think it was possible to love Cage any more than I already do but then he goes and says that. He thinks he struggles to understand emotion, although I'd say he understands it much better than he realizes.

"Yes, Daddy. I will."

He's right. I need to process everything. I haven't asked him outright if my father is dead. I don't need to. Cage isn't the type of man to give grace to anyone who hurts those he cares about. I'm not sure what it says about me that I'm not sad over it. Maybe the sadness will come. All I feel at the moment, is relief. Like a huge weight has been lifted.

"That's my good girl. Next rule. You have to tell me I'm handsome every day and that you love me."

Wrinkling my nose, I raise my gaze to his and giggle. He winks at me and grins, reaching out for me.

"Got you to relax a little. I do think that should be a rule, though."

I laugh harder and roll my eyes. He really is full of himself. In the best way. "Well, you are handsome, and I do love you."

He holds me between his thighs, his face buried in the crook of my neck. "You're such a gift, Ember. Everything I could possibly want."

Wrapping my arms around him, I sigh. "I feel like a mess. I have no career and no idea what I want to do in my life. I don't bring much to the table, Cage."

When he tenses and lifts his head to look at me, his eyes are almost black. "I don't ever want to hear you put yourself down like that again. I'm adding extra spanks for that."

A shiver runs up my spine. I really wish I had panties on right now so he doesn't notice me getting wet.

"I wasn't putting myself down," I argue.

He arches an eyebrow. "Really? Because it sure seemed like you did to me. You bring *everything* to the table, Ember Elizabeth. You don't need to know what you're going to do yet. You're just getting to start your life. And I'm going to be here to cheer you on with whatever you decide to do because that's what Daddies do. Do you understand me, baby? *You* are *everything*."

Sniffing, I nod, trying to swallow the lump forming in my throat. I don't think I'll ever get used to him praising me like he does. "Yes, Daddy."

"Good. I think we need to get on with your punishment since you now have two owed."

I squeeze my thighs together, trembling slightly. "Only one punishment, Daddy."

He raises his eyebrows. "Really? I'm counting two. One for getting out of bed when I directly told you not to. And second, because you just put yourself down."

Well... crumb.

"You're allowed to use your safeword during punishment. Since this is your first real spanking, I'm going to take it easy on you, but if it gets to the point where you need it to stop, you say red. You need to remember that even though I'm your Daddy, you still hold the power here. Okay?"

My heart races, and even though I'm facing my doom, I'm not scared. Cage would die before he truly hurt me.

"Okay, Daddy."

He puts me on my feet, then takes my hand and carefully helps me over one of his thighs. My chest rests on the oversized chair, and my feet dangle in the air. I can only imagine what I look like from his position right now.

"Part your thighs, firefly. Keep them parted the entire time."

Crap. He's definitely going to see my arousal. Maybe if i'm good, he'll touch me between my legs during my spanking.

He palms my bottom, making me jump.

"Ready, baby?"

I twist to look back at him. "Is the sun cold?"

His palm comes down with a sharp, loud smack. Holy crap, that was hard.

"You know, it's probably not smart to be sassy with Daddy when you're in such a predicament. Now, I'm going to ask you again. Are you ready?"

"Yes, Daddy," I answer breathlessly.

He spanks me again, this time not stopping with one. Again and again, his palm connects. He said he was going to take it easy on me. I think his idea of easy and my idea of easy are very different. Stinging pain radiates through me, and it's not long before I start wiggling, trying to dodge his hand.

"When I tell you to do something, I expect you to obey. Why did you decide to disobey Daddy?"

I bite my lip and whimper, trying to process his words while he continues to pepper my poor bottom with swats.

"Did you do it because you wanted to see what would happen if you disobeyed? I kind of think you did. Guess what? This is what happens. Naughty girls always go over their Daddy's lap when they don't listen."

"Owwie! Owwie! Owwie!" I hiss and kick, my eyes starting to burn with tears.

"You can test me all you want, firefly, but no matter how often you do it, I'm never giving up on you or sending you away. I want you to get that through your head right now. You're mine. I'm going to spank you when you're naughty. I'll never stop loving you, though."

Sniffling, I let out a sob. "I'm sorry, Daddy. I won't do it again."

He lifts his free leg and puts it over the back of both of mine, so I can't kick, then starts spanking me harder and faster.

"I wouldn't make promises you can't keep, firefly," he says, his voice amused. "I like my naughty, sassy girl. I also like spanking her. Fuck, I could spank this perfect ass every day."

After this, I think I'm going to try really hard to be a good girl. Although, despite my bottom being on fire, my pussy is throbbing.

Tears drip down my cheeks, but no matter how much I wiggle or fight, he doesn't stop. When I try to reach back to cover one of my cheeks, he grabs my wrist and pins it to my lower back. I'm completely at his mercy now.

It hurts. So bad. It's also cathartic. The longer he goes, the more I cry until I'm sobbing over and over. When I can't fight it anymore, my entire body goes limp and I give into it, letting the pain and tears wash everything away.

As soon as Cage stops, he pulls me up and settles me on his lap. I wince when my bottom connects with his pants. I have a feeling I'll be doing a lot of that for the next day or two.

"I got you, baby. Let it out. That's my girl."

He holds me against his chest and slowly rocks me back and forth in his arms for a long time. Even after my tears stop, he holds me, stroking my head and whispering praise. I'm sure I look like a train wreck right now, but I've never felt lighter. Maybe being spanked isn't all that terrible. Maybe it's exactly what I need to let go of so many unhealthy emotions I've been bottling up for so long.

"How's my girl? Where's your head at right now, baby?"

Tilting my head back, I gaze up at him and stroke his short beard at the same time. "I'm good, Daddy. I feel... light. And happy."

Cage scoots back in the chair and leans back, cradling me against him before he reaches for a throw blanket and covers me up.

"Me too, firefly. So fucking happy."

24

CAGE

3 weeks later...

"Thanks for your help. I owe you guys."

Theo adjusts one of the stuffies on the bookshelf. "Doing this reminds me of when we did Rowie's playroom. How happy she was. How safe it made her feel. I hope Ember loves this room just as much."

She will. If I've learned anything about my girl, it's that she's so fucking grateful for everything my brothers or I do for her. I guess when you've never had anyone go the extra mile for you, it makes it pretty special when people do.

"It's perfect," Cassian adds.

My heart swells, and once again, I find myself wanting to tell my brothers what they mean to me. Maybe Ember is turning me soft.

"I love you guys."

Rylan smirks. "Getting told you love me twice in a month. It's like I've won the lottery."

Narrowing my gaze, I flip him the bird. He's still been a total pain in the ass. Ember has declared him the mean uncle ever since he swatted her bottom, which makes me feel better. It's adorable watching him try to make nice with her, bribing her with candy and treats. Rylan is used to being loved by everyone, so this has been a humbling experience for him that my girl isn't putty in his hands.

Ghost grins. "Love you too, man. We're happy for you. Deke would be happy for you, too."

I nod, a lump forming in my throat. "I wish he could've met her."

Theo grins. "He would have fucking loved her. She would have had him wrapped around her pinky in a heartbeat."

It's true. Deke was the toughest guy I've ever known, but when it came to his Little girl or Rowie, he was absolute goo for them.

"Ember would have liked him too," I reply. "I wish I could thank him for saving me because if he hadn't, I wouldn't have found her."

Gunner pats my shoulder. "He knew how thankful we all were that he saved us."

He's right. We always made sure he knew how appreciative we were. Maybe it's why we trained so hard for him. Most of us had never made anyone proud in our lives until we met Deke Black. After he recruited us, there wasn't a day that went by that he didn't tell us in some way or another how proud he was of the men we became.

"I forgot to ask you." Cassian turns to me. "Did you do anything with those names I got you?"

Satisfaction spreads through me as I nod. "Sure did. By now, their lives should be well-ruined. One found out her husband's been cheating on her... with men. Another is now completely broke and being chased down by the IRS. Another had a little accident happen while she was at the salon and is now bald. And the last one just had her house condemned and has no place to go."

Ghost scowls. "With what those girls did to Ember, they deserve so much worse."

I grin. "This is just the beginning of their bad luck. I suspect they'll be hating life for the next twenty years or so. I'll let them start to get back on their feet before I slip the rug out from under them again. I figure they need to be punished for the same length of time that my girl has had to suffer because of their cruelty."

"Good. I hope they know how lucky they are that you're allowing them to continue breathing," Cassian says.

"Yeah, well, my girl asked me not to kill them, and I'm starting to learn I'll pretty much do whatever she asks."

Rylan snorts. "We hadn't noticed."

"Fuck off," I say, grinning. "I should go get Ember to show her the room before everyone arrives."

Theo laughs. "And you think you're going to be able to tear her away from here once she sees it? Good luck with that."

He's right. I can't wait until tonight for her to see it, though. We've been working on her playroom for weeks. It's been torture not showing her.

"Guess she'll come to dinner with a red bottom if she decides to have a tantrum about leaving it," I reply as I stride out of the room to search for my girl in the main house.

Giggling leads me toward one of the living rooms. As soon as I turn the corner, I come to a halt. Both Ember and Rowie are on their knees, coloring at the coffee table. At least they *appear* to be coloring, but what they're actually doing is trying to cover their laughing while continually pointing at Jasper, who is leaning back on the couch, fast asleep. With a smile drawn on his face in black marker.

"Girls," I scold softly.

Both of them gasp, their eyes wide as they look up at me standing in the doorway.

"Hi, Daddy," Ember says sweetly.

I raise an eyebrow at her, then Rowie. "What did you brats do to Jasper?"

Ember glances up at my brother and giggles softly.

"We just wanted to make sure he woke up with a smile, Daddy. He's been so tired and grumpy lately."

Rowie bobs her head in agreement, looking quite proud of herself.

Putting my hands on my hips, I let out a slow exhale. It's taking every bit of Daddy strength not to laugh right now because, honestly, what they did is fucking hilarious.

"You two are going to be in trouble when he wakes up and sees what you did. You're not even supposed to use markers without supervision."

Rowie holds up her hands and shrugs. "It's not our fault our supervisor fell asleep."

I glare at Rowie. "You know how much he struggles to sleep. Obviously, he felt safe to close his eyes with the two of you."

"Yeah, but he looks so happy right now," Ember replies.

Jesus. These two together are trouble with a capital T.

"You're both going to lose some Good Girl Points for this. Don't come whining to me when that happens."

Rowie and Ember look at each other and then back at me.

"We already discussed that before we did it and decided it would be worth it," Rowie tells me.

Ember nods, grinning proudly.

Unable to mask it any longer, a slow smile spreads as I look at my brother again. Poor Jasper. He's never going to sleep again.

I hold out my hand to Ember. "Come with me. I want to show you something."

She comes to me without hesitation, and when she slides her fingers into my palm, I'm whole again.

"Can I come, too?" Rowie pipes up, her gaze hopeful.

"Yes, brat. Let's go."

Jumping to her feet, she runs to us and takes Ember's hand and I think my heart just exploded. These two have been inseparable since I brought Ember home from DC. It's the sweetest thing ever. Not only has Ember learned to trust someone besides me, but Rowie is smiling so much more. It makes me feel shitty that I didn't realize she was lonely before. I probably need to talk to her about it and apologize. I should have picked up on it.

Both girls skip next to me, talking about all sorts of random things that pop into their Little minds. My baby girl is finding out just how much she loves being in this headspace. Seeing her blossom so much in these past few weeks has been the best thing I could have ever imagined.

She hasn't asked about her father once. Unless she does, I'll never speak about his existence around her. It will take time for her to fully know that she deserves so much more. And I'm going to give her everything.

"Where are we going? I thought your friends were coming over for a barbecue?" Ember looks up at me with confusion.

"They are. We're just going home for a few minutes, then we'll go back to the main house," I reply.

Ember's cheeks turn rosy. "Daddy, I don't think we should have brought Rowie with us if you want to sneak in a quickie before they come."

Jesus.

This woman. She is so sassy and quick witted. I love it. She's so damn perfect for me.

"Ember Elizabeth."

Both girls giggle and start skipping ahead of me. Sometimes, I feel a little ganged up on by those two. I'm not quite sure what I think about that yet.

My brothers, who helped with the room, are in the kitchen when we enter. They are about as excited as I am right now. Since my girl is still learning about what her Little likes, I had a hard time choosing a theme for her room. We ended up going with something simple for now so it will be easy to add to or change later on.

"What are they doing here?" Rowie asks, looking a bit nervous.

"Why do you look like you did something naughty, Row?" Theo demands with an arched brow.

Rowie gasps. "I didn't do anything!"

I tug on one of her pigtails. "Really? You want to stick with that story because it won't be long before the entire family knows what you did."

She shrugs. "Yeah, and they're going to think it's hilarious."

Shaking my head, I point a finger at them both. "You both better hope it was a washable marker."

The girls glance at each other. It doesn't take a mind reader to know that they *definitely* used a permanent marker. As a Daddy, I should probably punish them, but as Jasper's brother, I can't fucking wait to witness this show.

"Follow me." I lead them toward my office. Instead of going to that door, I go to the one right across the hall.

"We can make changes, but I wanted to create a special space for you."

As soon as they step into the room, they gasp and slowly turn around in circles.

"This is the most beautiful room I've ever seen," Ember whispers, her eyes filling with tears. "You did this for me?"

"Yeah, firefly. Just for you," I reply softly. "They helped too."

She looks at my brothers and then back at me, her bottom lip trembling. "I love it."

I hold out my arms, and she comes running, hugging me tightly. "I'm so glad. Go explore. We have a few minutes before we need to go."

Both Ember and Rowie walk around, touching just about everything. When Ember gets to the day bed, which has a safety rail on both sides, she blushes. I figured it would be perfect to make her feel extra Little during her naptimes.

"I love the twinkle lights. They remind me of fireflies." Rowie stares up at the wire lights strung from the ceiling.

"They do!" Ember squeals. "I love the pastel-purple walls. They're so soft and calming. Everything in here is so perfect, Daddy. Thank you. All of you. This means so much."

She goes to each of my brothers and gives them a hug. I barely resist the urge to growl at each one of them as they wrap their arms around her.

When she gets to Rylan, he almost looks nervous. "Does this mean you forgive me for spanking you?"

She tilts her head back to look up at him and smiles. "Yeah. I suppose so."

He lets out a relieved breath and pulls her in for a tight squeeze. "Love you, Little one."

"Love you too, Ry," she says right before I pull her away from him.

Theo pulls out his phone and looks at it quickly and then tucks it back in his pocket. "We better go. Declan and the rest of them just pulled up at the gates."

"**R**emind me why I haven't hired you guys for my personal security?" Declan asks when he gets out of his SUV. "It's like a fucking fortress here. Nice, though. No city noise."

Ember practically clings to me as several of Declan's men and their women get out of a line of cars.

"They're so pretty," she whispers.

"So are you, firefly," I say gently, stroking her back. "The most beautiful woman I've ever laid eyes on."

She gleams up at me. "Will they think I'm weird because I have a bow in my hair? Maybe I should take it out."

I grab her wrist before she can pull it out, then point toward one of the women. "She has a huge bow in her hair, too. They're not going to think you're weird. I promise these women are kind. They don't play as young as you, but they are still Little."

Ember raises her eyebrows. "Really?"

"Yeah, baby. Come on, I'll introduce you."

Cali, Paisley, and the other women are loud and excited as they all meet one another. It takes barely any time before Rowie and Ember are talking and laughing right along with them.

"Let's go inside and have drinks," I offer, motioning toward the house.

"Damn, dude, I kind of thought you'd live in an underground bunker or something. It's beautiful out here," Kieran says as he walks inside.

I chuckle. I also don't tell him that I do, in fact, have an underground bunker here. It's a bit odd having guests here. We've just never done it. The Ranch is the one place we've always kept sacred because it's the first place most of us have ever called home. I used to think I'd never trust anyone but my brothers, but I trust Declan and his men. They might be in the mafia, but they are good people.

My hands start to sweat a little as I pass out drinks. Why do I feel like I could vomit? Is this what feeling nervous is like?

As I give drinks out, Jasper comes strolling into the living room. Apparently, he hasn't visited the bathroom since he woke up.

Almost everyone does a double-take while Rowie and Ember burst out laughing, followed by the rest of the women.

"What the fuck happened to your face?" Declan asks him.

Jasper scowls at him. "What the fuck happened to yours?"

Cali snorts and doubles over; she's laughing so hard. There are very few men who would ever talk to Declan that way. It's pretty fucking comical watching his face morph into surprise.

"Nice to see you in a good mood," Theo says to Jasper. "It's about time you smiled."

"Oh my God. This is the best thing ever," Paisley says breathlessly.

Kieran glares at her. "Don't get any ideas, brat."

She sticks her tongue out at him.

"What are you staring at me for?" Jasper demands.

I go to him and slap him on the shoulder. "You should probably go look in a mirror."

He disappears, and a second later, he storms back into the room, pointing at Rowie. "You brat."

Rowie grins, not looking the least bit sorry.

"It was actually both of them," I tell him.

Ember's jaw drops. "Daddy! Tattletale."

Jasper glares at them. "You're both in trouble. I'm taking away Good Girl Points for both of you. Ten points each."

"They used permanent marker," I add.

"Daddy!" Ember hisses.

Cage!" Rowie says at the same time.

Jasper's gaze turns dark as he slowly approaches Ember and Rowie. "Fifty points each. And you're both helping me get this off my face."

"Fifty points!" they both cry out.

"Yes. Fifty. Now, unless you want me to take away more, come help me wash this off."

Ember sighs, and Rowie mutters under her breath, but they follow him from the room.

"Are you ready?" Theo asks me.

Declan furrows his brows. "Ready for what?"

Theo grins. "You'll see."

"Our girls are here," Declan growls. "If you do anything stupid or dangerous with them here, I'll kill you."

I shake my head and grin. "Paranoid much? Jesus. Calm down. It's a good thing. You're an ordained minister, though, right?"

"It depends. Will she be getting married against her

will? Because if the answer is yes, my answer is no," Declan replies.

My stomach twists, and that ill-feeling comes again. "I guess we'll know shortly."

He rolls his eyes, and I slap him on the back, chuckling.

The girls return with Jasper, who still has a faint smile drawn on his face. He doesn't look amused. Oh, well. Better him than me.

Ember's gaze lands on me first, and the rest of the room disappears as I stare at her. All my nerves disappear. All I can think about is how much I can't wait to marry her.

"Baby girl," I say as I start walking toward her. "I have something I want to ask you."

She draws her eyebrows together, confused. When I pull a small box from my pocket and lower onto one knee, she gasps softly.

"I know it's only been a few weeks since we met, but I've never been more sure about anything. Before you came into my life, I was existing, but I wasn't truly living. You've become the oxygen I need to breathe. I know I'm not easy, and you also have to deal with my pain-in-the-ass brothers, but I want to spend the rest of my days making you happy, giving you the love you deserve so much, and having the honor of being your Daddy. It's a big question, and I'll only allow one answer."

Ember laughs softly, tears dripping down her cheeks.

"Will you marry me, baby?"

She nods and throws herself at me, nearly knocking me onto my ass.

"Yes," she cries, letting out a sob.

The room erupts into shouts and congratulations. It's all background noise, though, as I lean in and lower my mouth to hers. She wraps her arms around my neck and kisses me back. That one word completes me. My brothers and Rowie mean everything to me, but there are only two people in the world who have truly changed my life with one simple word. Deke. And Ember.

"I love you, firefly," I murmur on her lips.

She sniffles and cups my face between her delicate hands. "I love you too, Daddy."

We finally pull away and everyone surrounds us while I slip the ring onto her finger.

Ember smiles up at me, "It's beautiful."

I rise and hug a bunch of my brothers as they congratulate me.

"Where's Declan?" I ask, trying to find him in the small crowd of my friends and family.

"I'm right here," he answers.

Taking Ember's hand, I pull her over and nod toward Declan. "Good. Marry us now."

Ember gasps and snaps her head to look at me. "What?"

I motion toward Declan, not sure what she's so

confused about. "He's ordained. He can marry us right now."

She opens her mouth and then closes it. She repeats this several times. Finally, she says, "We need a license, though. Don't we?"

"No. I don't need a piece of paper to tell me you're my wife. Though we will apply for a name change. Remember who you're marrying, baby. I don't exist on any database.

We stare at each other, and ever so slowly, the corners of her mouth stretch wide.

"You're crazy," she whispers.

I glance around the room and then back down at her, grinning. "Yeah, baby. So, are we doing this?"

She squeezes my hand. "Yeah, Daddy. Let's get married!"

25

EMBER

I can't believe I'm married.

Tonight was a dream. Only Cage would have an ordained minister on hand to marry us on the spot. Most people would probably think it's too soon. When you know, you know, I guess. He's my soulmate. I'm not sure if I ever believed in such a thing before, but I have no doubt now. It's a real thing.

"I have something else for you."

Tearing my gaze away from the sparkling wedding band, I watch him carry a plate to the bed with him.

"You already gave me so much."

He sits down and shows me the huge piece of chocolate cake he brought with him. The multi-layer fudgy goodness looks absolutely mouthwatering.

"Wedding cake?" I ask.

Using a fork, he scoops a bite and holds it to my

mouth. "No. Graduation celebration. You never got to celebrate your degree. I know things have been a bit hectic, but I haven't forgotten."

I stare at him, swallowing thickly. He remembered. It was important to me, so he made it important to him. This is one of many reasons why I know I made the right choice in marrying him tonight.

As soon as my mouth closes around the cake, I hum and close my eyes. "Oh my God, that's so good. It's almost as good as sex."

He laughs and takes a bite for himself. "Nah. Not even close, baby."

It's so rich and chocolatey that, by the fourth bite, I shake my head.

"I have one more thing for you. A wedding present."

"I didn't get you anything, though," I say sadly.

Cage cups my chin and presses a kiss to my forehead. "You already gave me everything I could ever want."

Then he pulls a long box from the nightstand and hands it to me. I stare at it for a second before I lift the lid and gasp, bringing my hand to my mouth.

"Daddy," I whisper.

"It's your mother's charm bracelet. I had it cleaned and inspected then added some charms to it. I hope that's okay."

I touch the cold metal, running the tips of my fingers over it. Tears burn my eyes as I look at each charm. The original two that my mom had are still on there: A baby charm she got from her parents when I was born and a candy cane for Christmas because it was her favorite holiday. There are five new ones. I smile when I touch one that's a dragon. Then, a firefly. A plane. A doll. And lastly, a black heart with a crack down the center, but it's been made to look like it's stitched back together.

"This..." I sniffle and try to blink back my tears. "This is the most thoughtful gift, Daddy."

He smiles as he pulls the bracelet from the box and proceeds to put it on me. "We'll keep adding to it."

I reach out to touch his face, my heart bursting. "I never knew life could be this good."

"Oh, baby," he whispers as he leans in to kiss me. "We're just getting started. It's about to get so much better."

Are you ready for Jasper's story?
Pre-order now!

Interested in reading more about Declan, Kieran, and the rest of his men? Check out my Syndicate Kings series!

ALSO BY KATE OLIVER

West Coast Daddies Series

Ally's Christmas Daddy

Haylee's Hero Daddy

Maddie's Daddy Crush

Safe With Daddy

Trusting Her Daddy

Ruby's Forever Daddies

Daddies of the Shadows Series

Knox

Ash

Beau

Wolf

Leo

Maddox

Colt

Hawk

Angel

Tate

Rawhide Ranch

A Little Fourth of July Fiasco

Shadowridge Guardians

(A multi-author series)

Kade

Doc

Syndicate Kings

Corrupting Cali: Declan's Story

Saving Scarlet: Killian's Story

Controlling Chloe: Bash's Story

Possessing Paisley: Kieran's Story

Keeping Katie: Grady's Story

Taking Tessa: Ronan's Story

Daddies of Pine Hollow

Jaxon

Dane

Nash

Dark Ops Daddies

Cage

Jasper

KEEP UP WITH KATE!

Sign up for my newsletter get teasers, cover reveals, updates, and extra content!

The kindest thing you can do for an author is to leave a positive review!

Made in the USA
Columbia, SC
19 December 2024

50147055R00180